# CODE OF HONOR

# CODE OF HONOR

## SANDY DENGLER

BETHANY HOUSE PUBLISHERS
MINNEAPOLIS, MINNESOTA 55438
A Division of Bethany Fellowship, Inc.

Editorial work by Penelope Stokes.
Cover illustration by Dan Thornberg,
Bethany House Publishers staff artist.



Published by Bethany House Publishers
A Division of Bethany Fellowship, Inc.
6820 Auto Club Road, Minneapolis, Minnesota 55438

Printed in the United States of America

**Library of Congress Cataloging-in-Publication Data**

Dengler, Sandy.
Code of honor / Sandy Dengler.
p. cm. — (Australian destiny ; bk. 1)
I. Title. II. Series: Dengler, Sandy. Australian destiny ; bk. 4.
PS3554.E524C6 1988
813'.54—dc19 88–18729
ISBN 0-87123-994-9 CIP

SANDY DENGLER is a freelance writer whose wide range of books has a strong record in the Christian bookselling market. She has authored almost 30 published books including juvenile historical novels, biographies, and adult historical romances. She has a master's degree in natural sciences and her husband is a national park ranger. They make their home in Ashford, Washington, and their family includes two grown daughters.

AUSTRALIAN DESTINY SERIES

*Code of Honor*
*Power of Pinjarra*
*Taste of Victory*
*East of Outback*

# CONTENTS

# With Memories and Regrets

A splintering *crack!*, the rumble of whispered thunder; the ancient mango tree by the garden fell unseen in the night.

Samantha Connolly, brave enough to circle half the globe and strong enough to make her own way once she got here, wedged herself in a corner, trembling. She covered her face and wished that her long slim fingers were fatter, that they might cover more. *Twenty-eight next month,* she thought, *and I'm acting like a four-year-old. Honestly!*

Crashing surf, normally a quarter mile away, flung itself across the front lawn to spend itself at the very doorstep.

Samantha pressed deeper into the corner between the treadle organ and the Regency bookcase. She was letting a mere typhoon reduce her to a gibbering idiot. She should be . . . uh, she should be . . . surely, she should be doing *something*! She should be taking command, as she so often did when a crisis struck. Logic ruled her life. Fear was, in certain circumstances, also logical—but this behavior certainly was not. For shame, Miss Connolly! She drew her long legs in tighter against her chest.

The eggshell of walls between her and the storm vibrated with every gust. Then the eggshell exploded as the pandanus palm that used to sway so gracefully above the house came slashing down through the roof to thunk against the organ. With an exuberant shriek the storm, victorious, slung its cold, stinging rain through the shattered shell.

Whatever strong reserve Samantha imagined for herself flew out through the roof into the whipping storm. Samantha Connolly was a person in control, a person to be trusted in a crisis situation. She always took care of things. Everyone knew that. But she had no control now; all the power lay in the hands and teeth of a mindless enemy; and that terrified her most of all. She was helpless, at the mercy of a merciless freak of weather.

Margaret had a comforting God to pray to; Samantha had none. Margaret had a young man to cling to; Samantha cowered here alone. If the storm destroyed her as it was destroying the house, no one would know until tomorrow, until this fiendish fury had passed—if it ever would. Samantha's tidy little paradise was ripping itself apart with an insane violence she could never have imagined back home.

Home. Ireland. Distant Ireland a world away. Gentle, soggy Erin with her misty hills, her boggy glens, her slick cobbled streets and muted beauty in grays and vivid greens. *Why, dear God, did you ever let me come here?*

CHAPTER ONE

# WITH GRIEF 1905

Once upon a time, so the storytellers claimed, when Ireland was young and her green face as yet not marred by cities, Dagda the giant built for the Celtic titans a series of magnificent palaces hidden away within great hollow hills. Their outside appearance, upon which anyone might gaze, was that of any hill—ragged, verdant, softened by mist. But deep inside, safe from mortal eyes, warriors and demi-gods made merry amid bright light and splendor.

Once upon a time, when the century had not yet turned and the world still tasted sweet, Samantha Connolly herself had climbed to the top of just such a hill palace in the mountains north of Cork. She knew her hill was one of the titan hills because Papa had said so.

But that was another century, another Ireland, and Samantha had been a child. She was an old maid now, already turned twenty-seven, and she no longer so readily believed whatever her father told her. Yet she still believed about Dagda's hill palaces, for they beckoned to her too strongly for denial. Her soul yearned bitterly for the brilliant light and warm cheer hidden from her mortal eyes somewhere within the wet, rolling, gray-green wilderness of Ireland's yesterdays.

When Dagda built, he kept the green. Ireland looked exactly the same when he finished as it had before he began. These days Ireland's fair face bore blemishes of gray, because mortal builders are not nearly so clever. Cork, a town made by men and practically devoid of brilliant light and warm cheer, perched like a lackluster scar on the edge of the sea.

Samantha was somehow, inexplicably, becoming bored with her native Cork. Today she walked nearly the length of Patrick Street without noticing a single patch of true Irish green. Blackish ragged moss between the cobbles sometimes showed a bit of color. Here an unkempt wisp of grass, there some plants in a window box—everything else sprawled beneath the overcast in shades of listless gray.

The wind shifted and gusted suddenly as she was crossing Connor Street; it dashed cold rain in her face and pushed her hood back. She grabbed the hood below her chin to snug it down close around her ears, then short-cutted through the little cobbled lane behind Marquardt Street and bounded up the back stoop into the house she knew best.

"There ye are! We were afraid ye'd miss supper." Grandmum Connolly creaked to her feet from the settle in the inglenook and began the laborious process of moving her aged bulk out to the dining table.

Samantha followed the little lady into the dining room, dragging her wool cape off along the way. "I be nae late, so supper must be early."

" 'Nuther meeting." Grandmum's voice rasped tight and thin. The sound and fury of this political fight over an Irish free state was accomplishing what the mere march of years could never do—it was making an old woman of her.

Papa was home already. He had loosely arranged his broad trunk and thick limbs into his overstuffed chair, all asprawl. With the barest smile of bemusement he watched Mum hack thick, jagged slices off a leg of roast mutton. He could do the carving better himself; he was a master carpenter whose cabinets and joinery were second to none; but as he so often claimed, he never interfered in Mum's trade and expected none of her interference in his.

Mum bent over the table with the sort of dogged determination that had forged a couple of small North Sea islands

lands into an empire. She spared Samantha a brief glance. "Where's yer sisters?"

"Margaret just happened to bump into Sean Morley—sheer coincidence, mind you, that they both chanced to be in the same street of a large town—so don't hold yer breath waiting for her. Where Linnet might be is anyone's guess. She'd already left the shop when I passed by there."

Samantha's strapping brother filled rooms simply by entering them. The dining room filled now as Edan came striding through. "How'd it go?" He plopped down at his place and stretched out a burly arm to help Grandmum with her shawl.

Samantha sat and scooted in her chair. "The ogre complimented me references and politely said he was considering someone else, thank ye anyway. 'Twould've served me quite as well to stay home."

"Hope ye told 'm what he can do with his stinking nanny position."

"No, Edan, I didn't. Perchance I'll have to seek employment from him some time in the future. Bridge-burning, ye know. Besides, one troublemaker in the family is already one too many. Grandmum said a meeting tonight."

"Griffith is making us official; organizing the cause, even giving it a name. *Sinn Fein.*"

Samantha translated mentally. *We ourselves*. Poetic, in a way. "Five years into the twentieth century, and already ye're trying to revolutionize it."

"Aye. We're getting together tonight to discuss it, see what we'll be doing next." Edan reached for a slice of bread. Mum rapped his knuckles.

"And what's yer own part in that newspaperman's mischief?"

Edan grinned. "Why, Sam, in the midst of the meeting, meself shall stand up straight and proud and announce to all Ireland's fine young men there that me three sisters be seeking husbands and ye can sign up at the back of the hall."

Grandmum hooted. "Ye want to help yer sisters find men? Best to tend yer own garden. Marry some lass yerself and set a grand example. Ye be only two years younger'n Samantha and men don't become spinsters. Twenty-five's more'n old enough to be settling down."

Samantha couldn't quite decide whether to laugh or scream, so she did neither. "Ye don't think I'll ever marry, do ye?"

"Ye haven't so far. Nae even a close call." Grandmum popped her false teeth out and rubbed with a finger at some imperfection in the upper plate.

Samantha studied the toothless lady, decided that you can't argue with an edentate, and buried herself in her favorite retreat, her own imagination. She thought of the nanny's position she had just been rejected for and how she didn't really want it anyway. She was hardly fond of children; they were, in fact, rather low on her list of tolerable necessities. She thought of the job she had heard about today, the one purchasing fresh fish for the inn down on Market Street. Come home smelling like a cod every day? At least it paid money. And she thought about the yellow paper pinned to the board by the meat market, the invitation with such bright and frightening promise.

Margaret at twenty-three was well employed as a typist, having mastered that new-fangled and mysterious printing machine. Linnet, barely seventeen, clerked in a tobacconist's. Edan, for all his caustic political polemic, still managed to draw a paycheck as an assistant in the Gleason law offices—prestigious, at the very least. Even Ellis, not yet fourteen, drove a wholesaler's pony cart down on the wharf. Why could Samantha never find a good, solid, comfortable position? What was wrong with her, anyway?

The rest of the family came straggling in and supper commenced. Papa intoned a blessing, crossed himself and picked up his fork.

Samantha crossed herself without thinking about it, for her thoughts kept drifting, as if drawn to a nightmare so horrible as to be absolutely fascinating. She was mad to even consider it. She'd better air it and get it out of the way, though. There was a pall over this meal, an ominous discomfort you could feel, and it was no doubt all Samantha's doing. Confession clears the air, they say.

"Papa, I saw an interesting notice at the butcher's today."

"Spare me more politics."

"Nae politics. Employment. A man named Cole Sloan seeks indentured domestics. Methinks I'll apply." There. It was out.

"Indenture?" Edan looked up from his dinner and laughed. "Sam, nobody does that anymore."

Her father snorted a whirlwind through his shaggy gray moustache. "T' America? Surely ye heard that letter Sean Galbraith got from his son in Boston. They treats the Irish like dirt in America, lass. 'No Irish need apply' sign in every office window."

"Australia."

That pall of discomfort had been nothing compared with this overcast of silence now.

Margaret's merry laughter broke the quiet. "Austerailia! Ah, sure'n that'd cure yer spinsterhood, Sam. Ye could marry one of them abba-driggidies."

"Or a convict." Edan wagged his head. "Better ye let me try to find ye someone here on yer own sod."

"One of yer fire-breathing political buddies? Nae. Besides, Margaret's on the verge of marrying Sean Morley, and he's a hothead after yer own heart. I'll let her be the one to put up with that nonsense."

Edan's doleful eyes skewered her and made her feel ashamed. "Ye think nothing of honor and freedom, do ye." It wasn't a question. It was a statement. And it was almost true.

"We get enough troubles in life without buying deliberately into more."

Papa's shaggy head wagged. "Hear the lass. She talks of bobbing across the wicked sea clear to Australia, as she accuses her brother of buying trouble."

Samantha sputtered a bit. "Let me rephrase. If one must invite trouble, wisdom dictates that one choose manageable troubles so much as possible. 'Tis the practical, logical way of dealing with life. These political upheavals aren't in the least controllable, nae even by the powers directing them. Too much blind emotion, too much obstinacy. They be nae subject to reason."

"Right." Edan washed down the last of his potato with a hearty draft of water. "Sure, and the ocean ye can control by reason. A ship out in hundred-foot swells is subject to reason. I see. Aye, I see." Edan pushed his chair back. "Ye ready, El?"

Papa's eyes squinted down and buried themselves somewhere within his bushy eyebrows and graying sideburns. "The lad stays home. Too young."

"He does a man's work, Papa. And 'tis his future; he should get a glance at it, ye think?"

"And if there be trouble. . . ?"

"Nae tonight. Just talking tonight."

"Mmph." Ellis jammed in half a potato, no doubt lest Edan notice that his plate wasn't empty and steal his food. Edan did that. His parents had named their son "Edan," a "consuming flame"—and Edan lived up to his name, consuming food like wildfire.

Papa flicked an eye toward Ellis, his grudging consent. "*Sinn Fein*; Australia; and what other delights have ye children to share, to gladden the heart of yer aging papa?"

"Ye'll nae find me floating round the world. I'll stay here and work on Sean Morley. Of course"—Margaret's eyes crackled—"I be nae so desperate as yerself, Sam."

"Meg, for shame." Linnet turned her sweet, glowing, gray-green eyes to Samantha. "Ye know, Sam, I don't think I could ever leave me home and country. Nae for someplace so . . . so different. So ungreen. So very unhomely. And I dinnae know how yerself can be thinking of it."

"The thing's nae said and done yet. Let it lie a bit, girls, and quit yer nattering." Papa folded his napkin, his unmistakable sign that the conversation was ended.

Edan and Ellis trooped off to their meeting of—what did he call it? *Sinn Fein*—and the house seemed empty again. It was Linnet's turn with the dishes, but somehow Samantha ended up in the kitchen. Grandmum settled back into the inglenook and took a nail file to her upper plate. All appeared normal on the surface, but the night still felt strangely out of joint, hanging dark and heavy on the spirit.

Papa traded his emptied teacup in on his cap and jacket and off he went without a word into the murky night for a round at the pub. He didn't have to announce where he was going—his routine was fixed and familiar, rutted and well-worn—unlike the future of his eldest daughter.

Australia. What could she be thinking of? A world that was a world away, literally; an alien world of freaky little animals and equally freaky little black semi-humans with spears; a world deemed so desolate by the British Empire that it hosted the Crown's ultimate penal colony. And she thought she felt some call to go there?

Well, she had nothing here; no marriage prospects, no job at the moment, no expectations. It could be no worse there.

But Samantha felt at home here. The sod under her, the gray sky above, the mist and rain between; they were as much a part of her as her dark brown hair. She couldn't rip herself apart and send half off to foreign soil while the other half remained, hopelessly rooted. It's not natural. It's just not done.

And yet she knew that millions of Irish lads and lasses like her, men and women with no prospects or expectations, had done exactly that. For the last sixty years, ever since the potato famine, more Irish had left the auld sod than had been born on it. There were fewer eligible men now than when she was a child. And the young men were still emigrating, chasing rainbows—and girls—across alien meadows.

The kitchen finally put in order, Samantha took a light up to her room and dug out her atlas. She hadn't looked at this old book in years. It hadn't been the biggest or most accurate of atlases when it was new, and Samantha had not purchased it new; she had no money for that sort of extravagance. But it contained maps, scores of maps, some in color, and it fueled dreams as no other book can. Samantha loved maps. What was the term? Cartophile. She might not be good enough to land a husband or a good job, but she was a grand cartophile.

The map of Australia was as she remembered it—a huge expanse of blankness. The artist didn't have the imagination to populate its vast unknown reaches with fantastic monsters the way medieval cartographers filled unknown oceans of yore. And no one had explored most of the continent, apparently. *Mossman.* The man purchasing indentures wrote from Mossman. But these map-makers had never heard of any Mossman. She tried to picture what this flat white surface must look like for real.

Here were some scraggly lines where Burke and Wills traversed the land a few scant years before the book was printed. Here was the penal colony, and there was Sydney. The great clippers had sailed from Sydney on the wool runs—*Cutty Sark, Thermopylae* . . .

A wail in the night—someone had cried out! Samantha tried to sit up straight, but a painful crick in her neck kept her S-shaped. Her lamp fizzed and flickered, nearly dry. She was scrunched in her chair like a ball of wadded-up paper. How long had she slept? Several hours, quite probably.

Her mother moaned. She could tell Papa's rumbling voice and even upstairs here, through two closed doors, she heard the anguish in it. She bolted downstairs.

The parlor was filled, but not by Edan. In the middle of the room stood a constable, shuffling from foot to foot, and a crisp young British army officer of some type. Papa stood rigid, his arms wrapped around Mum, and his cheek buried in her hair. Margaret draped across the divan sobbing. Grandmum sat on the ottoman by the clock and simply stared at the rug, rocking mindlessly back and forth.

Samantha almost missed Ellis. The stripling, devoid of his veneer of manhood, had melted into the corner under the staircase. It was his den, his hiding place, the hole he always curled up in when his world had gone drastically awry.

Linnet—Linnet's tender face told Samantha the news; she didn't need these bumbling talebearers. The shock and grief in Linnet's face told all.

"Edan. 'Tis Edan, aye? There was some sort of trouble and Edan was—"

"Trouble of the worst sort, yes." The officer's voice crackled, just as sharp and unyielding as his expertly pressed uniform. "Illegal meeting and public disturbance. Mr. Connolly here—you're the father, I presume?—called the army to fault. As I pointed out to him, the queen's army *will* maintain order, and by whatever means necessary to assure control. Persons fomenting disorder know that before they begin." He jabbed the constable's arm. "We've done our duty." They nodded brusquely. "Ladies—" and they were gone into the wet night.

Samantha stood transfixed, but only for a moment. *Edan . . . ?* She needed facts, she needed the truth, and Ellis, poor Ellis, had been there. He knew. She crossed to the boy and put her hands on his shoulders. "Please tell me."

Ellis stared numbly at her sleeve. "The meeting was all shouting at each other 'til some soldiers marched in unexpected. Then the yelling was at them. I was in back; couldn't see; after the shooting, there was . . ." The frail shoulders shrugged. "There was Edan and Sean Morley and one other fellow on the floor and all the blood . . ." The fragile voice drifted to silence.

Samantha wrapped her arms around her brother, and Ellis, flaccid Ellis, did not resist.

Margaret stirred on the divan. "Sam? I'll walk along with ye on the morrow when ye apply for that indenture."

Samantha shuddered, a wrenching sob-turned-sigh. Tears were coming now, at last, to help ease the pain. "Do ye suppose there's any place where warriors laugh, and are kind, instead of striking down our brightest and best? Bright light and warm cheer instead of . . . instead of this?"

CHAPTER TWO

# WITH FEAR AND TREMBLING

Did the storm seem to be dying a bit? It didn't matter. Samantha mourned her lost homeland, the gentle yesterdays of her youth, and nothing the wind could do now would mollify her. She'd return to her Ireland this moment if she could, but she'd not be able to do that for a long time to come. For the moment she had no money, no influence, no luck. She was trapped on an alien continent, in the claws of a typhoon the likes of which she had never ever seen.

Loose sheets on the galvanized metal roof started banging wildly. That was a good sign; until now they had been held to one stiff and unwavering position by the constant gale. Something in the darkness above her ripped away; rain pelted her face. Another tree went down in the garden.

Finally, by degrees, the storm was easing; Samantha could tell. The wild wind slowed. Rain by the gallon drenched the world and everything in it. Only here in the tropics did such dense deluges fill earth and sky. She curled tightly in her corner another hour as rain dumped on her through the ripped roof.

"Sam? Sam! Where are you?" The thick baritone came booming across from somewhere near the dining room.

Samantha's heart leaped. His plantation was ruined, his house broken, and yet it was she he thought of first! "Here, Mr. Sloan! I'm coming!" She squirmed to untangle her legs from her skirts, to stand erect. "I'm here."

"Hiding! Like the rest of this worthless help. I expected better of you. Come along."

"I can't see—"

"I sent Doobie to jury-rig a line from the power station. We should have lights in another hour."

Samantha stumbled across the ravaged room, following her master's voice through the blackness. She barely avoided colliding with the face. A stone cylinder nearly seven feet high stood in the middle of the parlor floor, more or less marking the end of the foyer and the beginning of the room proper. On one side of it was chiseled a hawk-nosed face. Granite eyes gazed unseeing out the many little panes of the big parlor window.

Mr. Sloan's voice rolled on. He was already entering the kitchen, headed for the back door. "The stable collapsed. I want you up there helping dig out the horses. Soon as they're all freed, run down to the mill and help Gantry. I want that mill operating tomorrow morning. We're going to have a blooming lot of downed cane to run through it in a hurry."

"Please, sir, me sisters? Meg and Linnet?"

"Meg's down at the mill. I've no idea where Linnet's hiding." Impatience. Harsh, bitter impatience robbed his voice of its pleasant lilt.

The kitchen appeared pretty well intact. Kathleen Corcoran, the big, bulky cook, had lighted kerosene lamps here and there. She bustled about now preparing hearty snacks to sustain the workers who would be struggling through the night. She seemed so efficient, so smooth. Even her white dust cap still looked crisp and clean. Sudden shame warmed Samantha's wet cheeks. While she cringed in fear, Kathleen had been working! Samantha didn't even have the excuse that Kathleen was accustomed to this sort of thing, for Kathleen had arrived with Samantha and her sisters; such a short time ago, and it seemed so long.

Cole Sloan paused at the back door and turned. The ruddy lamplight made his tanned skin glow. Samantha's very first impression of him, two months ago, multiplied itself now.

Here was a marvelous-looking fellow, tall and dark and well proportioned. He had shed the tropical white jacket he usually wore and had rolled his sleeves to his elbows. His shirt, dirty and sopping wet, gaped open now practically to his waist. There wasn't an ounce of fat on the man anywhere.

"Look for your sister in the morning, Sam. The horses come first." He wheeled and disappeared into the roaring darkness.

Obedience and shame mastered her fear. She plunged out the back door bravely. Rain like steel beat against her shoulders and stung her face. She followed the crashing footsteps ahead of her and hoped Mr. Sloan was returning to the stable area. She'd been a fool to think he'd worry about her. He had greater things to worry about than an indentured housemaid.

Filtered lights beyond the thrashing jungle foliage told her where the stable lay. Doobie the fix-it-all handyman had already set up electric lamps here. *The horses come first.*

Mr. Sloan, a hundred feet ahead of Samantha, stepped out into the circle of light. Instantly Fat Dog, the stable foreman, was at his elbow, pointing wildly, gesturing toward the smashed roof that lay all a-shambles across the collapsed walls. Fat Dog's shiny black face glistened in the yellow light. His eyes, sunk deep beyond the beetling aboriginal brows, caught the glint now and then as he turned.

"Here's Sheba!" called a cane-cutter. In the midst of the wreckage the chubby little bay mare staggered to her feet. The cutter gripped her nostrils with one hand and an ear with the other, holding the terrified horse in place.

"Clear this!" roared Mr. Sloan with a sweep of the arm, and many hands leaped to the work, Samantha's included. Two men with wrecking bars wrenched at this pile of splinters and that. Mr. Sloan himself helped heave and push shattered lumber until Sheba could step, shaking, to safety.

Samantha was up to her knees in wreckage now, pulling at broken joists. A splinter gouged into the palm of her hand, but she ignored the flash of pain and the oozing blood. She'd attend it later. *The horses come first.*

"Here's Glowworm, sir. Back's broke, I think."

A long gray head with rolling eyes appeared from between two timbers. The gelding struggled; the head disappeared.

Mr. Sloan pulled a pistol from his belt at the small of his back; Samantha had not noticed it before. "Stand on his neck, Vickers. Keep his head still."

She pinched her eyes shut and steeled herself; still the gunshot exploded like a cannon on her frazzled nerves. Her eyes grew hot; Glowworm's soft lips had nibbled crushed bits of cane off her opened hand a million times, and now . . .

If Mr. Sloan cared at all, he didn't show it. Instantly he was scrabbling again through the sorry wreckage. "Fat Dog, who's under here? Gypsy?"

"Yuh, Boss. Not much hope, eh?"

"Bring that light." The handsome face, wet with slathering rain, tilted and strained to see through the jumbled lumber. Samantha moved in right beside him. Gypsy was Linnet's special favorite. What would sweet and sensitive little Linnet do if Gypsy were a casualty of this hideous night?

Mr. Sloan shook his head. "All I see is blood." He reached behind him again for that pistol.

"Please, sir!" Impulsively, Samantha grabbed his arm. "She's Linnet's favorite, and nae such a bad horse. Please don't."

He glared at the hand on his arm.

She held steady. "Please, sir?"

He scowled. "She's too high strung; she'd never heal well, especially in this climate. I can't afford the time and cost of her, even if her bones be sound. Get back."

The master had spoken. With a sense of loss she would not have expected in herself, Samantha stepped back.

From the wreck, from nowhere, came a thin and flutey voice. "Nae! Dinnae hurt her, Mr. Sloan, please! Dinnae kill her!"

"Linnet!" shrieked Samantha. "Where are ye?!"

"With Gypsy here. Please, Mr. Sloan. I'll take care of her, I promise!"

A seldom-heard expletive burst from Mr. Sloan's lips. "Dig 'em out!" He jammed his pistol back into his belt.

Dig Samantha did, and frantically, though she had not the slightest idea what she was doing. These modern electric lamps put out hardly more light than any kerosene lamp. She could find no place to put her feet solidly; slippery palm-frond thatching and smashed lumber covered the ground. The roof had been thatch, the walls no more than a few poles to hold up the roof. How could so flimsy a building create such a frightening, hideous mess?

Samantha took one corner as black workers and white lifted most of what remained of the roof framing away in one grand chunk. That helped. Much of the stall divider came up in one piece. Samantha struggled with her share and nearly fell.

A shoulder far stronger than hers braced against her, supporting her, and arms far stronger than hers took over lifting the divider. She glanced aside to see who this was as Mr. Sloan's voice barked.

"Vinson! She's not here, so get out of here. Go preach to somebody else's horses."

The stall divider tipped aside and fell away. Other hands dragged it off into the darkness.

The man beside her stood his ground. "You can use me for a few hours yet, Sloan, and I'm happy to help. I saw your lights up here, knew it was the stable area and figured you must have a problem. No other reason to pour light on a stable in this storm."

Samantha knew Luke Vinson only as the preacher in the little church at the crossroads a half mile away, and as Meg's newest love interest. He was almost as good-looking as Mr. Sloan, and almost as tall—but not quite. He lacked, though, the rich darkness of her employer's coloring. He was light-haired, and so fair that no amount of tropical sun would ever darken him up.

No thanks, no appreciation for what was obviously a quite thoughtful gesture—Mr. Sloan glared at him up and down and then, without another word, again bent his back to the task of freeing Linnet and Gypsy.

And the Rev. Vinson (it was *Reverend*, wasn't it? Not *Father*. She was pretty sure of that) worked just as eagerly and earnestly. The little horse squealed when a timber broke loose and fell. Linnet's soft soprano purred in the darkness. Samantha could hear the horse thrashing.

"Linnet!" Mr. Sloan called. "Keep the horse quiet. Sit on her neck or something."

"I cannae." The small voice sounded even weaker than usual. "I'm stuck. I cannae move."

Samantha's heart thumped. She was afraid, now, and it wasn't a fear to be ashamed of. She was afraid for Linnet, for her gentle, fragile little sister buried in this dark chaos.

Mr. Sloan let fly another expletive, Reverend present or not, and put two strong backs to the wrecking bars. With a *crack* and the groans of spikes in wet wood, they tore aside the shattered manger. Gypsy convulsed and lurched to her feet. Mr. Sloan and Fat Dog grabbed her head to hold her in place. Two cutters joined Samantha and Rev. Vinson, and together they freed up a path to safety. Rev. Vinson pulled his belt from his waist and looped it around Gypsy's head and nose. Fat Dog led her carefully out of her splintered home to open ground.

Instantly Mr. Sloan dived into the wreckage until only his back showed. Here came Linnet, pallid in the sallow lamplight, and Mr. Sloan was holding her steady. Blood and tears streaked her face. She twisted around to face her master.

"I was so afraid ye'd shoot her. I heard them say 'here's Glowworm' and the gun went off, and then ye were working yer way toward us and I knew . . . I was afraid ye'd . . ." She sucked in air, a dry and shuddering sob.

"What in blazes were you doing here?"

She shrugged and studied her hands. "Sure'n ye know how nervous Gypsy can be. When the storm got bad I was afraid she'd panic and perhaps hurt herself, so I came up to try and keep her calm." The liquid gray-green eyes rose to meet Mr. Sloan's. "I dinnae finish stretching the strings for the peas like ye told me to, but the surf was coming up into the garden, so I dinnae think 'twas mattering too much anymore."

Mr. Sloan stood there in the seething, thundering rain, his face tight with rage, for a long tense moment. "Sam, take her down to the house, then return immediately. We still have three horses buried in this mess."

"Aye, Mr. Sloan." Samantha wrapped an arm around Linnet's shoulders and led her out the same cleared path Gypsy had followed. As they left the circle of light, Samantha glanced behind her. Rev. Vinson and Mr. Sloan were pulling at a thick roof beam.

Linnet snuffled. "Is Meg all right?"

"Mr. Sloan says she's working down at the mill. Linnet, that was so stupid!"

"Stupid? Nae. Gypsy was half out of her mind until I got there. She would've destroyed herself."

Wet leaves and branches slapped Samantha's face. Without Mr. Sloan to follow, Samantha had trouble keeping to the path. Then suddenly white light flared to life up ahead. Doobie had jury-rigged his line to the house.

Samantha pushed the kitchen door open and half dragged her sister through it. She pulled a chair up beside the stove. Linnet collapsed onto it with a plop.

Samantha started stripping wet clothes off the girl. "Is this blood yer own or Gypsy's?"

"Gypsy's, I think. Except for that piece of wood that was pinning me arm down, I was under her. She protected me."

Kathleen Corcoran stood herself squarely in front of Linnet, with arms akimbo. "I've seen mice in better shape after they've been carried in by the cat. Ye can go back up, Sam; I'll take care of this frail little bird."

Samantha stood erect. "Yerself has duties, too."

"Got a pile of sandwiches made, the coffee's on and the soup will be ready soon. I've time enough for this."

"Very well." Samantha watched Linnet a moment. The girl

did not seem to be in pain or difficulty, and a bit of color was starting to return to her cheeks. Samantha looked at bold, hulking Kathleen. "Weren't ye frightened during the worst of it?"

"Eh, nae." The cheery face grinned, and its round red cheeks bunched up into apples. She pointed to a wet spot in the ceiling. "Lose some roof? Nae matter; didn't even drip on me head to soil me cap. Besides, Sam, meself is young and that's next best to immortal. Naething's gonna kill me for a long time yet."

Samantha laughed suddenly, and her laughter surprised her, for laughter had been the thing farthest from her mind. Instantly it blunted the horror of this terrible night. "We're all young yet; how could I have fretted?"

Mr. Sloan had paid good money to bring her here, and in so doing he was offering her a brand new start in life. She owed him for that as well as passage. She would not cower again; she would not hide. Mr. Sloan from now on would get his money's worth.

She cast one last look at Linnet and hurried back out into the drumming rain. Darkness and a world of wet leaves encompassed her, pressing in tightly on all sides. Three years at the very minimum she would spend in this stifling, closed-in country. Three years. She put the thought aside. The matter at hand was to make it through the night.

A gaunt and bony gray kangaroo sprawled on its side under an acacia tree, propped on one foreleg elbow like a Roman at a banquet. It licked its wrists constantly, mindlessly, and paid no attention as one of the state's most successful pastoralists rode by not two rods away.

Martin Frobel, owner of one of the finest—and driest—cattle stations in Queensland, lifted his hat a moment to let the breeze dry off his sweaty brow. He drew his mare to a halt atop a low, gentle rise that, in this country, was as close as one got to a hill. He shifted in the saddle. Some said the Abos could see two looks away; from the back of his horse, Frobel could gaze nigh onto forever.

The vista pleased him, as it always did. This had to be God's favorite country, for the Almighty had bestowed it with open space on a scale as grand as heaven itself. The horizon sketched a thin, flat pencil line between gray and blue, between brigalow and sky. There was no land's end in this country. "Forever" here was not a theological time frame; it was a geographical description.

Martin Frobel loved this land; in a real way, he *was* the land, and he prided himself on that. No soft, foo-foo land, this, or delicate—it was tough, dry, uncompromising. It took a strong man to wrest a living from it, and Martin Frobel had met the challenge well. At least, until now.

The mitchell grass was long since nibbled away, and no new growth had come in to replace what had been grazed to the nubbin. Grass needs water to sprout. The acacia thickets provided a fourth the shade they usually do. Their gray-green leaves had all shriveled and fallen. Tightly gnarled branches curled in on themselves and waited patiently for rain.

There would be no rain today. Globs of fluffy white strewed themselves across the endless blue sky. None of them, though, sported dirty bottoms. These were empty clouds, waterless clouds, left over from some wild storm in the rain forest on the east side of the hills. They provided a moment's respite from sun if they happened to pass overhead just right, but they would give Martin Frobel and his tortured land no relief from drought.

Already the land suffered. Already the pulverized soil was literally disappearing into thin air. Frobel didn't have enough good soil as it was, let alone to lose it on the wind. The land—his land—could not tolerate much more of this.

Neither would his stock. The cattle stood about with blank expressions, or lay in the dappled shade of the acacia thickets and stared at infinity with hungry, vacant eyes. Their flanks had long since sunk in. You could count ribs from a mile off. None of them had enough meat left to make butchering them worth the water to wash the knife. The young and the weak were gone, and now he was starting to lose the prime stock.

Half a mile away a willy-willy dipped down to the earth. A dust cloud exploded where it touched and instantly filled its swirling cone. The miniature tornado bumped along a short distance and lifted again. Its dust thinned, and at last it disappeared completely.

A mere dot of a horseman appeared from behind the thicket east of Frobel's scenic viewpoint here. The dot grew larger. Now he could see it was a dark brown horse, and now he could see that the rider, too, was dark brown. The old gelding was nearing fourteen now, but he still moved like a five-year-old. Frobel had raised that colt by hand—practically raised the rider by hand, too, for turning a wild bush Abo into a top drover takes more work and patience than training a stock horse.

The horse jogged up this last little rise at the same speed he had jogged the distance around the thicket, without breaking stride. Jack pulled in beside Frobel. The horse's shoulders and flanks were wet, lathered at the rubbing spots, but he wasn't blowing.

"So what's out there, Jack?"

"No calves. I counted forty down and another fifty ready to fall over. Water wagon might save a few."

"They all in the thicket?"

"Yuh. Not eating, though. No grass."

"The mob over by the creekbed isn't any better off."

"Nothing left but bare dirt on the far side there, either. I took a turn around to the east a ways—thought maybe beyond the sand ridge." Gimpy Jack shook his head. "Not very good, Mr. Frobel. No good atall."

"No good atall, Jack." What was it that Luke Vinson had said? Prayer? Miracles still happen? Maybe. The preacher-lad claimed he'd found an Irish girl he really fancied. That rated as a miracle, considering the boy was pushing thirty without ever getting tangled up with a woman before. But rain?

Frobel took one last look at the sheer glory of uncut distance, and at the hollow sky with its drifting wool-balls.

Someone else, someone luckier, had gotten his rain again and left him nothing but a stiff breeze and sterile, mocking clouds. He reined his mare aside and led the way off toward home.

CHAPTER THREE

# WITH MALICE TOWARD SOME

Sure and Ireland was never like this. The sea stretched away forever, dancing. A million wavelets snatched bits of sparkling silver sun and tossed them playfully at Samantha's eyes. Dividing the worlds of sea and land, a thin ribbon of beach stretched itself between the green and the blue. No mere strand, this beach had once been alive. Doobie had explained to Samantha how the pale "sand," so called, was actually ground-up coral and that coral was a living animal—great colonies of tiny living animals.

Samantha paused and stooped down where the ocean meets the sand to study a chunk of coral cast ashore by that storm. It stank, for one thing, and its pallid gray was absolutely disappointing, not at all the bright red one calls "coral." Its upper face, no doubt the living part of which Doobie spoke, was not just rough and hard but sharp. The notion of a nearly flat surface being so sharp intrigued her.

As green as anything in Ireland, the forest beside her shimmered in the sun with a vibrating warmth unknown in Erin. In Ireland the constant green seemed a sort of backdrop to life, a landscape canvas against which the major characters of the drama of Samantha Connolly played their roles. This rain forest, though, was a living thing unto itself, a dense and brooding entity. It crowded relentlessly against the narrow white line of shore; in places, mangroves breached the line and brought the forest wading down into the very sea. Death lurked here, they said, and tangled resistance to even the most innocent of attempts to penetrate its ominous darkness. Samantha couldn't quite believe that; it was much too beautiful.

Sun. In her few short months on this Queensland coast, Samantha had basked in more sun than she had seen her whole lifelong in Ireland. And she wasn't even trying to bask—nor should she; her nose exhibited a pronounced tendency to peel.

Today she strode, inundated in brilliance, along that shifting, halting line twixt land and sea. The slurry of sand gave beneath her bare heels and squeezed up between her bare toes. Crystal ripples flung themselves up the beach where she walked and fell back to nothing, over and over and over. She tried to remember the storm and this surf crashing against the front porch a quarter mile beyond its normal confines. She couldn't anymore, not clearly, and that had been only a few short days ago.

Hoofbeats? Samantha wheeled. Here came Mr. Sloan along the beach. He was riding Gypsy today for the first time since the tragedy at the stable, and she appeared in rare form. She carried her nose high and her ears up. Her nostrils flared and snorted. Samantha almost wished Mr. Sloan would simply let her go and let her fly—let her run free and wild with her mate the sea—but he held her firmly to a brisk collected canter.

Gypsy was following the surf line, too, so Samantha stepped out into the water a few feet to give way.

But Mr. Sloan didn't pass by. He drew Gypsy to a reluctant halt in front of Samantha. "Out touring, Sam?"

"I suppose, sir, in a way. I just now helped Kathleen take dinner down to the men at the mill. She's driving the wagon back, but I thought it too nice an afternoon to bump along the road. 'Tis no farther, and slightly quicker, to return home along the beach here. And 'tis lovely, the day, aye?"

He swung down out of the saddle. Gypsy skitted aside and waltzed in a tight circle around him. He commenced a gentle stroll just above waterline, so Samantha fell in beside him. She shifted her shoes from her right hand to her left, lest they accidentally brush against him and make a dirt mark on his clean white jodhpurs.

His dark eyes held hers only a moment, then gazed off to far distance. "You seem t've become something of a mother hen to the house staff. You know your sisters quite well, I presume."

"Too well, at times."

He chuckled. "I understand; I grew up with two brothers. And how well do you know Amena O'Casey?"

Samantha considered a moment. "Not well, not really. We became acquainted, of course, on the voyage here. She indentured herself the very same day we did. But then and now she tends to explore her own pursuits and meself has other interests. And 'tis Linnet with whom she shares a room. I be nae her supervisor and she works outside the house for the most part, so we've scant contact."

"Her own pursuits. Byron Vickers?"

"The cane cutter with the black beard, aye. A jovial bear of a man." *Good friend of the Reverend's,* Samantha thought—but she didn't say that—not the way Mr. Sloan failed so obviously to tolerate the preacher, much less get along with him.

"Just wondering. I heard a rumor that she might try to break indenture."

"She's never mentioned anything to meself, but then, she'd have nae reason to."

"And Kathleen Corcoran?"

"Ah, now ourselves have become quite close, with her in the kitchen and I as housemaid. A delightful girl, that; always jolly and always helpful."

"Any romances on her horizon?"

"Romances? I've nae idea, but I doubt it, sir. She's not been acting moony or anything of the sort."

"How about you? Romance got you yet?"

Samantha's cheeks warmed instantly. Now, why should

that be? "I've an indenture to serve out first, sir. No use to think of romance yet."

"Your sister's not waiting."

At last she could see where this conversation was headed so obliquely. She stopped and turned to face him, which drew him up as well. "Forgive me speaking boldly, sir, but ye as much as asked. We Connollys be an honorable clan, and if we make agreement to something, we hold up our side of it. She agreed to work for ye three years and ye may rest assured she'll serve her full indenture."

"And if Luke Vinson decides the Connolly honor isn't worth the wait. . . ?"

Samantha began walking again. She was getting much too lippy with her employer; she must cool down, resume her proper place. "I admit Meg fancies the preacher, sir, but that may or may not come to anything. She's fancied any number of swains in times past. Besides, 'tis not Luke Vinson's honor to be maintained, 'tis ours. And we shall. Ye needn't worry about Meg." She glanced up at him.

He was watching her with a bemused, lilting twinkle in those dark, dark eyes. "Ah. Now I see what it takes to build a fire in Samantha Connolly. Challenge the family honor."

Her cheeks were hot again. "Honor bought with a heavy price, sir. Me father worked for a major cabinetmaker in Cork. When he refused to take part in a scheme to defraud a builder, he was fired. The best joiner and cabinetmaker in Ireland, and for years he could get nae work. And me brother Edan died for honor. Honor and freedom. 'Tis not a thing to be taken lightly."

"Obviously not." Suddenly he turned and vaulted into the saddle. Gypsy stumbled two steps back and danced in place, held to the spot by that firm hand. "I want you to tell me if you hear any rumblings about Amena quitting the crib." He twisted Gypsy's head around, and in a spray of stinging, flying sand they were off at a canter down the beach.

Samantha resumed her walk along the restless edge of the sea. *So. Cole Sloan certainly didn't pass the time of day with me merely to be friendly. He wants an informant. He pumps me of what I know and sends me out to learn more, eh?* She sighed. How she hated these intrigues employers seemed always to place upon the staff! *Tattle here. Spy there. Find out what my wife does tomorrow. Tell the gardener such and so. Let me know when . . .*

Somehow, she realized, she had almost thought she could put that sort of thing behind her when she put Ireland behind her. But no matter where she went, she could never escape human nature.

There were the loading docks in the distance. Samantha turned right onto the quiet little side path to the house. It angled from the shore up through the dim and sober forest to join the main walkway between house and stables. She found herself walking faster through this gloom. A dazzling little green pigeon with a red cap and yellow tail tip settled in a tree ahead and froze, as if by simply sitting quietly it could hide its lovely colors. Samantha stepped out into the walkway and headed left toward the house.

The house, like the pigeon, seemed to hold its breath as if in suspended animation, cool and dark and silent. Where was everybody? Without Kathleen's bounding good cheer the kitchen sulked, abandoned. Samantha inexplicably felt abandoned, too. She took a turn through the rooms, fluffing already-fluffy pillows, straightening doo-dads that were not in disarray, preparing the house to picture-perfection should unexpected visitors drop by.

Surely Kathleen was back by now. Perhaps Samantha ought to walk up to the stables to see if she could use some help unhitching. No, of course not; Fat Dog would be putting away the wagon team, not Kathleen; besides, Mr. Sloan was certainly there now. It might appear as if Samantha were chasing after him. That would never do.

Her stroll along the beach had been quite pleasant. Why did Samantha feel so irritated, so out of sorts? Nothing in the day should have put her on edge like this . . . unless it was Mr. Sloan's spy mission.

As Samantha returned to the empty kitchen, Linnet entered the back door. The girl looked like something a cat had dragged through a swamp. Chocolate-colored mud, green slime and putrid brown water spoiled her black skirt as well as her apron. Her hair hung in muddy strings where the bun had been teased loose.

"Linnet, whatever. . . ! Yer clothes are never going to come clean!"

She smiled broadly. "Fat Dog's wife, a woman named . . . oh, what is her name? I forget. Anyway, she was showing me how to dig out these roots along the creek. Ye find them in swampy areas, ye see. She says they taste good roasted, but what she uses them for is to make her hair glossy soft. She says ye pound them and then rinse the juice through yer hair after ye've washed it."

"Ye're supposed to be laundering the bed linen and mending the ripped seam in that blue dust ruffle."

"I'll get it done."

"Linnet, Mr. Sloan, he's not paying ye to pursue roots through swamps. The work comes first; ye know that. Now go clean yerself up. Meself's never seen such a royal mess. Sew up the dust ruffle and then start the washing. Perhaps if the man sees the ruffle's mended, he'll not think about the laundry. Run off now!"

"Meg's right, Sam; ye fret too much about work. Nothing wrong with a spell away from work. Kathleen's out enjoying a bit of a holiday herself, until time to start dinner. And she be as hard a worker as any."

"She was up before dawn and deserves the break. Ye slept in to breakfast. Go get busy. And set those clothes to soaking, though I doubt it'll do any good. They're spoilt, ye know."

Linnet almost left. But she paused in the doorway, turned and leaned against the jamb. "Why is it ye be constantly cross with me when ye never speak to anyone else in that tonc of voice?"

"Because ye're not pulling yer full weight. Ye lollygag too much. This isn't some lark ye set out upon, sailing halfway round the world to have a bit of fun. 'Tis hard work with much expected of ye. At the tobacconist's ye could slack off a bit. Not here."

"Slack off? Hardly! Me days be filled up."

"But not with anything productive. Ye could've stayed in Cork and done as much as ye're doing now, and Mr. Sloan wouldn't be out a boat passage."

"Sure and yerself sailed around the world just so ye could work harder than ye might in Cork. Balderdash, Sam; ye're here to find a man, same as Meg and I, for men be few and far between back home."

"And how would ye be knowing that? Ye left home before ye even tried."

A maddening half smile hardened Linnet's soft round face. "Ah, now I see the light. 'Tis more'n all right for Sam to go traipsing across the face of the earth, even though her dear brother be not but weeks in his grave. All right for Meg, too, perhaps, with her Sean Morley dead as well. But not Linnet. Linnet ought t' stay home and comfort the grieving parents so that Meg and Sam need not feel guilty about leaving."

"Guilty! No. This may well be me last chance at a full life, and Papa and Mum agreed. But yerself had nothing much to gain by coming. Ye're young yet. They begged ye stay."

"So I can drift along 'til I be a spinster like yerself, or fresh out of prospects like Meg? If it's so fine for yerself to begin a new life, why not for me as well? Why must I sit about waiting 'til I'm old and stodgy before I—"

The door slammed open. Mr. Sloan stood backlighted, his riding crop in hand. He scowled. "Has Kathleen returned yet?"

"Nae yet, sir." Samantha straightened. How much had he heard, if anything?

" 'Scuse me, sir." Linnet curtsied. "She purposed to take a little walk back the creek, is all. She's sure to return in good time to prepare dinner."

"How far back the creek?"

"Did nae say, sir. She fancies strolling in the forest, 'tis so unlike back home. Nae so far, I aver."

"When did she leave?"

"Straightway she returned with the wagon, sir." Linnet curtsied again and nibbled her lip.

The riding crop wagged at her. "Stay here. If she comes in, run to the stable and tell Fat Dog immediately. He'll send runners to me. Also, I don't ever want you near the estuary again, understand? That whole lowland is off limits. And clean yourself up. You're a disgrace." The crop pointed at Samantha. "You come with me." Mr. Sloan turned away, then turned back again. "And the two of you do your arguing some other place on your own time. I won't have nattering and squabbling in this house." He marched out.

Samantha glared at Linnet but she didn't have time to really skewer the wayward girl. She hiked her skirts and hurried out the door behind her master.

What was afoot? And why was Cole Sloan striding along in such a determined way? His long, strong legs swallowed distance yards at a gulp. Samantha fell into a jogging trot behind him, trying to keep up.

By the time they reached the stable the exertion had left her breathless. Samantha caught up to Mr. Sloan only when he stepped in under the makeshift thatched shelter-roof protecting the temporary horse stalls.

"Sir?" She dragged less air into her lungs than her body was asking for. "What's wrong?"

"Nothing, I hope."

Fat Dog led Sheba out of her stall. The chunky mare was saddled, ready to go. She stood patiently, resigned, in quiet contrast to Gypsy's prancing ways.

Mr. Sloan gathered up her reins, stuffed a foot in a stirrup and swung aboard. "Your nephews back yet?"

Fat Dog shook his head. "Still out there. Burriwi, he say it rains soon, better run fast, all the tracks gone rained away."

"Do we have 'til dark?"

Fat Dog nodded. "But not 'til morning."

Mr. Sloan wrenched the mare's head around and dug his heels into her ribs. She lurched forward at a decidedly uncollected canter, around the end of the shelter and off up the forest trail to the west.

Samantha felt absolutely muddled. "If he's in such a rush, why doesn't he take Gypsy? She's much livelier."

"Gypsy's tired; just been out. Sheba fresh. Besides, missy, Sheba's better forest horse."

"What is going on, pray tell? What's happening?"

"Missy Cook Kathleen, she go walkabout in the wrong place." Fat Dog waved an arm approximately westward. "Back valley there, pools of water, some sea, some other; bad place go to walk."

"Why?"

"Crocodile."

"But she's only been gone an hour or two. What can happen in an hour? Surely Mr. Sloan is acting hastily."

Fat Dog frowned. Apparently *hastily* was not in his vocabulary. "Maybe she comes home quick. So, I go tell Mr. Sloan run say it. But rain tonight, it . . ." He waved a dark hand, seeking to snatch the right word from the air. "Rain it beats away the track. My nephews, they go look, find her track, go to her quick before is rain."

"Mr. Sloan is really worried something might have happened to her?"

"Wrong place she walks. She don' know. Come too far away; she don' know where danger be's. Me, Fat Dog, I worry, too."

Samantha's heart thumped under her breastbone. From what little she knew of the aboriginal mind, worry was not a big part of their outlook on life. If Fat Dog was worried, the danger must be formidable.

Two young aboriginal men appeared instantly out of the forest gloom—invisible one moment and standing there the next. One of them leaned casually against a shelter pole and tucked up one leg as these people were fond to do. The other scooped up one of three canvas packs and started back the trail Mr. Sloan had taken.

Fat Dog handed Samantha a pack and shouldered the third himself. He took two steps, paused to adjust his load, and away he went. No word, no instruction. Apparently Samantha was to follow. Easier said than done. She struggled mightily with a bag of what must be lanterns; metal and glass clanked, and she could smell coal oil. No matter how she carried the pack, no matter how carefully she tried to move, angles and hard edges gouged at her, poked at her, rubbed on her.

Fat Dog was getting farther and farther away. Soon Samantha would be walking alone through this tangle, abandoned by those ahead, too far along to turn back. Linnet was young and sprightly; why didn't she ever get these sorts of chores?

The faint trail followed the creek, more or less, and never seemed to climb up and out of the slurpy, swampy shore, nor did it bother to avoid all the low and reedy puddles. Samantha's feet were soaked, and her black cotton skirt, like a wick, sucked fetid water up as high as her knees. Already she surely looked as muddy and forlorn as had Linnet just minutes ago. Silence closed in on the hot and heavy air. Where was everyone?

Wrenching fear forced Samantha's legs to move faster than they wanted, forced her poor back to ignore the drubbing the pack was giving it. Sweat formed salty beads and rivulets on her face. It soaked her underarms. She thought of the delicious green that made this forest appear so pleasant when viewed from the open, from the beach. The dark green, no longer sun bright, closed in around her ears now and reached toward her on every side, even from below. The long cords and buttresses of strangler figs stretched from the top of the world to the earth like prison bars. Myriad leaves blotted out the soft blue sky of waning day.

Men's voices ahead—how welcome they were! Or were they? She detected a frightening tone in them, a strange and ominous ring. The forest opened up ahead, and Samantha could see that Mr. Sloan was out of the saddle. He stood silent, grim, as Sheba shuffled nervously beside him—most unlike her. Fat Dog and the young man had abandoned their packs. The bags lay where they had been dropped in the mud beside a dark, quiet forest pool.

A charming pool it was, perhaps two acres in size. A vertical wall of jungle hemmed it close around, so that its flat surface could reflect only the fading light from directly overhead. Light green bushes hung out over the water here and there as if shoved beyond the shore by the crouching forest. Over on its far side, a jumble of logs and brush like jackstraws lay half in and half out of the water. Black flies buzzed all around its edge, and near Mr. Sloan a great cloud of them swarmed.

Samantha unceremoniously dropped her burden beside the other two packs. She looked from face to face and approached Mr. Sloan, for it was his tanned face she could read best. What she saw terrified her. He glowered at the pool surface, dark as a winter storm, while Sheba, normally so placid, fretted behind him.

She stepped in close to his elbow. "Sir?"

He gestured toward the ground with his quirt, flicked angrily at the buzzy swarm of flies. Roaring, the chaotic cloud lifted into the air. Beneath it the mudbank was slathered in a broad splash of bright cherry red. A yard farther, where the dank waters lapped at the greasy black mud, lay Kathleen Corcoran's soiled, lace-trimmed cap.

## Chapter Four

# Victor

Gloom. Tight, nerve-jangling, on-edge gloom. Samantha stood numb and listless in the gray morning half-light, on the shore of that morbid dark pool. She watched the rain dash dimples across its face. Mr. Sloan thought the earthly remains of Kathleen Corcoran lay somewhere beneath these black waters. Samantha didn't. She couldn't bring herself to think that. Kathleen was next best to immortal. She herself said so. She had become lost in the mysterious thickness of this forest, that's all. She'd find her way out any time now.

The rain had long since soaked Samantha to the skin. She was too distraught to care. Unlike chill Irish rain, this downpour was more like a warm bath. According to literary symbolism, rain cleanses. Rain pounded upon Samantha so earnestly she need never bathe again. Green symbolizes hope and the renewal of life. She was surrounded by green—bushes, trees, moss, the stinking slime along the shore all abuzz with flies. Life could not have been cut off so viciously, horribly, unfairly. Samantha had no desire to move or speak.

Speak she needn't, but move she must. With the cook missing, cooking chores now fell to her. Back at the house she had prepared the household's breakfast—no big thing, getting up long before dawn; she hadn't slept a bit last night—and now she was the official camp cook here at poolside.

Mr. Sloan was riding Sheba the forest horse again today.

What was a forest horse? Samantha felt too drained to care, let alone ask. The patient old mare came kaplopping up the muddy trail at her rocking-horse canter and drifted to a lackadaisical halt beside the rain fly. Mr. Sloan didn't have to hurry dismounting and ducking in under the canvas. His ride out from the house had soaked him thoroughly. Samantha stepped in under the rain fly beside him and poured him a mug of tea unbidden.

He accepted it absently and stood at the very edge of the shelter, studying the little knots of aborigines standing here and there around the pool. "Anything happen this morning?"

"Nae, sir. That Wurra Somebody thinks one or two may lie among the reeds on the far side there, but he's waiting for the beaters, he says. He apparently kept watch here all night."

"Boats and beaters are on their way." He sipped at his tea. The air was warm and muggy, as it always was here, and yet a curl of visible steam rose from the mug. The steam reminded Samantha of the hard-working dray horses back in Cork—how, on cool days, mist would rise from their sweaty backs. She almost expected such a gentle mist to rise from Mr. Sloan himself. His sopping wet shirt stuck to his skin so tightly she could feel his body warmth radiating.

"Uh, sir? How do ye, uh . . . If there be more than one, how do ye tell which crocodile, uh, performed the dastardly deed? I mean, sir, if indeed the deed's been performed."

"It has. Kill 'em all and slit bellies until we find trace of her."

Samantha's stomach rebelled for the hundredth time. He said it so nonchalantly. And yet he appeared obviously and visibly shaken. Angry. His face and hands, his carriage—all bespoke anger. Not sorrow, not fear, certainly not hope. Anger.

He stiffened as his head snapped around toward the trail. "What the bl—?"

From the dank darkness of the forest stepped, of all people, the Rev. Vinson. His blond hair looked darker in this rain, plastered to his head as it was. With a grim half smile he strode straight to the rain fly and ducked in under the shelter. He nodded to Samantha and extended his hand to Mr. Sloan.

Mr. Sloan declined. "Like a vulture, Vinson. You smell trouble and come soaring in from thirty miles away."

The Reverend shrugged boyishly. "These are state lands back here. Anyone can wander about."

"Rotten weather to be sightseeing, isn't it?"

"Rotten weather, yes. Both sides of the mountains. We get all this rain, and on the far side of the hills the sheep and cattle are wasting in drought. I received a letter this last week from a pastoralist friend near Charter's Towers. Martin Frobel. It'd better rain there soon, he says. His cattle can't take much more. And his brother down by Longreach is even worse off." He stuck his wet hand out into the rain, palm side up. "And we get all this."

"Why are you here?"

"To help, if there's something I can do. Also, I'm assuming Miss Corcoran was Roman Catholic. There's no priest or other cleric in the area to perform extreme unction."

Samantha found herself smiling in spite of her sorrow. "Why, Reverend, 'tis most gracious of ye."

The man looked teen-aged when he smiled, albeit sadly. "I'm not an official cleric of that church, but apparently I'm better than nothing." With a nod to Mr. Sloan he stepped out into the driving rain and wandered down to the shore.

"Extreme what?" Mr. Sloan frowned.

"Last rites for the dead or dying. One of the more important offices of the church. I'm ashamed to say I'd not thought of it 'til he brought it up. Me ties with the church be nae too strong; naething beyond duty, ye might say. I've nae idea what his own church thinks of it. 'Tis a blessed comfort, though, I tell ye, to know there's someone about willing to do such a thing, whether ye belong in one church or another. Very thoughtful of the man."

"Right. Not to mention a fine excuse to come snooping and meddling." Mr. Sloan turned to study her squarely, as if he were looking for an argument.

Samantha dipped her head noncommittally. She knew better than to rise to the bait. Whatever the friction was between these two, it was none of a housemaid's concern. "As ye wish, sir." She turned away.

The water in the big soup kettle looked hot enough now. She flopped a haunch of raw beef down on a makeshift chopping block/stump and began the mindless task of cutting it up. Just this small bit of blood nearly turned her stomach over again. The chilling memories of yesterday came back as vividly as if it were happening all over again. She tried, but soon her hands began to shake so violently she had to put the knife aside.

Larger, steadier hands than hers picked up the knife and balanced the haunch on end. Luke Vinson whacked off a thick slice of meat and started chopping. "How big?"

"That size is good, right there. Ye were once a butcher, aye? Or a cook?"

"Once upon a time, I was a chemist."

"One who dispenses medicines."

"So they're called in England. Over in America, they're called druggists. I wasn't a druggist. I was one who studies chemistry. A laboratory scientist. Also dabbled in physics. I'm certain they're two departments of the same discipline. I looked forward to unraveling the mystery of the molecule, the harmony of the elements, the secret of the sun's heat . . . pure research. But then I got redirected, you might say."

"Into the pastorate."

He nodded and expertly whacked off another chunk. "Born and raised in Canada, educated in the United States. Learned about the risen Christ when I happened onto an evangelistic meeting. A tent meeting." He spread his hands. "And here I am."

"A much more colorful past than simply spending one's life in County Cork. So now instead of unlocking the secrets of the universe, ye're filling in for priests, aye?"

He chuckled mirthlessly. "That's happenstance and a

tragic one. No, I have goals. To right wrongs, to preach the gospel. There's much to be done, and few workers to do it. For example, the plight of the South Sea islanders who—"

Commotion in the forest stole Samantha's attention. Here came Doobie and Mr. Gantry with a small army. Samantha recognized some of the faces, both black and white, as mill workers. On their shoulders they carried boats—a dugout canoe, a little punt, a small dory, a strange flatbottom rowboat Samantha could not even guess at identifying.

Some of these men were not from Sloan's estate at all. Apparently word of Kathleen Corcoran's probable demise had spread through Mossman as well; half the town was here. Like vultures, knots of strangers arranged themselves along the shore and peered absently across the water.

Amena O'Casey, Meg, and Linnet came slipping and sloshing into the camp, as burdened with extraneous parcels as Samantha had been. Samantha cast a quick glance at the minister. He smiled radiantly. Quite obviously, Meg's infatuation was not unrequited.

The smile wasn't lost on Sloan, either. He snarled, "Do your courting on your own time, Vinson. She's working."

Gantry, the mill foreman, came slogging over to the shelter, his craggy face absolutely morbid. He accepted a tin cup of coffee from Samantha without so much as a smile or a nod. "The last thing we need is this."

"Did you close down?" Mr. Sloan held his cup out for a refill.

"Might's well. The few men we got there now can't handle it. Nobody can handle it, Mr. Sloan. We can't salvage a half of what blew down. And that what we're squeezing's poor quality. *Poor* quality. Y'll not get a third of your value out of the whole crop."

"Chestley come up from Sydney yet?"

"Aye. Dipped one hand in the soup and left again. Says he's not interested."

"We'll be done with this by nightfall or I'll know the reason why. When you get back, shut down completely. Get rid of what's left and lay the workers off. Cut our losses right now."

"That's a whole lot of cut cane, Mr. Sloan. Get rid of it where?"

"Dump it in the sea. Dump it in the forest. Get rid of it."

Samantha translated mentally. Get rid of what cane? The cane not yet processed, probably. Also, she felt pretty certain she remembered the name Chestley as being a sugar buyer from Sydney. Surely Mr. Sloan was wealthy enough that the loss of one year's sugar harvest couldn't scuttle him. And surely Chestley wasn't the only sugar wholesaler in the world. And surely the situation couldn't be too serious or Mr. Sloan would appear more bothered by Mr. Gantry's report. Yet, if all these surelys were true, why did she feel such a tension here, such a heavy cloud?

The boats were in the water now, and laden so heavily with beaters, black men and white, that only a few scant inches of freeboard kept them afloat. Bearing drums and poles, the men lined their rickety little boats out along the far shore. They beat the drums, they yelled in singsong, they thumped on the boats' gunwales with sticks, they thrust the poles deep into the water before them.

All the usual little forest noises disappeared in the din, even the constant rustle of rain in the leaves. Samantha walked down closer to the shore, watching faces more than events. The beaters out in the boats showed an exuberance, a heady thrill of the chase. Amid certain danger they were out to catch a croc. The Rev. Vinson watched from shore with a grim sadness to his boyish features.

And Mr. Sloan? The plantation potentate stood close beside her, as grim as the preacher, but there was no sadness about him, none at all. Fury tightened every muscle of his face, as if this ancient reptile had personally affronted him. He had picked up his high-powered rifle, the sort of gun with which a hunter would go off in pursuit of elephants. Samantha had never liked guns; her mind flitted to memories of Edan. She abhorred guns now.

At the far end, men in two boats hollered at once. A loud

shotgun went off, both barrels, and one of the aborigines in the farthest boat stood, raised a spear and drove it straight down.

The quiet pool erupted in a wild spray of water. Thrashing, churning mayhem boiled up and tipped one of the boats over. Men screamed, splashing in white froth. Samantha saw a gaping snout thrust high, saw the huge tail whip the water. More spears sliced home; the froth turned red.

The pandemonium changed from fear to jubilation, though the shouting and hooting were quite as noisy as ever. As the upset boat righted itself and its soggy crew clambered back in, the farthest boat began to move this way, poled by eager hunters.

The aborigines among them laughed and sang. Samantha knew that to the aboriginal mind, "louder" meant "better by far," and this whole boatload seemed in high feather. The rest of the line of beaters paused along the far shore as this boat brought the prize to Mr. Sloan.

Mr. Sloan transferred that hideous rifle to his left hand and gestured toward the butcher block. "Bring the knife."

Samantha grabbed it and followed her master down to the water's edge, as caught up in the chase now as anyone.

Four black men jumped out of the boat into the pool to drag their trophy ashore. Two yards of crocodile emerged from the dark water and still they hauled. Ten feet at least, and now twelve. Here were the limp hind legs—stubby, scaly little things for such an enormous monster. And the tail! When the men paused for breath and stood erect, a foot of the tail still lay in the water, its tip flicking absently. Samantha stood not four feet away from it and she couldn't begin to fathom the horror of the beast.

"Leviathan," murmured Luke Vinson beside her, his voice filled with awe.

"Oh . . ." Meg pressed close to the preacher's arm, her eyes wide.

Mr. Sloan flourished the butcher knife, but Doobie held up a hand. "Wait." He whipped out a carpenter's rule and unfolded it rapidly, expertly. The crowd pressed tighter. Samantha was being squeezed between Mr. Sloan and Mr. Vinson and she didn't care.

Silence reigned while the end of Doobie's rule splashed against the twitching tail. The handyman stared through the water. "Nineteen feet, seven inches." He stepped back.

Samantha closed her eyes. She didn't have to watch to know what Mr. Sloan was doing. Hideous smells boiled up around her face and literally forced her to look.

Mr. Sloan was poking about with the knife blade inside the slashed belly. "Couple small bones, a bird beak. Fish and a goose is all he's had lately." He stood up straight. "Fat Dog, give it to your nephews for their clan."

"Too right, Mr. Sloan!"

And the hunt was on again. The boat took its place in the line. The beaters thumped and drummed and yelled with an enthusiasm worthy of schoolboys on holiday at the beach. Inch by inch the boats moved forward across the tortured pool.

Meg and the men seemed to be drifting off to the left, closer and closer to the action. Samantha felt no desire to be a part of the scene. She had already seen more crocodiles than she cared to, ever again. She wandered off to the right along the shore. She should go back and start the stew, but she certainly wasn't going to use that knife, and there was no other. She ought to start another pot of coffee, but she had no energy to walk back to the shelter.

The horror of all this and her lack of sleep worked in concert to turn Samantha's brain to mush. She should be thinking deep, important thoughts just now and she couldn't apply her mind to anything at all. Poor Kathleen. Jovial, bouncing, hard-working Kathleen. *Young yet; the next best thing to being immortal.* Ah, Kathleen . . .

The beaters were halfway across the pool now and approaching Samantha foot by noisy foot. There was Mr. Sloan, his rifle ready, striding along the mud nearly at the waterline, coming toward her.

The important thoughts finally surfaced in her weary mind. She should have moved off behind the party, not across the pool from it. She had walked in the wrong direction to get away from the action; the action was coming to her. Quite possibly, in the water between the beaters and herself there lurked a large and lethal reptile and here she stood watching the whole hideous hunting party come this way. And how reliable were those howling, trigger-happy hunters? She might well be right in their line of fire.

A twinge of terror cured her weariness instantly. What exactly might a cornered croc be expected to do? The unfocused shapelessness of the peril, her ignorance about it, multiplied her fear. She must get back away from the water. She turned and started hastily up the bank, slipping in the rain-slick slop.

Then the world exploded. As one the beaters screamed and pounded, Mr. Sloan shouted, his rifle roared—the pond burst high behind her, a great crashing wall of water. She dived forward without thinking into the slime and flung her arms over her head. Her face pressed tight into the mud as all the cannon of the Crimea thundered and volleyed.

Many footbeats came pattering toward her, but she dared not move, much less raise her head. Samantha Connolly, Mum's little helper, the chief domestic of Sugarlea's household staff, the woman in sure command of herself at all times, began to weep. She choked on mud and still she couldn't stop her wild and violent sobbing.

"Sam!" Warm and powerful hands gripped her shoulders and pulled her to sitting. "Are you shot? Did I hit you?"

She shook her head; it was the best she could do for the moment. She tried to say "I'm fine, really," but all that came out was a coughing fit. Against her better judgment she raised her eyes. The long, pointed nose and pallid gorge lay at her very feet. If crocodiles have eyelids, this monster wasn't using them; the glassed eye stared unseeing at her shoe.

She forced her eyes higher. Mr. Sloan's face was tight with concern, his dark eyes studying her anxiously. She tried again to ease his mind but only blithering came out. And then in the aftermath of her terror, he utterly surprised her. The master of Sugarlea wrapped his long arms around and gathered her in firmly against him. She was tear-streaked and muddy; her nose was plugged and slurpy from crying; and he didn't seem to mind a bit.

Another heavy sob or two and she began picking up the pieces. She sat erect and drew a deep, shuddering breath. "Thank ye, sir. I'm all right now."

One of the beaters, a black fellow, approached the beast. Mr. Sloan twisted swiftly toward him and snarled, "It's mine!" The man backed away instantly. The strange little vignette struck Samantha almost exactly like a lion laying claim to its kill—or a dog defending a bone.

She struggled to her feet, her legs all tangled in her skirts, and his strong hands steadied her. He left her then, and straddled the carcass. He rolled it to its side, its back toward her. The stubby little foreleg flopped limp. She couldn't see the belly as he ripped it open, and just as well.

He stabbed and poked a moment, then stood erect. "The hunt is over." Almost carelessly he tossed a black handful of something into the mud beside the beast's snout. He dipped his head toward Gantry nearby. "Go find her."

The mill foreman stared scowling at the black lump for a moment and turned away. He walked off toward the boats, shouting orders.

Mr. Sloan handed Samantha the knife. "Wash it off in boiling water first."

"Aye. Of course." She looked at him and didn't feel the least ashamed of the hot tears in her eyes. "I dinnae understand, sir. Kathleen's gone, aye? Ye're certain?"

He turned toward the rain fly, so she walked beside him. He rubbed his face. "Yes, I'm certain."

"The black thing?"

"Her shoe. Guess you didn't recognize it. You see, Sam, a croc's jaws are murderously strong, but its teeth aren't really all that sharp. So it seizes its victim and drags it underwater 'til it drowns. If the prey is small enough to swallow, down it goes. If it's big, the croc will simply hold the body in its mouth until it softens up—decomposes—or stashes it away underwater for a while."

"And returns to it later when 'tis nice and tender." Samantha shuddered. She stepped in under the rain fly and glanced at the chopping block. A curtain of noisy black flies had descended upon the beef haunch. She took a deep breath and met Mr. Sloan eye to eye.

"I wish to thank ye—express me gratitude—for coming to me rescue moments ago. I should never have walked to that part of the shore; 'twas pure foolishness. I would have gone the way of—" her voice stuck a moment— "of Kathleen, had ye not dispatched the beast so promptly and skillfully."

He laughed. He threw his handsome head back and laughed so heartily even Samantha could feel a wee bit of his pleasure, though she hadn't the foggiest notion why. "You were safe that far up the shore, Sam. I didn't save you from as much as you think." He sobered. "Kathleen must have waded out into the pool, probably with her shoes in her hand, much the way I saw you on the beach yesterday. She probably almost escaped its first attack—the blood and hat on the bank."

"So that's why ye forbade us going near the estuary. Linnet and meself. And Fat Dog said . . . I see now." She closed her eyes, but she couldn't close away the constant, hideous buzz of the flies. "I am grateful anyway, Mr. Sloan, for yer concern."

"And you're very, very sorry you came."

She opened her eyes. "Aye, I am that. But as I've already told ye, a Connolly can be trusted. I made the deal and I'll stick it out to the end."

"You're a good woman, Sam." He laid his warm hand on her shoulder and gave it a gentle squeeze and shake. "A good woman."

From the far side by the jackstraws, a man's voice called out. "We found her."

Mr. Sloan strode back out into the rain.

And the good woman sat down beside the buzzing butcherblock and buried her face in her apron and wept.

## CHAPTER FIVE

# ROTTEN CANE

For years now, postal service had been the responsibility of the new federal government, although each state still issued its own postage stamps. Unfortunately, no higher level of competence prevailed despite the change of leadership. Luke Vinson didn't trust the postal service any further than he could finance it. He sent Martin Frobel a letter. He also sent a telegram. And at the last moment, almost certain something would go awry, he went himself.

An hour west of Townsville, Luke perched on top of a load of fetid green sugar cane as the sun beat on his head, and watched the flies work the sticky sap. He had abandoned chemistry and physics but they had not abandoned him. *In spite of myself,* he thought, *I can never help pondering a sticky, excuse the pun, problem in physics.*

This was an open slat-side railroad car and the train's velocity had to be close to thirty miles an hour. And yet, unless a fly flew above the top rail where the wind caught it and whipped it away, that insect, unattached to any surface, could zig and zag, hover or cruise, as if the train were standing still. There was a defined physical principle involved here, and Luke was certain that at one time he could have quoted it, but he could not for the life of him remember it. And while he racked his memory, the flies nonchalantly ignored the fact they were hurtling west at breakneck speed.

The fellow named Josip popped up like a jack-in-the-box

from the back end of the train. He had worked his way forward, hopping from car to car, staggering drunkenly across the shifting loads until he could join Luke here.

Josip settled cross-legged on the pile and grinned. "Goot ting dis cane going in stakesides. Stink to high hebben. Inside closed boxcar, build up, and *poom*."

"*Poom!*" Luke chuckled. "The dreaded cry of the chemistry lab. I'm contemplating flies and physics, but you've offered me a more pressing question: why don't you fall off the train? This cane is treacherous footing indeed."

"Fall off! Not yet. Tricky going is when you haf the open car of cows. Walk on cows' backs, den it gets snakey. I don' unnerstand why preacher-man rides on stinking cane. Come back to dem caboose. Haf a little drink, relax, don' stink, eh?"

Luke grinned and spread his hands. "But I'm having a wonderful time up here. Blue sky, wide open spaces, wind in my face—"

"Also all dis smoke and soot. You don' ride train much maybe, tinks is great, eh?"

"I rode the train constantly in Canada. That's the way to get around there, especially in winter."

"Snow. Snow, eh? Lahssa snow in winter there, right?"

"More snow than any man deserves."

"Been long time I don' see snow. Since old country. Miss it, sometimes."

"No, not I. Look at me. It's late April, we're coming on winter here, and I don't have a coat on. I don't even own a winter coat anymore, Josip, and it's glorious! No shoveling snow, no bundling up. No calculating the coefficient of friction of glare ice when all you want to do is get across the street. This is *my* kind of winter."

"So you shovel cane. I seen you. And sit on stinking bundle. You hopeless." Josip rearranged his seat in vain pursuit of comfort. "Where your friend? West a piece?"

"About a hundred miles out from Charter's Towers, give or take some. Quite a cattle station he has, he and his brother. Both of them dinkum Aussie."

*Native Aussies, good colonial boys.* The distinction was still being made, but not as much anymore. A generation ago most of Australia's population, barring aborigines, had been born under distant fealties. Today most Australians knew no other flag. History. And lack of it. It intrigued Luke. When the Hudson's Bay Company was turning Luke's native land from a wilderness into a civilization, this country had not yet begun.

Gentle slopes and open woodland gave way to prairie and broken patches of gray-green acacia. Six at night, dinner-time, they pulled into Frobel's siding. Possibly someday it would be a town—Frobelsville, or Frobel's Corner. Martin's Landing, perhaps. Right now it was a siding.

Beside the stock tank, Martin Frobel himself sat astride his horse and watched the modest engine huff to a stop. He urged his old mare forward to meet Luke halfway.

Luke hopped off the car and crossed to him. He offered a hand and received a warm, friendly shake. "Which got here first, the letter or the telegram?"

Martin looked a bit blank. "Didn't know you were coming. Just rode out here in case there was any mail. You're welcome, though. More'n welcome. Hope you can stay awhile." He nodded toward the train. "What's all that?"

"Cattle feed. The letter will make things clear—if it ever arrives."

Martin studied him a moment and rode over to a car. He stood in the stirrups, sniffed and touched. "Some larrikin's got himself a lucky streak longer'n my line of credit."

Josip yelled, "I get to do dis alone, eh?"

"Coming." Luke would let Martin figure things out unaided. He could barely stand not staring at the old stockman's face.

The weight of this wet green cane bulged the gates out and made pulling the pins more than a little difficult. *Talk about your basic coefficient of friction!* Luke thought. He was sweating profusely by the time they sprang the gate open on the first car. He and Josip let tumble out what would and pushed the rest out with coal shovels. One car unloaded, four to go, and it had taken fifteen minutes. They'd be here all night, and Luke was starved.

Josip must have been reading his mind. They took a breather before tackling car number two, and the railroader leaned on his shovel, grinning. "Look the goot side. You do dis on a railroad in New South Wales, eh? Different gauge. Irish gauge. Dese tracks tree feet six, but New South Wales, the tracks five feet tree. Trains twice as wide, hold twice as much. Take twice as long. We're lucky, eh?"

"Aren't we. On to the next."

The engineer stepped down from his cab, in no hurry at all. The engineer does not, as part of his job, load or unload. "Marty. You got two letters and a telegram here. One from the Townsville Bank and one from some fellow named Vinson. And a package from your sister in Brisbane. Gotta sign that you got the package."

"It's the letter from that drongo Vinson that I wanna see."

Luke cast an occasional glance toward the stockman and almost lost his thumb when the second gate gave way while he wasn't paying attention. He watched Martin read his letter. He saw Martin wipe his eyes, but squatters are tough old cockies who would never in a million years admit to being misty-eyed. And then Martin, strong as new hemp, was in there helping with the unloading, and it all went much quicker.

The train departed and Luke had no idea where Josip was going to eat his dinner; he knew only it would be late, for the sun cowered close to the flat line, ready for the plunge. It was nearly seven by now.

Martin beamed like the noonday sun upon his long, long pile of cattle feed. "Still don't quite understand where it come from."

"I overheard a sugar grower tell his mill foreman to dump it. It's apparently not good quality. I got the mill foreman aside and offered to take it off his hands, all of it. Knew you could use it. And the foreman was grateful. Didn't have to bother with it."

Martin grunted. He pulled a rifle from his scabbard. "You take the horse home, Luke. Send Jack to me with the hay wagons. All of 'em. Tell Grace I said she's to feed you a seven-course dinner by candlelight. Tell her I'm gonna count the courses when I get back and it better be the full load and it better be extra grouse or there'll be he—" He cleared his throat. "Sorry. Keep forgetting you're a revrin now."

"You ride and I'll walk, Marty. We'll dine together."

Martin grinned suddenly. "I ain't leaving this pile of gold. It's dusk. The kangaroos'll be abroad now, and they'll find this stuff in no time flat. But ain't no 'roo in Queensland gonna get a taste of it. Go on now."

Luke climbed on the mare. He didn't even have to turn her head. She started off home with a relieved sigh. When he looked back over his shoulder, Martin was standing on top of the highest stack of cane looking for all the world like the bronze statue on a military monument, his rifle cradled in the crook of his arm. And he was smiling the smile of a hopeful man.

*Not a bad place, Sloan, considering. Not a bad place at all. Assuming you can just hang on to it. And you do have to agree, the European women on the house staff make it a lot homier. You got clean socks when you want them, the place stays cleaner and the food's better. Sloan's harem. There are worse things to have, Cole, boy.*

He simply sat on Gypsy awhile and let her squirrel around in place as he admired his major possession. From down here at the bend, with the house just barely in view up ahead, it looked majestic, almost a manor. Soon as he got a little further out of the hole, he'd fix the place up. Add to it. Patch the roof better where the pandanus blew down, maybe even replace the treadle organ. He didn't play—didn't know anyone who did—but it looked good sitting in the parlor there.

He could just barely see Linnet out in the side yard hanging bed sheets on the line. Cute little number, but a bit young for his taste. She seemed fragile—a delicate orchid you almost didn't dare touch. On the other hand, youth is its own excuse for being desirable.

Margaret came up the side path with a basket of mangoes on her arm and continued around back, no doubt to the kitchen door. She couldn't have been down visiting the minister again; Vinson was out of town. How should he handle this? Just let her go awhile and see if the infatuation faded? If he forbade her to get near that wowzer, she might set her hackles and slip around all the more. The Irish were noted for their temper and stubbornness and with her reddish hair she looked as Irish as a shamrock.

The postman had gone rattling up the lane in his pony cart just ahead of Cole. He reached the front door, then climbed down and knocked. Strange. Until recently he simply blew his horn and expected someone to come to him. New postal regulations? Sam answered the door, smiling. They swapped goodies, the mail for a slab of bread and jam. No, not new postal regulations. Greed. The woman did bake good bread.

The old galah climbed awkwardly into his cart, holding his bread high, and went his way. Sam leafed briefly through the mail, her willowy body draped against the doorjamb. Surely she must have a past. She was too good-looking to have escaped every suitor's clutches over the years. What kind of man warmed up this cool, efficient housemaid with the razor-sharp mind and overworked sense of honor? She lurched erect and walked inside, closing the door behind her.

Cole eased up on the reins, and Gypsy needed no urging. She pressed forward, homeward. He paused again halfway up the lane. The house definitely needed something along this south wall. It looked flat, blank, unattractive. Plain. That's it. Plain was for people who couldn't afford fancy or didn't care.

Bushes. He'd plant some sort of ornamental bushes there. Something imported.

Sloan dismounted near the corner of the house and swatted Gypsy on the rump. She cantered off up the hill toward the stable. He stepped from bright sun into cool gloom and had to wait in the foyer a minute until his eyes adjusted. The house even smelled homier. The aroma was bread fresh from the oven, and the postman had beaten him to it.

He stuck his head in the kitchen door. "Bring me a pot of tea and a slab of that bread."

"G'day, sir. Jam or marmalade?" She was whacking apart a large orangish fish at the kitchen table. The fish was dinner, probably. And probably in mornay sauce.

"Better bring 'em both; it's too important a decision to make casually."

She grinned, bright as the coral sea. Did she have a crush on him? She seemed to perk up when he was around, but then, he didn't know how perky she was when he wasn't around. And she kept up this facade, this mien of servanthood. Hard to tell, not that it made much difference to him. The girls he hired often did. Kathleen had been the boldest in letting him know.

Sloan's harem.

Sam had left Sloan's mail in a neat stack on his desk. It waited for him, simply smacking of efficiency and businesslike procedure. He had seen her dossier with her employment history, but he couldn't remember that she had ever performed office and clerical duties. Too bad. She'd be a natural.

He popped the top straps on his boots, swung his feet up on the desk and scooped the orderly stack into a haphazard pile in his lap. The Brisbane bank. *Now,* what did they want? A note from Chestley, the Sydney buyer. Probably bunging on an act about how bad things were and why Cole shouldn't expect him to pay full price for raw crystal this season.

His mind froze in mid-thought. A plain envelope, the same as that other one. Postmarked Townsville. Addressed to the son of Conal. He should throw this rubbish away without even thinking about it. But even as his mind resisted, his hands ripped the envelope open.

THUS SAITH THE LORD!
JEREMIAH 32:18!

THOU RECOMPENSEST THE INIQUITY OF THE FATHERS INTO THE BOSOM OF THEIR CHILDREN AFTER THEM. VENGEANCE IS MINE, SAITH THE LORD

"Sir? Be ye ill?" Sam hovered over him like an anxious hen counting chicks.

He looked at her eyes, glowing gray-green eyes like her sisters'. Gorgeous eyes. "Yeah, you might say so." He flipped the note onto the desk in front of her. "Here's why I don't want your sister anywhere near that preacher in the chapel."

She picked it up and studied it a moment. "I cannae believe the Rev. Vinson would send this."

"Posted in Townsville two days ago."

"Have ye any notion what it means? Your father?"

"I had some labor problems a couple years ago, and my father did also, back when he was getting Sugarlea started. Our Bible basher there fancies himself the champion of the downtrodden."

"Meg tells me 'tis a favorite theme of his. Something about white laborers resenting colored laborers and causing them grief. She says here in Queensland, according to the Reverend, was the worst of it, with the plantations bringing in men from abroad."

"Favorite theme of his. Right." He shrugged. "That's about all I can come up with."

"Pity. Likeable chap, that."

On to more pleasant things. "Jam or marmalade? Marmalade or jam? Fix me one of each."

She smiled suddenly, and Jeremiah or God or whoever that was faded to nothing. "You'll never forge an empire, sir, if ye keep vacillating so."

"On the other hand, by not choosing between, I get both. Cut yourself one, and sit a minute."

"As ye wish, sir, and thank ye." She carved off a modest slice and slathered it in the marmalade. She settled into the wingback chair. She looked tired, drawn, weighed down upon.

"What kind of bushes shall I plant along the south side there? It looks plain."

"Were we back in Erin, sir, meself'd be quick to recommend box or privet. Neat habit of growth and stately texture. But I've nae the slightest inkling for here."

*Neat and stately.* Sam. Of course. Neat and stately. He should be pursuing her romantically right now. She appealed to him more than he would have thought, and he wasn't sure why he didn't, except that he thought he knew how she'd take it. And he hated being refused. He didn't mind claiming what he considered his in most situations, but there are some situations where simply seizing the moment doesn't work.

"Sir? Be ye sure that note was sent by our Reverend?"

Now, why did she have to go and change the subject? "Who else?"

"And 'tis the first such?"

"Second. First arrived two weeks after he got here. Less. Caught up on local history quickly; or else he did his homework in advance and came with the intent of causing trouble. Now that I think about it, I don't want you mentioning these notes to Meg. To anybody. See if he mentions them first. Understand?"

"Whatever ye say, sir." She stood up, refilled his cup and left. The room suddenly became empty.

He went back to the rest of the mail, to Chestley's fatuous note and the banker's letter from Brisbane. Buyers and bankers. There could not possibly be a God in heaven; he was certain of it. No halfway decent God would let this mob of silvertails twelve hundred miles away control the fortunes and destiny of Cole Sloan's Sugarlea.

# CHAPTER SIX

# RUIN

"Sam?" The door opened a bit. Meg's tousled red head peeked in. "Ye be up yet, aye?"

"Aye. Writing to Mum. Come in." Samantha laid her pen aside.

Meg closed the door behind her. "Ye nae be mentioning that croc, I hope."

"No. Of course not. The tea's gone, sorry. And how do ye like yer new job?"

Meg flung herself casually across Samantha's bed. "Eh, being housemaid's much better than what I was doing down at the mill, but of course there be not near so many men up here."

"No matter, when ye have the Vinson lad at your beck and call."

She giggled. "And yerself the Sloan lad, no less."

"Hardly."

"Meself has eyes." Meg flipped around onto her stomach and elbows to face Samantha squarely. "That's why I've come, Sam. For a favor. Ye're in good with Mr. Sloan, more so than I . . ."

"Only because he doesn't know ye as well yet."

"More'n that, I aver. And I wish ye to sound him out about selling back me indenture. See what he says sort of, aye?"

"Ye promised a promise, Meg. I'll not be a party to ye breaking yer word. Nae."

"I said naething atall about breaking me word. I'll pay him off, every penny. Ye know that. Just ask. Please?"

"And where might ye find this money? Luke Vinson doesn't make enough to buy a cat out of hock."

"Just ask, aye? There's a good girl!"

"Perhaps, on the morrow or sometime when the mood seems right."

"He's still up now, ye know. Ye could ask him now."

"Ye're in a blooming hurry."

Meg popped to her feet. " 'Tis important, Sam, please? G'night." She blew Samantha a kiss and bounced out the door.

Samantha sighed as she wiped off her pen nib. Why? Why did she not simply say a firm no when Meg or someone came up with something like this? Mr. Sloan told her to spy on the hired help and now the hired help was seeking her collusion. She hated this sort of intrigue. So why was she standing up and taking off her apron? Besides . . .

Why should Meg think that she had a stronger "in" with the master of the house? Why didn't Meg ask Linnet? She and Linnet were much closer companions. Because Mr. Sloan was not particularly well pleased with Linnet's frequent failure to get all her chores done in a day, that was why.

And was Mr. Sloan satisfied with Sam's work? Seemed so. That pleased her in a warm, funny little way. She always took pride in her work, always did the best she could, but this was somehow different. She enjoyed immensely pleasing Mr. Sloan.

She walked slowly down the dark stuffy hall, listening. Mr. Sloan had more or less tacked his office onto his house. The L-shaped house, almost a bungalow, sprawled out ever so casually, with lots of windows and airy light. The kitchen and servants' rooms comprised the back leg of the L and the house proper—parlor, dining room, Mr. Sloan's private rooms—formed the front leg. Making the L into a lop-sided U, the office stuck itself to the back of the far end.

The only light in the dark corridors was the yellow line

below his office door. Dare she? She got within two steps of the door before she came to her senses. Of course she dare not! Let Margaret sound out her employer herself. Samantha was neither above nor below Meg and certainly not her sister's keeper. Meg had indentured herself—Samantha had nothing to do with that—and now Meg could handle her own affairs. What could she have been thinking of?

Someone was knocking on the door out front. Samantha frowned. She seemed to be the only servant out and about; funny how the new housemaid disappeared so conveniently. She hurried back the hall and out through the parlor to answer it.

The man was no more than a black shadow under the porch roof. Samantha could not make out his features. "John Butts to see Mr. Sloan, please."

"Come in." Samantha led the shadow through the foyer into the parlor. "I'll see if he's receiving guests, sir." She curtseyed and walked smartly back to the office door. She should have provided Mr. Butts with a light; why did she not at least light the little electric lamp by the window?

She rapped at the door and pushed it open cautiously.

Mr. Sloan sat in his big chair with arms and legs draped at casual angles to each other. His sprawl reminded Samantha of Papa back home and her heart pinched just a bit. Papers alone and in stacks cluttered the floor in a broad circle around him.

"Mr. Sloan, sir, John Butts to see ye."

"Bring him through and serve us tea."

"Aye, sir." As she turned away, from the corner of her eye she saw him leaning down to tidy up his papers. When she returned with Mr. Butts, though, he had ordered only a little of the worst of the mess.

He stood up and offered his hand. "John, been a long time."

She left them. The coals were still warm, the water still hot. She didn't need long to bring the kettle up to boiling. She had served the Fortnum and Mason black pekoe, Mr.

Sloan's favorite, at dinner. Tonight she'd prepare a pot of the Murchie's Queen Victoria blend. Perhaps there would be some left after Mr. Butts departed, and Queen Victoria was her own favorite.

When she entered the office with her tray, John Butts had made himself at home. The leather-covered chair had been pushed back into a corner and the visitor slouched in the brocade wingback chair immediately in front of Mr. Sloan's desk. Mr. Sloan now sat erect in almost prim repose, his elbows on the chair's arms, his fingertips forming a peaked cage.

Mr. Butts tugged at his tie, loosening it until its knot lay beside his second shirt button. "Frankly, Cole, I'm at wits' end. This last storm ripped the roof off my storage shed and soaked over a thousand pounds of tea. Good tea, ready for market. Spoiled now. With that ergot or blight or whatever it was, I didn't show a profit last year and I'll not again this year. And the new lot I planted won't be ready for at least another eighteen months. The bank learned somehow about the ruined tea and refuses to advance me any more until I service my outstanding loans." He raised his hands helplessly. "It's all gone against me."

Samantha set out the cups and saucers.

"Pity." Mr. Sloan's eyes followed her, probably without seeing her. "Can't you dry out that lot and dump it in America?"

"Not since they passed their good-tea law back in ninety-seven. Very picky about the tea they import now. You can't sell just anything to them anymore."

Mr. Sloan sighed. "I was really behind you, John. If this area is going to thrive and prosper, we need a rich variety of produce. Not just bananas, or my cane or your tea or whatever, but a wide range of enterprises. We all need each other if any is to do well from year to year. Broad labor pool, all that."

"I agree. Diversification. That's why I feel I've let you down—that I've let us all down, for that matter."

"Hardly, John. You did your best. A few bad breaks." Mr. Sloan shrugged and watched his teacup fill. "Miss Connolly, bring us some of that fruit bread you served for dessert at dinner."

She left as Mr. Butts continued his tale of woe. When she returned with the coffee cake and two dessert services, the man seemed considerably more relaxed.

Sloan watched her hands as she sliced off generous slabs.

"I should have waited until morning, but I—well, I guess I'm just too distraught. I finished my books tonight and simply had to go out and commiserate with someone. Ah, but you—" Mr. Butts waved a hand. "It doesn't look like the storm did you much hurt. Sugarlea appears to be rolling right along."

"We've been fortunate in many ways—save for the tragic loss of my cook a few days ago."

"My foreman told me. Dreadful." Mr. Butts took his first bite of the coffee cake.

"And yet even that black cloud has a silver lining. Miss Connolly here took over the cooking and is doing splendidly, as you just now learned. Delicious fruit bread, is it not?"

"Mmbph. Crrtphly ifsh." The man nodded vigorously and smiled at Samantha.

She refilled teacups and tried to hide her own delight behind a stoic servant attitude. He was praising her before strangers and almost sounded like he meant it!

Mr. Sloan sat forward and the look on his face startled Samantha. It reminded her of his appearance when he stood on the shore of that listless pond, determined to destroy a crocodile. He wasn't grim now, or angry—and yet, the look was there.

"Have another piece of the fruit bread, John. It's been a long day. Miss Connolly, we'll probably use another pot of tea. How about the Fortnum and Mason black pekoe this time round?"

The corners of her mouth tipped up a bit in spite of herself. "Certainly, sir."

Mr. Butts could speak again. "There, you see? You must import the tea you use because I can't provide it for you—you and the rest of Australia. And yet the clim . . ."

She left the flowered china pot of Queen Victoria on the tea table and returned a few minutes later with the speckled blue pot.

" . . . keep you going awhile. So what do you think?" Mr. Sloan sat back and extended his cup for Samantha to fill.

"Cole, this is exceedingly generous of you." Mr. Butts was studying a hand-written sheet of heavy paper.

As she topped off Mr. Butts's cup her eyes dropped almost involuntarily to the paper. The script was Mr. Sloan's hand, very largely written, no doubt to be read quickly and easily by an older man without his spectacles. The sheet mentioned the amount of a loan—a very large loan—and in a few telling words and phrases, none of them a coherent sentence, listed terms of repayment should the tea crop fail again. And if she interpreted the hieroglyphics rightly, it blatantly transferred ownership of the land to Mr. Sloan.

She feigned disinterest and cut two more slices of coffee cake. She could hardly wait to hear how Mr. Butts would tell her employer where to discard this ridiculous offer.

Mr. Sloan spoke first. "There are limits to my generosity; the title transfer there would be insurance for me. I'm happy to advance you the loan. Your tea plantation is nearly as important to me as it is to you, as we were just discussing. But should you ultimately go under, heaven forbid, I need some means to recoup at least part of my money. Once your land reverted to the bank I'd be left out completely. You understand."

"Absolutely. You're quite wise to ask for title assurances. Were I to go bankrupt, my land would be tied up who knows how long. And you'd have to share the debt burden with the bank and my other creditors. You'd be lucky to come away with a few stray shillings on the pound. No, I agree. I want you covered."

"But you're not going bankrupt. I have every confidence

that your run of bad luck will end soon, if it hasn't already." Mr. Sloan extended his hand. "John, this is the beginning of your success; I feel it."

Mr. Butts positively glowed. He reached over, shook hands warmly with Mr. Sloan, and returned to his second piece of coffee cake. He waved his fork. "My accountant is going to howl, you know. He'll say I'm giving away the farm."

"Does he realize how close to insolvency you are?"

"Oh, yes. He advises selling out while I can." Mr. Butts snorted. "And why shouldn't he? It's not his blood, sweat and tears that went into it. Draws his pay and goes home. If I were to sell out, he'd simply hire on with the next bloke. I'm foolish to struggle, I suppose, but my tea plantation means so much more to me than simply a business enterprise."

"I understand what you're saying. I didn't build up this cane patch and mill because I like a little sugar in my tea."

Mr. Butts laughed, and the fear and worry had fled his face. His shoulders were squared again, his head high. He was not the same man who had stood in the shadows under the porch a half hour before.

After fifteen minutes more of happy small talk he left. Samantha saw him to the door and returned to the office, then started gathering up the dishes.

"Sit down, Sam. You look tired."

She obeyed and within moments, found herself relaxing, melting back into a chair still warm from Mr. Butts's presence.

Mr. Sloan was studying her with a wry, bemused look on his face. "Butts didn't notice you, but I did. You gave more than passing interest to that little offer I made him. So tell me: what do you think of it?"

"None of me affair, sir."

"I know, I know. You've a quick mind, Sam; you're capable. More than capable. Just for curiosity, I'd like to know what you think. So forget indentures and master-servant and such for a moment here. Tell me what you see."

Should she be a quiet, perfect little know-nothing servant, or should she answer truly, since he asked? One of the reasons she could never keep a position long was her honest mouth. It opened now almost against her wishes. "If the final agreement includes the terms on that draft, I cannae believe he'd sign it. In essence it hands his whole property over to ye."

"Have some tea and pour me another. You put Queen Victoria in the flowered pot and Fortnum in the blue one, correct?"

"You've a good sense of taste."

"And Butts has none. There are a few things a tea grower must have, and a delicate sense of taste is one of them, because the people who purchase tea can taste good from bad. The climate here in Queensland is too warm to grow really tasty tea. You need high elevations with cool weather for that. He complained about not supplying Australia. If his plantation produced a million pounds, I'd still buy my tea out of England and Canada because I can taste the difference."

"Ye think tea cannae be grown commercially here."

"On the contrary, it can. Most people don't care about the subtle nuances of flavor, provided the tea is inexpensive."

"Which tea grown locally would be. Nae transport." Samantha nibbled at the coffee cake, but her heart wasn't in it. She must work to keep her tongue in check.

"Spill it."

"What?"

"Whatever's bothering you." Mr. Sloan polished off his third slice of cake.

"Methinks ye're taking unfair advantage of Mr. Butts in his extremity and it bothers me immensely."

"You, ah, failed to mention your school in your letter of introduction. University?"

"I've had nae schooling of that sort, sir."

"Butts has. You've been in charge of a large business operation, I trust."

"Nae, sir. Supervised two dozen other girls at a woolen mill once, but then it closed."

"Butts's tea plantation is an ambitious undertaking—

more complex than a woolen mill."

"Oh, meself wasn't in charge of the whole mill, sir. I—"

"Right," he interrupted. "Just a small part of it. Do you see my point?"

"Nae, sir."

"Butts has chosen to play the game with the big boys, so to speak. Major investment in a large operation. No one forced him into tea growing. It started as a lark for him. And he's well educated. Now, here's a simple Irish servant girl without that education or ambition, and she sees right through my offer."

"In short, I was wrong to speak out just now, let alone peek at that paper."

"Not at all. Your indignation amuses me. In fact, I admire your principles. Now consider, Sam. I did nothing illegal or underhanded. I laid my offer right out front there, for him to take it or leave it. Apparently he's choosing to take it. If an untrained servant can make a wise decision about it, shouldn't I expect a trained businessman to know what he's doing?"

"If he takes yer offer, ye'll be the rich robbing from the poor. A sad twist to the Robin Hood legend."

"Not quite." He waved an arm over the melange of papers. "He says Sugarlea wasn't hurt. Another wrong guess. What I'm telling you is for your ears only. We're closer to insolvency than he is. That lost sugar crop will put me under unless I play my hand very carefully."

Samantha studied those dark, dark eyes for the longest moment. Somehow the master-servant division had blurred in these last few minutes. In Ireland she would never in her wildest imaginings expect to sit across from the master of the house and talk about business as if she were an equal. Was this strange, tenuous equality something unique to Australia or simply an anomaly of this particular household and the late hour?

She poured the last of the Queen Victoria into her cup and didn't care that it was cold by now. She stirred in a dollop of sugar and sat back, still thinking. "It seems to me, sir, if I read that rough proposal correctly, that your notion of diversification and Mr. Butts's be not atall the same."

"Explain."

"Ye both agree a variety of crops and enterprises be beneficial to the local economy. Mr. Butts has in mind a variety of entrepreneurs. Yerself, methinks, has in mind all the crops under one ownership. Your own. Sugarlea, raising more than just sugar."

His eyes danced; their corners crinkled up. Was he bemused again, as he had mentioned once before, or was he simply playing her along, a cat with a mouse? "Explain further, Sam. Why variety?"

"That I needn't think about. Should a single crop fail, the whole plantation's gang aglee. But 'tis nae likely that several crops would all fail together in a given year; 'tis the good crops carry ye over, so to speak."

"Very good."

"I should think, too, that a diversified district would be less likely to suffer doldrums, and would therefore attract ambitious people and thrive further; prosperity begetting prosperity, if ye will. I should think it well behooves ye as a businessman to attract our brightest and best."

And she froze. *Brightest and best.* When had she used those very words? When Edan's shrouded body lay outside their door cooling off. Not that many months ago. Here she sat talking about attracting the brightest and best of Australia even as her Ireland, her beloved Ireland, was slaying them. She shuddered.

"Sam?" His sharp voice sounded worried. "You all right?"

"I'm sorry; me thoughts strayed. The late hour, no doubt."

"I doubt it. You're thinking very clearly. I'm impressed. And you're right on all counts. Butts's tea plantation is a boon to the whole district. *But*—John Butts is making a muddle of it. He's not a tea grower. Poor businessman, doesn't know the tea trade. Do I sit back and let his farm go under, to the detriment of the whole area, or do I step in and save it? Make it pay off, to the benefit of the whole region?"

"Sir? Why be ye addressing all this to me? Why confide our financial state? Why encourage me opinion? Why any of this?"

He studied her a moment and rubbed his chin. "I'm not sure. You're a good servant, probably the best I've ever had, and I—"

"Kathleen Corcoran was the best ye've ever had, I daresay."

He nodded. "True. Until she went wading. And I think I see in you far more than a mere indenture. You're good. Very good. Even better, you know your place. You'll not betray confidences. I can trust you."

"Sir, ye've asked me, in essence, to spy on the likes of Amena O'Casey and me own sister. If ye really trust me, please dinnae ask me to betray the chance confidences of others."

"Carrying tales is part of the job, my dear. From the servants to me, that is; but not what I tell you in confidence."

"I was afraid of that. But how can the girls' romances and such be your concern?"

"I just said Butts is no businessman. He thinks more money will save him. If he can just buy his way out of this hole, he won't fall into that hole. No. Competent people—a good staff—are what keep you going. If I'm to save Sugarlea, I must expand her productivity beyond just sugar. Broaden her base. And for that I need workers, even more than I need money."

"I see. So when ye bring in a working girl, sure'n ye don't want her marrying and running off right away." Samantha drained her teacup. *No, fair Meg, ye need not bother asking; he'll not buy back yer indenture no matter what the price.*

"Precisely. When I hire, I've bought a proprietary interest in the hiree. He—or she—is mine, and I won't have what's mine ripped out of my hands."

Samantha stared at him and couldn't stop. "The crocodile. Ye were so visibly angry. Ye seethed fury. But 'twasn't because a poor woman be lost. The brute took something ye considered yer own. It bruised yer pride. 'Tis its effrontery that galled ye, and nae its ghastly deed."

"That bloody croc deprived me of a good worker."

Samantha set her cup on the tray. "I see, Mr. Sloan. I see a great deal." She gathered in dishes and crumbs and napkins quickly. "Our conversation tonight will go nae further than this room so far as I'm concerned. But I shall mourn poor Mr. Butts, for I can see what's coming."

"I expect that of you."

She stood erect with her tray. "And I mourn yerself, Mr. Sloan. This be surely not the last time ye'll grasp a questionable business opportunity, nor probably is Kathleen Corcoran the last good possession ye'll lose. I see more anger in yer future and more hard-heartedness. But nowhere in yer future do I see any happiness coming from all this." She dipped her head, because carrying a loaded tray makes a curtsey next to impossible. "G'night, Mr. Sloan."

CHAPTER SEVEN

# UNANSWERED QUESTIONS

Samantha plopped a dollop of sugar into her tea and crossed the kitchen to the woodbox. Luncheon was completed and dinner was not yet close enough to demand her energies. She sat down carefully on the blanket folded across the stove wood, lest the wood beneath shift and send her sprawling, and stretched her legs out full length. Her feet were tired. Her legs were tired. Her arms were tired. Her shoulders were tired. Her brain was very, very weary.

The walking. So much walking. She thought about Ireland, dear old Ireland, so far away. By contrast, Erin was such a small country, and pinched together. Houses were tight, compact, stacked story on story. Town house shouldered against town house, and shops waited close at hand. Here the house sprawled casually out across its acres (it seemed) of floor space, and kept itself hundreds of feet aloof from its own outbuildings. The nearest neighbor lay at least half a mile distant.

But it was more than the walking. Domestic work back in Cork drained her at times. And certainly Mr. Sloan maintained the accouterments of civilization as best he could. Yet somehow work here was infinitely more taxing. There was a pervasive wildness to the land, and that wildness had to be dealt with constantly.

For one thing, Samantha was becoming a crackerjack wood-splitter, for the aboriginal lad assigned the job was more often than not nowhere around. Splitting this hardwood took skill and muscle. Samantha was developing the skill, but the work part wore her out. So did keeping this dense wood burning. No glowing peat fire, no gentle coal heat.

She was getting pretty good at cutting up dead animals, too, for there were no butcher shops at all. She could dress out a sheep in no time flat now, right down to sawing through the bones. She had even served cassowary once, for that had been the only meat available. Just once. A tougher and less palatable bird she had never tasted.

But it was more than that. Strange noises and alien calls put her on edge day and night. The rain forest brought unrecognized jungle creatures to her very doorstep. The forest crept in close, always closer, always trying to reclaim its lost ground, challenging axe and machete and cane knife.

*That's it!* she thought. *Much of this constant weariness is surely nothing more than unfamiliarity with this new land. When I become better attuned to the forest and the sea, I will undoubtedly feel more relaxed and less wary, as Mr. Sloan and Doobie and the others have become.* She left her teacup at the sink on her way out.

She walked up the path toward the stable. It had been trimmed and cleared just recently—chopped leaves and branches still littered the ground—but already the forest was reaching out with new growth to close the wound. She passed Fat Dog and the horses all dozing in the midday heat, and continued back the trail along the creek.

The dark green and the boggy ground and the tall bars of the strangler figs were as she had remembered them. Her shoes got soaked, and they squished where the path was marshy.

She arrived eventually at that infamous pool. Did antediluvian monsters still lurk in the flat dark water, posing a threat to life and limb? Perhaps the beaters and the hunters had not killed them all.

Silence. Peace. Samantha tried to picture Kathleen walking along this shore, disturbing the buzzy flies. *With her mob cap a bright white spot in a dark world, she takes shoes in hand and wades out into the water—tepid water, so inviting. Suddenly, from out of nowhere . . .* Mr. Sloan said Kathleen struggled. *Screaming, flailing, she tries to return to shore. She almost makes it! But inexorably she is drawn back, back and down, beneath the dark water. The beast stuffs her limp body into its lair somewhere in that jackstraw pile of logs and swims away.*

No! Samantha could not imagine such a thing. Her mind would not even consider it. This place was too serene for such a horrid event to happen.

An overwhelming sense of loss engulfed her. Edan. Kathleen. Even her Ireland, her lovely, familiar land, was lost to her, for she had no means to return, even if she could. The brooding rain forest—hot, muggy, close, confining; in short, everything Erin was not—pressed in upon her heart. It was gone, it was all so hideously gone.

On the crook of a branch overhanging the water, a brilliant blue bird with a long beak perched. Suddenly it darted out over the pool, dipped against the surface and soared up to a distant perch, a silver fish flapping in its bill. Slow, lazy circles moved out from where the bird had touched serenity and left its mark. The circles faded to nothing; serenity prevailed.

"Kingfisher. It's a relative of kookaburras."

She shot straight up and wheeled. Cole Sloan stood not fifteen feet away, leaning against a tree with his arms folded. And he was grinning! She closed her eyes and took a few deep breaths, trying to convince her heart that it didn't have to beat its fists against her breast. She walked over to what had once served as a chopping block and sat down.

" 'Tis lucky ye are, Mr. Sloan, that this humble servant girl nae would dream of punching ye for scaring her out of her wits."

"What's this humble servant girl doing out in the bush?"

"I dinnae know." And she caught her breath, for she realized that she truly did not know.

He moved in closer and leaned against a tree very near her. "I saw you leaving the compound. I was going to call you back but I changed my mind. Followed you, instead."

"And silently. I dinnae hear ye." She stared out across the dark, silent pool. "She was young. Next best to being immortal, she said." *And Edan, too.*

He was watching the silence also. "Death is a fact of life, Sam. Strong ones win and weak ones die."

"Aye. Death and life. And fain would I understand either one, but I cannae." She wagged her head and studied the dense, enclosing forest, pretending she could see beyond the trees. "I knew when I agreed to come that 'twould be different here, but . . . The map of Australia in me atlas back home has such broad blank spaces, including where we sit this moment. Yet I've heard 'tis nae all like this. That somewhere the closeness opens up and ye can see yer future nearly."

"None of it's like this. You're sitting in Australia's only rain forest, that we know about, at least. Most of the country; small trees or none at all, low hills or none at all. Mostly it's very dry, and flat forever."

"Meself cannae picture that—flat forever, I mean. 'Outside the city' means hills. Me father and me, we'd tramp the hills up behind Cork, and to the west. The Boggeraughs. Now and then we'd take a three-day holiday over to the Killarney lakes."

"Just you two?"

"Aye. Meg be not one for tramping. Edan was working by age fourteen and Linnet and Ellis were too young."

"Your mother?"

"Eh, she relished the time to herself, she said. Sent us out with a basket of lunch and a heigh-ho. Then she'd shoo Grandmum off to the park with the wee ones and put her feet up a bit." Samantha sighed. "The hills of Ireland be nowise like these, of course. Wild and misty, and cool always. Nae trees, though they say Ireland once had her forests. And windy. But ye knew that close at hand be Dagda's hill palaces, with the mirth and the brightness—somewhere. Ye might even be standing upon one. Ye never knew. And that was the charm of it, ye see."

"Hill palaces?"

"Myth. Naething but myth."

"I read somewhere that myth is what binds a people together. And no one's bound closer together than the Irish."

"When they be not a-slaying one another, aye."

"You mentioned a brother who died for honor and freedom."

"Ye've a fine memory."

"When?"

"A fortnight—no, nigh onto three weeks—before we sailed."

He stirred. She looked up to see him watching her, and his arms weren't folded now. He dipped his head toward the pool. "And now this."

"And now this. Recently meself has come to doubt there be a God in heaven—or anywhere else. Isn't that a dreadful thing to say? And raised in the church I was, too."

"If there is a God, I've never met Him."

"Meg's Rev. Vinson claims he has. Got God and Jesus right at his elbow, so to speak. He preaches it to Meg. She's commented upon it."

"Preaches God and sends threatening notes. Bible bashers—never met one I liked. The missionaries were the ones who'd squawk loudest when my father hired Kanakas. Howled from Cairns clear down to Melbourne. People up here knew the truth, but the farther away you got, the more others would pick up the howl. Like dingoes. To stay competitive on the world market, we had to bring in colored labor. Not enough whites willing to do it. Oh, they liked seeing the export figures, but they yelped blue about colored feet walking Australian soil."

"Ye mentioned having labor problems like yer father's."

"All the work you see done by machines used to be done by hands. They earned a few shillings a year where they came from. Or nothing atall. Most of them didn't make a brass razoo back home. But bring them here and the missionaries claim they need pay like a factory worker. Already getting more money than they ever saw in their life, but to the missionaries and the church people it was never enough."

"Perhaps ye'd like Mr. Vinson better were he in another line of work."

"An ocker's an ocker whatever his trade."

"Ocker?"

"Opinionated mule who wants to run everybody's life according to his own rules."

"Eh, on the other hand, wouldn't it be lovely if God were truly as the fellow preaches Him? But I cannae see that being so, nor can I see meself believing in such a one, more's the pity." She sighed. A confused, scurrying column of little black ants pittered in the duff at her feet. "Time to commence dinner. I must be getting back." She stood up, and the ants paid her no mind.

She raised her head and turned to leave, but he was standing squarely in front of her.

"Why did you come to Australia, Sam?"

"To get away." Her lips had just spoken without consulting her mind, and she was shocked at what they said. "But it did nae work." That surprised her, too.

His warm dark eyes like melted chocolate penetrated to the very heart of her. "I'd love to just send you back to Ireland and let you heal, or settle whatever seems to need settling, but I can't. I'm sorry. I need you here. I need competent, dependable workers and you're good. Very good."

She meant to mumble something appreciative, like "That's very nice of you" or whatever, but it came out garbled. Her eyes were hot; they spilled over into scalding tears. Heal. Settle. Yes. And escape. Escape this hideous wilderness that had gobbled up, most literally, the bright and lively Kathleen.

He wrapped his warm, strong arms around her and pulled her in close, pressing her head against his shoulder. Even as a part of her was trying to control this embarrassing outburst, another was trying to apologize for it. Neither part succeeded. By bits and pieces she brought herself back together.

She blew into her hanky and stepped back.

He was smiling. "If God is up there, He'll take you when it's time. The good go to heaven."

"I, uh . . . thank ye. I must go now. 'Tis past time to start dinner, ye know."

He studied her intently for a moment. She wanted so badly to read his thoughts, his intents, and she could not. Not a glimmer. Then his arms fell away and he stepped aside. She forced a false, fleeting smile, and she stepped aside. When she made her legs begin walking, he followed at a respectful distance, as if he were the rear guard.

What did this mean? Surely Mr. Sloan had far better things to do than to follow an errant servant out into the bush. More than once had Samantha encountered some lout with immorality in mind, and she could see that sort of thing coming from afar off. That was clearly not Mr. Sloan's intention here. Or was it? Did he really care? Or was he simply and shrewdly practicing some direct diplomacy to assuage the hired help's emotional problems, lest he lose another worker? She was so confused, and the more she sorted thoughts, the worse her confusion tangled them.

Questions. At a time when most she needed answers, she kept getting more unanswered questions.

The sun hung very low by the time she entered the back door into the kitchen, and the forest had turned dark with shadows. Her legs had been tired at noonday. They ached now. She lighted a lamp and paused to consider a menu. She would cook the potatoes by boiling them skins and all. Quicker that way. She dug the imported potatoes out of their bin.

Meg parked in the doorway with a maddening smirk on her pretty lips. "Have a good time with Mr. Sloan?"

Samantha stood erect, the better to face her snide little sister. "The man may have a caring heart, or else, perhaps he is a very shrewd and cynical employer, but he be nae a lout."

"Of course." She giggled. "Well, now, if he's going to go romancing, he'd best use his charms on Amena O'Casey, and stop wasting them on you. Keep all his pretty mares in his stable."

Samantha took a deep breath and counted ten. She must not let Meg do what Meg did best: get under her skin. "Ye think Amena may be leaving?"

"Might be gone already. When ye packed up Kathleen's belongings and sent them home, and Amena moved into the room, she bothered nae to move in proper. And now most of her things be gone and herself has nae been about all day, and that cane cutter's disappeared."

"All the cane cutters are gone. Mr. Sloan dismissed them days ago."

"Eh, but this one hung about 'til now."

"I hear the door, Meg."

Meg pushed herself erect and ambled off, though not nearly as quickly as Samantha thought she ought go. Samantha started a tea kettle. Mr. Sloan would likely want tea, with guests appearing like this, and quite possibly extra mouths at the table. She tossed a couple more potatoes into the pot.

She walked out through the house in Meg's wake, to receive Mr. Sloan's instructions firsthand. Meg tended to be lax in her transferral of information.

The Rev. Vinson and a tall, gaunt stranger were being ushered back to the office. A moment ago Meg had slouched lackadaisically. She was all starch now, smart and snappy as an Oxford dean. Samantha reversed herself and returned to the kitchen. This was one order Meg would get exactly right. She had the tray set and was bringing the water off as Meg came hustling in.

"Three for tea, Sam, and that raisin bread. Oh. Ye've got it. Here. I'll take the tray out."

Samantha slapped her hand. "At the risk of running yer fine romance through the sheep dip, this is one tray meself shall serve. Ye can hold the door."

Meg swung the door wide and let it swing shut on its own

as she followed at Samantha's heels. "Ye know who's here?"

"Yer Reverend and what looks for all the world like a solicitor."

"Aye, representing a law firm, he said. How'd ye know?"

"Yon Cassius has a lean and hungry look."

"Ye're such a frustration with the airs ye put on!" But Meg had to lower the rest of her crabbing to an inaudible whisper, for they were coming too near the office door.

Meg shoved the door open onto a war. Mr. Sloan stood rigid in absolute rage. The Rev. Vinson looked grim and determined, which he usually looked, and the lawyer appeared indifferent to it all.

The lawyer was rifling through papers in a briefcase or portfolio of some sort. "And this, Mr. Sloan, is the cease and desist order over Judge Bothner's signature. You are herewith forbidden to make any overture regarding ownership of the property in question until such time as the courts have completed a judicial review."

Those eyes that had once reminded Samantha of melted chocolate were crackling anthracite now. "Butts signed of his free will. Miss Connolly, you were present. Was there any duress, any misrepresentation?"

"Nae, sir. He seemed quite comfortable with the arrangement, even eager to take part in it."

"A simple Irish peasant in your employ is hardly corroboration, Mr. Sloan. I shall be by in a few days with the writ of tort. Be advised that legally, in essence, your hands are tied. Good evening, Mr. Sloan, Mr. Vinson."

And the lean and hungry gentleman left. Meg disappeared with him, showing him out.

Mr. Sloan took a deep breath. "Vinson, I warned you before about your interferences."

"I can't stand by and watch you ruin Butts, and that's exactly what it will be. If legal recourse is the quickest way to stop you, that's the way we go. The man's a fine Christian who sees only the good in everybody. I won't let you take advantage of him."

"Out."

The Reverend nodded. "Good evening, Mr. Sloan, Miss Connolly." He turned on his heel and strode out, not the least cowed.

Mr. Sloan sank into his chair. "Seen Amena?"

"I hear rumors she may have eloped with the cane cutter."

He rubbed his face. "Your sister's privy to Vinson's coming and going. Pump her. I want to know everything she can come up with. Plans, people he's meeting, women he's been cozy with, everything."

"Ye run a risk in that, ye know, sir. If Meg be encouraged to associate with him, she might become so entangled she'll go the way Amena O'Casey may well have gone. I cannae control her; never could." Samantha hacked a thick slice of raisin bread. "Here ye go, sir, to tide ye 'til dinner. Jam or marmalade?"

"I'm not hungry." As he cast more than a few aspersions on the Reverend's cleanliness and ancestry, Samantha spread the bread with marmalade and poured tea. ". . . That he has the nerve to bring a lawyer in on this."

"Did ye see credentials, sir?"

"What?"

"I steeped the Fortnum and Mason, sir; thought ye might could use it." She passed him his cup. "The lawyer's credentials? Did they seem sound?"

"Why would you question him?"

"I be nae certain, but I believe an injured party must bring his own suit, and the Reverend is not injured. Mr. Butts must be the plaintiff. Since he is not, perhaps he is still amenable to yer agreement more so than the Reverend would like. Also, I don't believe that torts come in writs, nor would they apply here."

"Where'd you get this?"

"Me brother clerked for Gleason's law offices in Cork. The vernacular rubbed off a bit, ye might say."

Whatever could Samantha be thinking of? Heart and soul she had been on poor Mr. Butts's side. And now here she was trying to help out Mr. Sloan. Why couldn't she keep her overactive mouth in check? She was painting a minister of God in black and whitewashing this callous and greedy schemer.

The broadest, wickedest grin spread across the man's face. "Good on you! Sam, my dear, you're a beaut!" He scooped up his raisin bread with marmalade and took a giant bite. "Delicious. You're a good cook. And a good woman."

Good. She was good and she was helping him oppose Rev. Vinson, which made the minister bad and the ideals of justice and fair play she shared with him not good.

No, Mr. Sloan, she was not good. Not inside. Fortunate, that the existence of God was in question. She'd never pass muster if He could really see inside her as some claimed.

"When's dinner?"

"The potatoes will nae be ready for a while yet. I just put them on."

"Then cut yourself a slab of this. It's good stuff."

She did so, and her breastbone tickled just a bit. Samantha Connolly might not be the paragon of goodness others claimed she was. But Mr. Sloan was right in this regard: the not-at-all-good Samantha could bake a good loaf of bread.

CHAPTER EIGHT

# CORAL REEF

"Is that it?" Luke Vinson pointed at a distant green blob on the line between sea and sky.

"Mebbe so." Burriwi shrugged and grinned with what looked like four dozen huge teeth. Luke often wondered if the aboriginal mouth contained the normal complement of thirty-two. Sometime, when the moment was right, he'd ask one of these people if he could please count his teeth. It probably wouldn't harm his relationship with them; they all thought he was nineteen and six to the quid anyway. One more crazy request wouldn't matter.

This was not the moment, however. Their little one-master thunked along from swell to swell, hitting the wind chop exactly wrong for a smooth sail. Keeping one hand draped over the tiller, Burriwi slackened the boom guy the slightest bit and studied the results aloft with a critical eye. He let it out a mite more. The trim looked perfect already to Luke, but then Lucas Vinson, native of Manitoba's Red River country, was hopelessly a landlubber, painfully at sea when on the sea.

Burriwi's blue-black potbelly burgeoned up over his loincloth. When he worked for Sloan, Luke noticed, he wore pants, unless it was a difficult tracking job. If his forest skills were the talents needed, he reverted to the forest ways, became at one with the dark and moody jungle. Today his equally prodigious skills as a seaman were on call, and he was as casual, as bright, as lighthearted as the coral sea over which they bounded.

The other sailors on this cruise, introduced to Luke as Burriwi's nephew and two grandsons, giggled and yabbered like school chums, and indeed this was something of a school outing. What these youths learned today they would one day show their children and perhaps their children's children—if the race survived that long.

And the race's survival was number two on Luke's list of priorities, a very close second place to the gospel itself.

Luke nodded toward the three up front. "Do you ever let the boys sail?"

"Sure." Somewhere behind the beetling brows, dark eyes twinkled. "Day like today, perfect. Wind's right, sea's easy, everything's apples. Anybody can sail today. *You* can sail today. Me, I'm gonna enjoy this easy sailing. Have a good time. Now rough days, when you're tacking against the wind and everything's going rats, that's when I give them the tiller. They learn how to sail best then y'see, eh? Wouldn' learn nothing today."

Luke smiled. "Don't you suppose they might enjoy this fine sailing once?"

"Let 'em take the boat out then. Today's mine." And indeed the man looked consummately content, a sailor attuned to the sea. Luke felt a sudden stab of envy, not at all a Christian attitude. Luke had never felt at ease in a place the way this man so obviously did, not even back home in Manitoba. And Burriwi was equally at comfort in the forest. Could it be that this unlettered aborigine would have fit in just as easily in Manitoba or Princeton or wherever else the Lord's inscrutable hand happened to drop him? Was his unity with his world a phenomenon of the so-called primitive mind, generalized, or of the man himself?

Social philosophy was pushed to the wings of Luke's thoughts, for the sea itself had just taken center stage. They were in very shallow water here. The blue sea color had altered itself to a random patchwork of blues, greens and grays. The shining surface ripples prevented a clear view, but Luke could make out a fantasy below of yard-wide coral blobs and ridges.

"Dibbie, which way's the tide going?" Burriwi called.

One of the youngsters studied the water. "That way."

Burriwi's nephew scrambled in beside him. "Naw, that's the way the wind is rippling the top, Dib. Look under at the way the stuff on the bottom is bending."

"That way!" Dibbie corrected himself.

"That's good!" Burriwi chuckled. He glanced at Luke and the smile faded a bit. "You don' think so, mebbe?"

"Sorry. Didn't mean to stare. It just occurred to me that you and your boys there speak English just as well as any white man. And yet, when you talk to whites and they talk to you, you use that broken English, that blackfeller jibberish. Why?"

Burriwi shrugged. "Whitefellers, they expect it. They use it on me, don' make me no difference. Makes 'em feel above me better mebbe. Who knows?"

"That doesn't bother you? That they feel and act so very superior to you?"

The toothy grin burst forth again. "Superior. Tha's the word I couldn't think of." The easygoing grin hardened just a little. "When Mrs. Perkins' boy, four years old, wandered off, they called me. Getting dark, not much time, no good light no more, and I found him. Gave him back to Mrs. Perkins safe. When the cook wandered off, they call me. I tracked her to the pool. Couple places she coulda gone, but I found where she went."

"And as I recall, with the rain coming, you had to do that one quickly, too."

Burriwi nodded. "Eight years ago—longer—a ship got off the way and broke up, couple miles down south here. They call me. Nobody can get out to the reef with a boat, pick off the men hanging there; too much wind, rain. I did it. I got there. Got 'em back safe. Y'see, Lucas? They act superior, sling off at me, talk silly talk. Big-note themselves and mebbe even believe it. But when the land is too much for them. When they can' make it. Who they call? Who's the real superior, eh? I know who. If they don' know, tha's their problem."

"Looka da ray!" The smallest boy practically fell in the water with all his gyrations.

A broad, dark, triangular shadow drifted by below the boat. The trailing edges of its five-foot wingspan rippled as it glided along, barely moving.

Luke watched it disappear into the sun-glare. "What does that thing eat, do you know?"

"Preachers."

Once only a blob on the horizon, the little island lay hard before them now. A narrow white beach defined the line where sea ended and land began. A dozen coconut palms clustered along this nearest shore. Bushes and trees crowned the rest of the tiny drop of land with a thick mound of green. Was this how Eden looked?

Burriwi dumped the sail. They skidded to a halt. "Got the tubs, boys?"

Luke had assumed the three tubs stacked by the mast were sponge tubs; they seemed about the size. They weren't. As Dibbie whipped one up and over the side, Luke could see a glass bottom in it. Dibbie pressed it into the water as he hung over the gunwale and exclaimed nonstop in two languages.

Burriwi's nephew brought his uncle a tub and scurried forward again.

Burriwi handed it to Luke. "Try it. Tub, it takes away the sun from the surface, you can see like thin air. You boys, you pull the boat over, you swim home, eh?"

Luke mashed it against the water, tipped it slightly to free a trapped bubble, and gazed. They floated in extreme shallows. Inches below the boat, the coral grew in mounds and blocks. A profusion of other forms studded the coral and the brief snips of sandy floor here and there.

And life. Everywhere, life. No matter where Luke looked, no matter which way he tilted the tub, he saw fish. Silver fish, gaily painted fish, somber fish, tiny darting things. Clumsy looking greenish-blue fish two feet long scraped at coral with thick lips. By sticking his head deep in the tub,

Luke could actually hear, however faintly, the gritching sound they made.

He sat erect and looked southward to the horizon. "This is overwhelming. The whole reef is like this, isn't it?—all the way down to Sydney. And north—all the way up the coast. Fish and coral everywhere, for thousands of miles."

"Out beyond the island there, same for mebbe an hour's sail. Another island out beyond. Same that way, that way as far as I ever been."

Luke hauled in his tub. "Here. Your turn."

Burriwi shook his head. "You look. I seen it." The smile came back. "You tell me things I never hear before. Jesus, heaven and hell, sin. Some of the things I know about but called them other names. Everything you tell me you get out of a book. Everything you say I need, you got them out of a book. I ask you a question, you show me the answer in a book.

"This. This is my book. We came here today because I want to show you not everything in the world is in your books. Some of it is in my books. Not everything a man needs is in your books; some is in mine. And I read my books as good as you read yours."

Luke turned his back on the grandeur of Burriwi's book in order to think. The thoughts fell into line easily because of the beautiful simplicity of Burriwi's figure. Phrasing his response was the hard part.

He didn't get the chance, for Burriwi's elder grandson spotted a shark below. Luke caught a glance of it—a slim, graceful gray shadow perhaps six feet long, cutting a lazy S-curve. White tips on its fins made it a bit more easily followed, pale smudges gliding deep in the water. As the boys clamored encouragement, Burriwi swung the boom out and caught the wind. Their little boat eased forward, leaned aside, took off in gentle pursuit.

The casual *pas de deux* lasted at most five minutes. Then the final white-tipped gray vestige of their quarry disappeared and they were abreast the south side of the island. With a terse warning about coral cuts, Burriwi nosed the boat onto a patch of sand. Here was a holiday and an adventure, not a theology seminar. Luke abandoned philosophical discussions for the moment and joined the boys as they clambered ashore.

This was not, technically speaking, a shore. It was a reef, coral so near the surface that low tide almost uncovered it. Luke strolled across its jagged flatness with never more than his ankles getting wet.

A score of silver seagulls had just sat down to lunch. They rose and glided away on gleaming wings. They settled a hundred yards off to resume their interrupted dining. A dark, smoky-gray seabird with a white skullcap flew to the far side of the reef.

How Luke wished Burriwi could approach the gospel of Jesus Christ with the same awesome wonder Luke felt upon reading Burriwi's book. Slim starfish of the most intense blue clung to the shade sides of coral chunks. Dazzling royal blue! An amazing little white clam of some sort had buried itself hinge-down in solid coral rock. It lived in a slotted hole apparently of its own making.

From pictures, Luke identified this nine-inch black, sausage-shaped glob as a sea cucumber. When he picked it up it draped limp in his hands, then exuded a tangle of long white filaments. Before it did that he had no idea what to do with it; now he had even less. Baffled, he laid it carefully in a puddle and continued his exploration.

"Shark! Here's a shark!" Dibbie stood staring at the coral, fifty feet from the nearest open water. Shark? Impossible. The water was nowhere deeper than eighteen inches on this reef. Luke sloshed and staggered his way to Dibbie's side.

The nephew crowded in beside him and grinned. "Whitefellers call it a epaulette shark. Jus' one of the little wobbegongs. Lotsa kinds of wobbegongs. Don' hurt nobody."

At first, Luke couldn't make out anything resembling a shark amid all the blobs and splashes of earth colors. There it was, a skinny, yard-long fish, tan with brown blotches.

Rounded outsized fins broke up the shape even more. It lay motionless in a gentle S-curve among the shallow globes of coral. The water was perhaps six to eight inches deep here in its little pocket of safety; its dorsal fins just barely broke the surface. In textbook discussions of cryptic coloration, Luke had never seen an epaulette shark mentioned. It deserved citation as *the* classic example.

Burriwi's grandsons erupted simultaneously. With lightning speed the shark wiggled and whipped away as the boys leaped forth to catch it. Luke found himself ten years old again and caught up instantly in the heady thrill of the chase.

Why were the boys holding back? They were surely quicker than this, and the nephew just said the thing was harmless. Luke made a wild grab; for a moment only he touched it as it slid out from under his fingertips. A startling sensation it was—cool skin, shiny smooth and yet rough, perhaps like greased sandpaper. The very name shark, this slim fish with the outrageously floppy fins, its presence on this exposed reef and its texture all screamed "unreal!" Nothing in this confusion resembled what Luke would have expected, were he simply reading about it in a book.

The coral mounds and flats rose above the surface here, and the lithe little shark ran out of tidepool water to scurry through. It curled around full circle and came snaking back. Luke dived for it and the world spun out.

Salt water lay in puddles in his lungs. It burned his nose. He coughed, hacking and choking, and didn't budge the puddles the least bit. Whoever was pounding him on the back finally, blessedly, quit. Cradled in warm gentle hands, his head bobbed. Was the owner of those hands laughing or crying? Laughing. He could see now, however poorly; it was Burriwi's nephew, with a toothy grin spread across his dark face.

Burriwi himself hovered overhead, and he wagged his head even as he smiled. "There you are. Ready to sit up? Wanna wait awhile more?"

Surely this nightmare would right itself if viewed from

the vertical. Luke struggled to sit up, but he wouldn't have made it even that far without strong hands helping. Not just his nose burned. His left arm blazed. His ribs ached. Fire tortured his left shoulder. Blood kept trickling down into his left eye. He sloshed a handful of seawater on his face to wash it clear and looked to Burriwi for some sort of explanation.

The loincloth-clad aborigine hunkered down in front of him. "Coral cuts, they don' heal up for forever. No worries. Jus' tell your grandkids is 'nitiation scars like these." He thumped the pattern of cicatrices on his own chest. "Is true, eh? Now you're 'nitiated about coral."

"You can afford a little optimism. It's not your blood." The confusion abated and anger took over as he realized what he had done—and had not done. He would never have made such an off-kilter lunge among rocks back home. Too dangerous. And yet these rocks were just as hard; worse, they claimed the paradox of being at once rounded or flat and very, very sharp. They had torn his left sleeve nearly off in their eagerness to lay open his arm.

The two grandsons, with gleaming grins on their black faces, brandished the little shark between them. Out of the water, it looked even less like a shark, not even a brown-blotched parody of a shark.

Why had Luke worked so vigorously for *that*? Had he not moved a muscle, the lithe boys would have caught it all the same. His efforts were not only useless but damaging—to him.

Luke gestured toward them. "Dinner tonight?"

"There's better-tasting fish than that one. But that one is caught; that makes it better than all the fish swimming in the coral, eh? Here. You think nothing's broke mebbe, I give you a hand up."

Luke surveyed the visible damage and identified by its pain that damage not easily seen. "I don't read your book very well, Burriwi."

The bright grin widened. "Naw, is okay. You jus' skipped a couple pages, eh?"

# CHAPTER NINE

# BY HOOK OR CROOK

Viewed from afar, from out in the open, the rain forest was not just a smooth green carpet to cover the angular mountains. It was a very nubby blanket, a globby patchwork of many kinds of green. Here and there at random, deep green trees with white limbs stood head high above the jumble. They seemed out of place, too tall for the forest they found themselves in. Palm trees studded the steep slopes with frothy mounds of pale green.

Samantha stood at the south end of Cole Sloan's latest clearing near the water's edge. From here she could see not just the clearing but the clearing process. Very near her, workers were churning up the rusty-black forest soil. Moldy loam that had not felt the heat of direct sun in millennia began immediately to dry out under the unbroken sky. Over there they were ripping out brush, pulling big stumps with the big draught horses and smaller roots with Sheba, hacking at mangled low growth with cane knives. On the far side they were just now cutting into virgin forest.

The measured cadence of *che, che, che* ended. An expectant silence, the passage of a long moment, and one of the palms shimmied. Slowly, gracefully, with an air of disbelief, it tipped out over the clearing. It slammed into the underbrush. Almost instantly the axes' *che, che, che* commenced again.

Samantha gave the pot of rice a stir. She dipped out a few

grains and pinched them. Ready. "Meg, put the bread and cheese out. Linnet, be the fruit bowls on the table?"

"Almost."

Samantha rolled her eyes skyward. The easiest job of all, and . . .

She motioned to Fat Dog and stepped up to the open fire. The aboriginal stable foreman gripped one end of the spit and Samantha took the other. Together they swung the side of roast mutton onto a wooden slab. Fat Dog commenced whacking it apart with his big machete. He was far more efficient with that thing than Samantha could hope to be with a properly honed butcher knife. She cut the savory chunks into serving pieces.

Meg rang the dinner gong just a bit prematurely, but no matter. It would take the workers at the far end of the clearing a while to get here.

Laborers brown, white, and black came crowding around, laughing, jostling, boasting, sweating. None seemed interested in washing. They queued up, tin plates and spoons in hand. Meg plopped great dollops of rice on the plates and Samantha served the mutton. She tried to do it properly and in sanitary fashion, but her apron and hands were greasy in moments.

The line dwindled. The last of the crew arrived, accepted their food and wandered off to eat. There was no such thing here as a properly laid table. The bowl of jam and the bread, cheese and fruit were set out on split logs on the ground, a puncheon table without legs. Men filled their plates and sat about anywhere the notion struck.

By the time Samantha could fill her own plate, the ants had found the jam and cheese, and flies covered the mutton. She was almost accustomed to picking off the bugs before dining. Almost. It would never be easy. She seated herself on the tailgate of Fat Dog's wagon and ate just as eagerly as the rest.

From beyond the forest wall came Mr. Sloan, riding Gypsy along the rough track. Samantha put her plate aside quickly and tossed a chunk of mutton onto the embers. By the time Mr. Sloan arrived and dismounted, she had warmed up his meat and filled his plate. He perched on the tailgate and watched her curiously.

She hesitated not at all. He knew where she had been sitting. She picked her plate up and settled back into her place.

He poked at the rice. "What's in it?"

"I've nae idea, sir. Fat Dog's wife showed Linnet this herb and it smelled as if it would complement rice well. So I tried it out because rice gets rather boring after a time."

"Tastes good." He smiled. "Very adaptable of you."

"Until I choose the wrong herb and we all turn shoe soles up one dreadful morning."

He chuckled. "I'll risk it for some decent food." He waved his arm toward the ruined forest. "Not what you're used to, is it?"

"Meself sat here thinking the very thing when ye rode in. Unimaginable to this Irish city girl. Nae proper furniture, nae proper tableware, few kitchen implements, open fires. And all these mouths to feed. A side of mutton roasted whole, and see—it be nearly gone. What frightens me, may I be so bold, is that 'tis not nearly as alien to me as it ought be. I *like* the refinements of civilization. I dinnae want to become inured to savagery."

"Adapting and becoming hardened aren't the same thing."

"Too close for me comfort." She set her empty plate aside and studied for a while the flat wall of forest at the far side of the clearing. "Curious. Here's meself, preferring all the trimmings of the civil life, and yet . . . and yet, there be a profound sadness about watching the forest die."

"Die? Poor choice of words. The forest isn't dying any more than a caterpillar dies as it turns into a butterfly. 'Transform' is the word."

She looked at the tangled green wreckage and the fallen giants, and kept her tongue in check.

Mr. Sloan pronounced an ugly word. He was staring at the track. From the forest trail came a mill worker pushing a handbarrow heaped high with something. Samantha couldn't see what, for the barrow was covered with a wet sheet or tarpaulin of some sort. The man brought the barrow almost nigh and unceremoniously dumped it. Short thick chunks of green wood they were. He tugged at the wet sheet until it more or less covered them and turned to leave.

"What's going on, Dakins?" Mr. Sloan demanded.

"Sir?" The burly man put his barrow down. "Your bananas."

"I know. Why a hand barrow?"

"Mr. Gantry told me to, sir. Only thing about."

"Send him up here."

"Aye, sir." The man picked up his barrow handles and trundled off, in no hurry.

Samantha looked at her employer quizzically.

Mr. Sloan scowled at his mutton. "Gonna take 'em forever to bring up the banana stocks with a handbarrow. What can he be thinking of?"

"Ye might use Fat Dog's wagon here, sir, if need be. Meself need not take things back to the house just yet."

"We have wagons and oxen. Gantry's out of line."

The mill foreman appeared in person with the next barrow load, followed by that same burly man and another wheelbarrow. "Ye wished to see me, Mr. Sloan?"

"What's going on?"

"All our oxcarts are on the road, sir. This is what we got left to haul your rootstocks."

"On the road carting what?"

"Your downed cane. You said get rid of it any way I found. I tried dumping it in the sea but it floated back in and the boys say it messes up the fishing too much. Since most of them live on fish, I figured I best find someplace else. I was gonna just go dump it in the bush somewhere, but the oxcarts have trouble getting off the road with it. Then Vinson came along with th—"

"Vinson!"

"Aye. Took it off m' hands for free. Only charged me for the stuff we'd chopped, because it's so hard to transport, he says. And so I loaned him use of some oxcarts, since he's doing us a favor more or less. Carts should be back in a few days."

"Took it where?!"

"Don' matter by me, sir. Took it. Between the oxcarts and the sugar trams, he sent it all down to Townsville, I think."

"And we're left with two wheelbarrows to plant forty acres of bananas and twenty of cane!"

"Three barrows, sir. And I might with your permission use Fat Dog's wagon here a few hours. Uh, you say you want to put twenty acres more into sugar?"

"Told you that weeks ago."

"Aye. Forgot. I think we still got enough if we dig some out of the established fields."

"You got rid of *all* the fallen stuff?"

"It's whatcha said, sir. Don't worry. I'm sure I can come up with enough good joints to put in twenty acres." Hastily Mr. Gantry dipped his head and snatched up his empty barrow. Away he went.

Mr. Sloan stared after him. "Vinson!"

"Excuse me ignorance, sir; what would a preacher wish with a mountain of useless green sugar cane?"

"I plan to find out."

"And ye feel nae gratitude that he solved a weighty problem for ye? Even admiration?"

"Do you admire a fox for his skill at reaching the hens? The meddler's up to something." And Mr. Sloan returned to his herb-flavored rice.

In Ireland one might prepare a plot for planting by first removing the tons of rocks and stones. Then one would plow the whole, disk or harrow the rough furrows, and perhaps hand rake it as a last touch. Of course, in that last pass one would remove further tons of rock and stone.

Not here. Stones like bald white heads lay wherever they

appeared. The ground remained all chopped up and lumpy, for no one took the trouble to smooth it in any way. Sticks and leaves and severed branches stuck out of the tortured dirt, and you just knew that in a few days the weeds would be back—the forest's first steps toward reclaiming its own. In this jumbled plot that could nowise be called a garden a score of hands planted the banana stocks.

Samantha the cook found herself pressed to service as farmhand as well. Under penetrating sun they worked, burying in the disturbed soil each chunk of banana plant along with a few fish for fertilizer. The scrambled mess which Mr. Sloan called his banana patch was completed by evening, but supper would be late.

Finally, after an eternity in the broiling sun, Samantha could return to the dark and quiet kitchen. Her nose would probably never forgive her for frying it so today. She tried to wash her poor roughened hands. They smelled of thoroughly dead fish, no matter how hard she scrubbed. Her fingernails were broken back to the quick, and yet they still tenaciously held dirt that could not be brushed out, try as she might.

Why did Mr. Sloan hate Luke Vinson so? Was it those notes or something else, something deeper? And what could the preacher man ever want with all those oxcart-loads of useless vegetation? Such a disquieting place this was! Samantha felt even more an alien and she couldn't explain why. Nothing seemed to fit right; nothing lined up correctly with what she had always assumed was common sense.

She tried to write a long letter to Mum that night. She said they planted bananas but there she stopped. How could she describe the lackadaisical way they halfway cleared the land? Her parents would think this place even more savage than it was. Mum's letters already as much as accused Samantha of living in a grass hut and eating insects. Or would they, after all, be right?

She found herself wandering through the darkened house. She rapped softly at the office door and obeyed the call to enter. "Would ye be liking tea or such, sir, before I retire?"

"Your father's a cabinetmaker, you said." His sleeves were rolled to the elbow and his shirt open. He looked even wearier than Samantha felt.

"Aye, sir."

"What does he pay for planed ebony and mahogany?"

"I've nae inkling, sir, but I'm writing to them tonight. I can ask."

"Do that. I want the retail price he pays as a workman. All the major hardwoods, particularly imports. A steamboat will be leaving Mossman Friday morning. Make sure your letter's aboard her and request a prompt reply. Tell him I asked."

"Aye, sir. Tea?"

He rubbed his face. "Why not? What's in the pantry?"

"Meself'll prepare ye a tray as the water's heating."

He nodded and stared at his desk. "Serve me an extra five hundred pounds sterling along with tea while you're about it."

"I'll check the pantry, sir, and fetch whatever money I find there."

Their eyes met and for a delicious moment shared the escape that friendly banter provides. She returned to the kitchen with a lovely, strangely warm feeling. For a few brief minutes at least she was shaking that miserable sense of alienation.

The fruit bread was gone so she sliced fresh fruit itself and arranged it on a platter. She thought long and hard about putting two teacups on the tray and decided on one. Two would be presumptuous. Then genius struck. She would leave a teacup and saucer on the mantel in the parlor halfway between kitchen and office. Should he suggest she get a cup and join him, she could do so quickly. Delighted by her own cleverness, she returned to the office and poured tea for her master.

He sipped at it. "Queen Victoria."

"Y're out of the Fortnum and Mason, sir. 'Tis this or the Murchie's Lapsang souchong."

"Lapsang souchong smells like a burned barn."

"Aye, the dry stuff does. But the brewed tea be tasty." She glanced at him hastily. "Me own humble opinion, sir."

He burst out laughing. "Sam, you should be the mistress of a vast plantation. You've too many strong opinions for a servant."

"Me brash and forward tongue be a vice, sir, which mehopes to conquer. A woman's tongue is the most unruly part of her."

"I'd be a fool to argue. So tell me, brash and forward servant, what Vinson is doing with his dead cane." He chose a slice of fruit without really looking; she noted he seemed attracted more to red than to cream or green.

"The ox drivers should be able to tell ye before too long."

"One of them's already returned. Gantry was right. Townsville. Railroad head."

"And no hint where from there?"

"The driver claims there was a lading order with a name on it, but he can't read."

Samantha smiled. "Perhaps ye ought hire only laborers out of university."

"As strong as the labor unions are getting, it may come to that." He paused and frowned. Someone was pounding on the front door.

" 'Scuse me." Samantha curtseyed and hurried out and down the hall. She felt vaguely disappointed that Mr. Sloan had not asked her to sit and join him. Silly Sam! Why should he do that? And yet, the disappointment persisted. Perhaps if they had not been interrupted now by this late-evening caller . . .

She opened the front door.

In the gloom under the porch a chunky man in a tunic removed his helmet. "Constable Percy Thurlow for Cole Sloan, please."

"Come in." She made a brash, forward decision and conducted the gentleman straight back to the office. She stepped inside the door. "Constable Thurlow, sir. Another cup for tea?"

The constable extended his hand to Mr. Sloan. "Not for me, thank you. Can only stay a moment. We've received word, sir, that your cane-cutter—Vickers is his name?—is being held down in Cairns as regards your verbal complaint. Until you sign a formal complaint against him, however, they can't hold him long. Thought I'd tell you tonight without waiting for morning."

"I appreciate your extra effort, Constable Thurlow, very much. I'll get right on it. Go to Cairns myself. Thank you!"

The man hesitated, head atilt. "Your complaint said something about suspicion of theft? You think he stole from you when he left?"

"Something like that, yes." Mr. Sloan came around his desk to escort the man out personally.

This was none of Samantha's affair. She should remove the fruit dish and tea, but was Mr. Sloan finished with it? She ended up following the men at a respectful distance.

Mr. Sloan closed the door and pivoted. "Sam, get Fat Dog up. I want Gypsy saddled now. And tell—"

"You're leaving for Cairns tonight, sir?"

"Moon's in first quarter. Light enough. And tell him he's to—no. I don't want Gantry, I want you. You'll ride Sheba." He headed for his rooms.

"Sir?" She ran up behind him. "Ye be telling meself to ride upon a horse to Cairns with ye tonight? *Me?*"

Ridiculous!

He turned so abruptly she nearly bumped into him. "Why not?"

"For a start, sir, meself has never ridden horseback, save for a few gentle rides on a plow horse at an uncle's. And I've me duties here and all."

"Your duty is to serve my needs, and I may well need a woman as a matron, possibly even to go places men can't go. Tell Fat Dog to fetch the horses down, now."

"Aye, sir." Samantha was halfway to the stable before she had worked out what was really happening. Vickers the cane-cutter had run off with Amena O'Casey. That was the theft in question. Mr. Sloan would bring Amena back, by hook or by crook, because she was his. His was a prior right even stronger than the tug of true love. His was the right by reason of economics. The crocodile had robbed him of one servant. That upstart Vickers would not deprive him of another.

And Samantha? She who hated intrigue was right smack in the middle, and about to make an utter fool of herself. Horseback. Fifty miles.

Sure and she should have emigrated to Boston.

## CHAPTER TEN

# JUST PLAIN PAIN

When Samantha was young and carefree (though she didn't know then just how carefree she was), she used to ride the great Shire mare named Molly on her uncle's village farm behind Ballincollig. That broad, flat back would wedge her legs nearly straight out. But even when Uncle Colin urged Molly to a lumbering jog, Samantha had no trouble staying on; she would simply grip the nickel-plated hames tightly, one in each hand, and laugh as she bounced up and down. Much as she liked horses, that was the sum of her experience as a horsewoman.

Until now.

The first four hours of the ride south, with the rising moon splashing black and silver on the road, wasn't all that bad. They pounded on the door of a tiny inn until the sleepy-eyed owner fed them bread and cheese as their horses rested.

Samantha's first major error on that journey was climbing back in the saddle after those four hours. Precisely at the joint where leg meets torso, pure, unadulterated pain stabbed her. She assumed it would abate. It did not. Three hours further into that hideous night, she became aware of a new seat of pain, literally: the places where her hip bones most closely surfaced.

Mr. Sloan seemed not the least discomfited. He kept Gypsy at a smart, even walk as Sheba rambled along behind. The eastern sky turned from charcoal gray to misty silver. There would be no bright sun today—a blessing to an Irish girl whose nose tended to peel. Hazy overcast dulled the light and muted the forest greens.

Samantha tried to shift in the saddle. No position, no change of weight distribution helped. Raw pain. Raw, unmitigated pain. She made her second error an hour past sunrise as they stopped at another of the country's ubiquitous roadside taverns: she dismounted.

The dismount began innocently enough. She tipped her weight onto the left stirrup and hauled her right leg up and across the horse's back. She must have watched riders do that a thousand times. She herself had done it more than once. Not this time. Her knee buckled. Her ankle relaxed and her foot slid out of the stirrup. She grabbed the pommel and a fistful of Sheba's mane, trying wildly to catch herself. Her right leg, as useless as her left, came sliding down like a falling log; its heel gouged poor Sheba's flank. The startled mare threw up her head and sidestepped. That ended it. Samantha's grip melted and she flopped in the dirt, a defeated, pain-racked parody of a horsewoman.

She couldn't move her legs. She couldn't even sit up straight for the aching stiffness in her bottom half. She sat leaning at an angle with both hands in the dust; she snuffled, and she tried to keep the tears from coming. It took several moments for her to muster the courage to look up.

He stood towering before her, leaning casually against Gypsy, watching. It wasn't a smile; it wasn't even a smirk; but the look on his face maddened her. As if she didn't know already, his eyes told her that he was in complete control and she was in absolute shambles.

He extended a hand. "Haven't been riding much of late, I take it."

She didn't move. "On the contrary, sir. I've been riding twelve hours too much of late." She looked at that warm, waiting, steady hand. " 'Tis nae good, sir. They won't work. Me legs have gone on strike and I dinnae blame them the least bit."

He chuckled as he shouldered Sheba aside and stepped in behind her. The long, sleepless night hadn't sapped his strength at all. He hooked under her arms and hauled her swiftly, deftly to her feet. She clung to Sheba's mane and tried to make her legs stiffen up and behave. Why did she always end up with all the suffering and inconvenience? If there really was a God, He had a dismal way of playing favorites.

Mr. Sloan piloted her to the door and her legs actually began to function on their own as they entered the little tavern. He pointed to a wicker chair with arms, at a table in the middle of the room. "Sit there." He left her to lower herself carefully (very, very carefully) into the seat and crossed to the door behind the bar.

She heard him discuss what was undoubtedly breakfast, but she paid no attention to the words. She ached so all over that surely she could not sleep even if there were opportunity.

But there would be no opportunity. How far had they come? How far need they go? She sighed and her ribs hurt.

He flopped down in the chair at her left and stretched his long legs out. "Breakfast in five minutes. He has the hostler up to look after the horses. And he's bringing you the pillow off his bed."

"The pillow—?" She felt her cheeks flush. "Meself hardly doubts that ye're very sorry ye brought me."

"Sorry? No." Those dark eyes sparkled. "Amused."

The heat in her cheeks turned to rage. She must keep her tongue in check.

He waved a hand. "The first day, you're afraid you'll die. The second day, you're afraid you won't. The third day is apples. Very few horsemen die of saddlesores."

"Ye can well afford a cavalier attitude. No doubt ye grew up riding horses."

He smiled and his voice softened. "No. I was once right where you are, pillow and all. I'm a city boy; grew up with streetcars and omnis and a racy little Stanhope gig of which I was extremely proud. Never sat a horse before I came to Mossman."

With a big, white, fluffy pillow in his hand, the tavern keeper came waddling out. "As ye requested. Ye want molasses for your porridge?"

"Brown sugar, please." Samantha stood up oh so cautiously and arranged the pillow in the chair. She lowered herself. Ahhh. "And so, Mr. Sloan, if ye be such a city fellow, how do ye do so well as a farmer and pastoralist?"

"By doing what Mr. Butts will not do—learning and adapting. He thinks he can grow tea without becoming knowledgeable about tea. Before I took my first step north from Sydney, I made sure I knew what cane needs to grow, and what I would need to grow it, and where my transportation would be found once it was milled. I didn't send for those banana stocks until I knew they'd produce in this climate. I can tell you more about growing tea than some Chinese can."

"So ye do intend to relieve Mr. Butts of his plantation."

His face changed slightly and she could not read the expression. "I forgot how sharp you are. I'll not make that error again."

And then the sausages arrived, followed closely by the porridge, and Samantha quickly learned that her churning stomach was eager to accept whatever she sent down. They lingered over tea. Samantha talked about Uncle Colin's farm and Mr. Sloan actually seemed interested. He paid for breakfast and, bless him, bought the fellow's pillow.

The pillow didn't make much difference at all; riding Sheba hurt as badly as ever—maybe even worse. But the pillow was so fluffy with shelduck feathers, Samantha could convince herself that it surely must make a vast improvement. *Ergo,* it did. The human mind, properly flummoxed, is a wonderful thing.

They arrived in Cairns not long past one in the afternoon. The only evident life was the ever-present flies buzzing in clouds around whatever might in the least way attract them. The sweat on Samantha's brow attracted them. The horses attracted them. Garbage middens, tangles of seaweed on the shore, horse plops in the street, fishy grease spots on the wharves—hundreds of things in Cairns proved interesting to flies.

The houses intrigued Samantha, and almost made her forget her suffering. Most of them perched awkwardly on stilts, a story above ground level. Everything from buggies to hogs occupied the shady spaces below the floors. Were storms so wild here that stilts were the only way to keep the surf out of your parlor? Was this particular architecture simply an extension of the thatched-roof huts of nearby island habitations? Houses well uphill of the shore were built thus even as stores and homes on the very beach hugged the ground on conventional foundations. Most curious.

They passed a knot of aboriginal hovels near the shore. Nondescript gray dogs lolled in the shade with their tongues out and watched the horses pass. Out on the end of a pier sat two black girls in simple cotton shifts. They dangled their legs, kicking idly as they talked—such a . . . a . . . *human* thing to do. How many times had Samantha and Meg sat like that talking, on a lake pier or waterfront quay or the loading dock where Ellis worked his pony wagon?

Samantha assumed Mr. Sloan would be seeking out a nice restaurant. No such thing. They passed several without pausing. He dismounted finally in front of a shabby horse barn on a back street. But of course. Sheba was stumbling and Gypsy had completely lost her prancing lilt. *The horses come first, Sam. The horses always come first.*

The *Livery* sign had weathered to a few flecks of paint. Lining one side of the shed were buggies Samantha would not trust to make it around the block. Ramshackle fences pretended to be strong enough to contain the dozen brumbies dozing in the paddocks. No one had done a thorough cleanup lately.

Samantha slid cautiously to the ground and clung awhile to the saddle, until her legs regained their starch.

Mr. Sloan picked her pillow up from where it had fallen into the dirt. "This stays with her saddle. I'll expect them to be ready an hour after sunrise tomorrow."

The hostler grunted. "Do I lead 'em away now or do I stand about while the lady hangs there some more?"

Samantha drew herself up and risked stepping back. To her relief, her legs still functioned. "Ye best hold yer tongue or else speak respectfully, sir. Meself has just ridden fifty miles farther than ever I've ridden before in me life, and I daresay I've reached this far end of the sojourn in better shape than many a woman might. I've naething to be ashamed of and yerself has naething to make fun of."

The hostler mumbled something apologetic and led the horses away.

There, her mouth had spoken out rashly again. It was Mr. Sloan's province to reprimand the man, if he was to be reprimanded—not hers. She glanced guiltily at her employer as she assayed a few trial steps toward the street.

Mr. Sloan's hand was clapped over his mouth. He sputtered. He suppressed a laugh. He roared. "Sam, you're a wonder! And I couldn't agree with you more." He led the way downstreet.

"If we be in such pleasant agreement, perhaps we might be considering lunch soon, eh, sir? 'Tis two hours past midday."

"Down to the gaol first, then lunch."

She fell in behind him and didn't really care that her slow, shuffling gait was holding him back. She ached all over, some parts far more than others. The filtered heat from the overcast sky bounced off street and building to press upon her on all sides. Her eyes sagged, so heavy she was quite literally falling asleep on her feet. They arrived eventually at the dressed-stone gaol house and she could not for the life of her remember the way they had just come.

They stepped from hot tropical breeze under the masked sun into hot tropical stuffiness under a close, dark ceiling. Despite open windows, the stagnant air made Samantha sleepier than ever. Mr. Sloan spoke to the man at the desk as Samantha tried to keep herself alert. Mr. Sloan had brought her for a reason surely, and right now she wasn't sharp enough to cut pudding.

Several minutes later chains clanked in some distant hall, and Samantha thought briefly of Dickens's *A Christmas Carol*. One of Scrooge's ghosts? Hardly! Byron Vickers, his black eyes blazing behind the beard and eyebrows, emerged from the far door. Chains hung from the manacles on his wrists.

His deep scowl sent a chill up Samantha's back. "Ye did me muckle wrong, Sloan. I took nothing of yours."

"Amena O'Casey."

"Eh! Should've guessed. She's a piece of meat, that I stole her from ye? Perhaps y'd like to tell these gentlemen how ye own her in the first place, that a thief might take her and then be charged with thievery."

"She's under contract to me and you participated in her decision to break that contract."

The dark face glowered, black as a tropical storm. "I found me a good job here cutting cane. Wind didn't topple it here like it did up north. Top pay. Then at your behest these people came to arrest me and I was fired. Like that. No words of explanation would do. I've been branded a thief because the high and mighty Mr. Sloan claims I stole from him."

"And you did. You—"

"I served ye every season since ye took over Sugarlea, and when I was a mere lad I served yer father before ye. Served ye well, too. Now ye've ruint me. Ruint me! On whim! On the off chance I might lead ye to some woman ye thought ye owned. I tell ye this, Cole Sloan: Every cutter in Australia's gonna hear how ye wronged me. Next season, when yer cane is tall and oozing sugar, see how many cutters'll risk ruin to work for ye."

"Amena O'Casey signed an agreement to work for me, and now she's gone. I want her back to complete her contract and you know where she is. It's as simple as that."

"Simple! Even if ye get me my job back, I still carry this black mark. Arrested for theft. Accused of stealing from the employer who fired me because his cane blew down."

"Mr. Sloan," the gaoler interrupted. "Who is this O'Casey

woman? What is her legal status specifically?"

Sloan said "Indenture" even as Vickers burst out with "Free woman in a free country!"

"Indenture?" The turnkey wrinkled his nose.

"A formal contract for labor in exchange for boat passage, room and board, and a modest stipend. She owes me two and a half years."

"It's illegal! An anachronism." Mr. Vickers glowered.

Sloan stiffened and moved in closer to the chains. "Now where'd a cane-cutter ever learn to use the word 'anachronism' in casual conversation?"

"They did it a hunnert years ago. More. But it ain't a thing for this modern age we be in—not the twentieth century."

"We're five years into the twentieth century and a contract is still a contract, Vickers. Who've you been talking to?"

"Vinson's lawyer explained how ye can't enslave a person, and that's what it be. Him and Luke see alike on it."

One moment Mr. Sloan was hot with rage; the next he chilled. Samantha had read of such transformations in novels, but never had she guessed she would see it. "Vinson!" His voice cut, icy sharp. "His lawyer isn't a real lawyer."

"I know that. But the principle's true, all the same."

Mr. Sloan wheeled to look at Samantha and his eyes were gloating. *Aha! You were right!* He turned to the gaoler. "I'll be in tomorrow to finish the matter. Some people I have to confer with first."

"As you wish. Sure you don't want to file your charges now? We can only hold him three days."

"Tomorrow." Mr. Sloan turned his back on the man in chains and walked outside into the gray light. A drizzling, indifferent rain had begun. He paused at the curb to study the sky.

Samantha stepped in beside him. "Sir? Ye'll not reach Amena through him, I'll wager. He defended her cause and he accused yerself, but he dinnae at any time so much as admit to knowing her."

"He knows where she is."

"Aye, but his back's up now. Meself can't fancy him being the least bit cooperative with ye. And he's a strong man."

"I'll break him."

She watched rain patters make dents in the street dust because she knew her mouth was speaking out of turn again and she couldn't stop it. "Mayhap ye already have, sir." She forced herself to look at him. "Should ye not have him released now? Ye've naught to gain from leaving him locked in that cell another night."

"Let him rot." Mr. Sloan stepped off the curb and started across the street.

Samantha should be following obediently. She stood in place.

He stopped in mid-street and turned to look at her.

She lifted her voice enough to carry it over the sound of passing horses. "And when can I expect ye to see some wrong in meself, real or fancied, and cast me off to rot as well?"

He stared at her the longest time, with no hint in his expression as to what might be going through his mind. He drew a deep breath. "Don't bother worrying about it until you've served out your contract. Come along if you want to eat." He turned and walked away.

The clink of Vickers' chains haunted her memory like the ghost of Scrooge's past.

She remembered Edan's accusing voice: *Ye think naething of freedom, do ye?*

*I'm sorry, Edan. What can I do?* She stepped off the curb and followed Mr. Sloan through the rain.

## CHAPTER ELEVEN

# THE THRILL OF THE CHASE

Sheba mashed her thick, velvety nose against Samantha's bodice and hinted broadly for a chunk of sugar cane.

"I've nae cane with me today, lass, sorry." Samantha rubbed the hard forehead.

"There ye go." The hostler slipped his fingers inside Gypsy's saddle girth, tugged experimentally, and stepped back. "Your master ought check the girth before he mounts. She blows up some."

"I'll tell him so, thank ye." Samantha had no idea what that might mean. She took both horses' reins in hand and led them away from that shabby little stable. Were she a true horsewoman she would ride Sheba and lead Gypsy. Not likely. The painful stiffness where her legs joined her body absolutely forbade her to consider getting into a saddle.

She led the horses downstreet as instructed and tied them to a rail near the bank. She watched the gaol on the far side of the street, halfway down the block. Here came Mr. Sloan. He walked away up street and disappeared suddenly between two buildings.

Minutes later, Byron Vickers stepped out into the street and drew his first breaths of freedom. *Don't come this way. Go that way. Let Mr. Sloan be the one to follow you. Don't come this way. Please don't come this way . . .* The dark bear glanced this way and that and then, to Samantha's great relief, walked off upstreet.

Mr. Sloan was far more bush-wise than Samantha. Sloan could follow a man undetected. Samantha could not. And yet, had the ex-cane-cutter come this way, Samantha would have had to keep him in view at least until Mr. Sloan caught up to her. Her master reappeared from between the buildings and walked upstreet.

Samantha had little to do now except wait. Mr. Sloan knew where the horses were. He obviously knew where Mr. Vickers was. It was all Mr. Sloan's game. She might as well have a cup of tea. She would cut through this alley (she was becoming quite knowledgeable about this dinky town on the brink of the sea), cross Severin Street and find that little tea shop in Fearnley Street.

She paused to admire a bold cotton print in the window of a dry goods shop. She studied the bonnet styles in a milliner's shop and almost considered a sweet roll in a baker's window. This is what she most missed in the months of her Australian exile—the fascinating little shops that are the real accouterments of civilization.

Wait! There was Byron Vickers, walking rapidly this way on the far side of the street. Samantha turned her back quickly, lest he see her and realize he was being followed. She watched his reflection in a shop window as he continued northward. She kept an eye behind him, waiting to spot Mr. Sloan.

No Mr. Sloan. Mr. Vickers turned a corner and still no Mr. Sloan. Samantha broke into a run, north along the street. Obviously Mr. Sloan had let his quarry get too far ahead somehow. She must keep Vickers in sight until Mr. Sloan could catch up. There was Vickers. She'd better get a little closer.

She was sweaty and panting heavily when she finally drew to within half a block of their quarry. Vickers glanced about and then stepped out to a sorry-looking bay horse tied near the curb. He was adjusting the saddle girth. He was going to ride away! Samantha would never be able to keep up with him if he were on horseback and she afoot. And yet, no way could she go back for Sheba. She was blocks away by now.

A young man with a rather vacant smile was polishing one of those new bicycles right across the street here. Samantha had attempted to ride one of those infernal things once. Bicycles do not do well at all on the cobbled streets of Cork. Would they do better on the damp dirt streets of Cairns? She crossed quickly to the far side of the street and tried to keep an eye on Vickers.

She smiled as charmingly as she could and thickened her accent. "Awr, now there's something meself has read about. One of them bicycles. Be they as thrilling to ride as I hear?"

The gangling young man leapt to his feet. "They sure are! Yes, ma'am! Here. Try it out. Oh. My name's Bob. Bob Wilkins."

Samantha dipped her head. "Bob, me pleasure. I'm Samantha."

"Nice name," the boy cooed. "Hop aboard here and take a spin. You'll see how sweet she is."

"Meself'd love to! How kind of ye." Samantha purred, "Sure'n I'm beholden to ye, Bob."

"No worries. Here ye go. Foot here. Aye, that's it. Now so long as you keep your speed up, you should have no trouble."

"How do I stop?"

"Eh, the brakes are a bit shaky. Just keep turning corners and ride around the block."

Vickers was climbing onto his horse.

Samantha pushed off. She giggled as the front wheel dipped and wavered. "This is glorious!"

Bob ran eagerly alongside."Perhaps you'd like to join me for lunch somewhere."

"I'd love it." Samantha pedaled harder.

There went Vickers around a corner. Samantha headed for the same corner. Bob stopped, winded, and called cheery encouragement from the middle of the street. She was on her way.

How fortunate she was that this wasn't one of those bicycles with the huge front wheel on which you rode atop! On this machine the rider's position was more or less slung between the two wheels and she wasn't much higher off the ground than if she were walking. Difficult as this was, it was much faster than any gait afoot. Every time she hit a bump, the little saddle reminded her of her recent folly on horseback, and there were ruts and bumps aplenty on this ragged road. No matter. It was far, far better than a horse's saddle.

Vickers left town practically at a lope and try as she might Samantha could see no sign of Mr. Sloan. The game had become hers. She rounded a curve just in time to see Vickers turn his horse aside onto a dismal forest track. She barely made the turn herself. One advantage to horses; they more or less self-steer.

Vickers' horse was the only animal to take this track recently. She could see his one set of hoofprints. She saw also, in the thick and clinging mud, that his horse had cast its right front shoe. Good! If she lost the trail, Mr. Sloan might perhaps find Aboriginal trackers who could pick up the unique trace.

The forest closed in, pressed down, shut out the filtered light. It was beginning to rain; she could hear the patter in the treetops even though no water was as yet reaching the ground. She could hear also the steady beat of the horse up ahead.

Dark forest like this always bothered her. Why was she feeling so elated? She almost giggled aloud as the answer came to her; her bit of charm on the boy named Bob had worked. Amazing! Samantha was not a charming woman. Charm never worked on people who mattered, like prospective employers in Cork. And yet, a smile and a nod had played young Bob right into her hands.

She would return the bicycle, of course, at the earliest opportunity, and perhaps she could even convince Mr. Sloan to pay some sort of fee for it. It was, after all, a godsend.

Godsend. Godsend? She could not imagine God being involved in this sort of flummery, assuming there was One such. Was God involved at all with Mr. Sloan? Luke Vinson was the man trained in godly matters, and he was constantly at odds with her master. Did that mean Mr. Sloan was ungodly? Quite probably. She had watched Byron Vickers' face yesterday, the face of a man dreadfully wronged. Godly people do not ruin others.

Her legs were getting very tired; muscles she had never known existed began to chide her. They were not the same muscles used for horse riding, either. And the muscles where her shoulders met her neck were tight and aching, too.

The hoofbeats ahead had stopped. She let her vehicle coast to a halt; it slowed quickly in the clinging mud. Silence, except for the rain patter above. She waited, trying to see everywhere, unable to see anywhere for the dense growth and darkness.

The hoofbeats began again, moving away. She pushed off and with great difficulty got rolling again. The road was very steep here, and up is not the best direction to take with a bicycle (another advantage of horses!). Shortly she got off the machine and walked rapidly, pushing her bicycle and keeping an eye on the fresh tracks cut in the mud.

She was tired, oh so tired. Mr. Sloan had provided her with a tiny garret room to herself and she had slept the clock around. But twelve hours' rest does not make up for a preceding night spent in a saddle. She was hungry, too, although she doubted Bob would be particularly enthusiastic now at the notion of buying her lunch.

The forest seemed lighter up ahead. The hoofbeats either stopped again or were muffled somehow. She left the bicycle in a clump of ferns and moved forward carefully. The rain was penetrating to the forest floor now. It came not in the usual filter of little raindrops but in the huge clunky blobs that collected on myriad waxy leaves.

Vickers had ridden out into a grassy sort of clearing. At the far side of the glade, tucked against the rain forest wall, stood a shanty of unpainted boards. Its shake roof was green and hairy with moss, its stovepipe rusty red. Mr. Vickers swung down, tied his horse to a bush and entered the lopsided front door.

Samantha looked and listened for any sign of a dog. It seemed safe; she stepped cautiously into the clearing and paused. The horse raised its head slightly to watch her from the back of its eye, but it made no noise. She hurried along the edge of the clearing to the shack's windowless wall and pressed in close.

". . . Listened a couple times," Vickers' voice was saying, "but I didn't hear no horse. Nobody followed me."

"I was so frightened for ye." Amena O'Casey! "Perhaps Luke was wrong. Perhaps I best go back and finish out at Sugarlea. If Mr. Sloan can get ye thrown in the dungeon for no reason, there's nae seeing the end of what he can do."

"They couldn't keep me."

"Three days they kept ye. Three days without ye. Ah, Byron, ye cannae imagine what ye mean to me! Me whole life long have I yearned for the man who'd be mine. A strong man and noble, and a gentle lover. Ye be it all and more. Byron, I love ye so."

Vickers mumbled something reciprocal and appreciative, but it was Amena's words that tore at Samantha's heart. For over a decade she herself had been seeking that very thing, without finding a man who so much as approached those ideals. *Nae even a close call,* as Grandmum said.

Amena had found her man. Samantha could tell by the warmth in her voice. What was pure joy, Byron Vickers had found his woman; you could hear it in every word. Now here was Samantha ready to rush back to Mr. Sloan, tattling, wreaking further havoc with their lives! Amena was breaking a vow made Mr. Sloan. But Mr. Sloan had broken Amena's man, damaging his good name. When did all this horrid breakage end? When did the books close, the sides declare even-steven, the slates sponge clean?

Amena was giggling. "Byron! None of that now. Should we not be on our way south, making our escape? Byron—"

"We will, we will. Later. After bride and groom business be taken care of. Three days without ye's a lifetime, Amena."

The past spoke to Samantha. Edan: *Ye care naething for freedom, do ye.*

*Yea, Edan, I do care for freedom*. So far as Samantha was concerned, the books closed now. She stepped back and turned away. She would return to the bicycle, roll down the hill back to Cairns and report . . . report what?

The horse stirred and nickered as she moved within its view. Rain whispered all around her.

"Halt!" Vickers' voice sent her straight up a foot. She wheeled.

The dark bear stood shirtless in the doorway, a rifle or shotgun of some sort leveled on Samantha. He took a step forward, out into the drizzling rain. "I shook Sloan, but I wasn't expecting you. Ye're good, Miss Connolly, to follow me clear out here without me knowing."

Why didn't that great black gun muzzle gaping at her heart frighten her? Why wasn't she hysterical? " 'Tis appropriate to congratulate the bridegroom, I believe. Me congratulations."

He dipped his shaggy head. "Luke Vinson married us 'fore we left Mossman."

"I wish yerself and yer bride a happy life together."

"Yer boss cocky's made that bloody difficult for us, but we'll try." He took another two steps forward. "I've dealt with the blackest of the blackguards in my day; there's none tougher than them that cuts cane. But ye're a brazen one. No fear atall, not even in yer eyes. Not like any woman I ever knew."

"I wondered about that meself, but I know why now. Ye be nae bushranger. Ye're an honest and decent fellow, or ye'd not feel so outraged when yer name was impugned. I've naething to fear from a good man in the throes of true love."

The great bear laughed and tipped his gun muzzle skyward. "A good man in the throes of true love. Aye and again aye. And with the best woman in the world, I trow. Get yerself down the hill, Samantha Connolly, and tell yer boss where to find me if ye've the mind to."

"I don't have the mind to, but I do owe him me loyalty. Sure and by the time he brings others, ye two will be long gone."

"Aye, long gone. We've nothing left here; Sloan saw to that with his accusations. But we'll make a go of it elsewhere. And ye tell yer slave master that one day Byron Vickers'll return. And on that day, Cole Sloan'll be paid back full and running over for the misery he's caused us."

"Misery? Were it not for him, Amena would still be in Ireland. And many Irish girls never find a good man. They die spinsters. He owes ye, I warrant, but Amena and yerself owe him, as well. All the blessings of the saints fall upon ye, Byron Vickers, and on your bride. G'day." She turned her back to him and walked through the wet and rustling grass to the track, to the darkness among the trees.

She dared glance over her shoulder only as she was digging her bicycle out of that clump of ferns. He had gone back inside, he and his gun. She perched on the narrow seat and pushed off. Oh, she was sore!

What did that Bob fellow say about brakes? Nothing, as Samantha could recall. There were no hills this steep in Cairns. She tried to slow herself by pedalling backward but of course that wouldn't work. Her speed picked up.

The track ahead moved; some sort of brown snake was slowly uncoiling itself, stretching forward to cross the road. With a yelp Samantha lifted her feet high. The snake, lightning fast, jerked itself back into a tight pile as she bucketed past it.

Now she couldn't get her feet back where they belonged. The pedals revolved with a mind of their own and slapped her feet and ankles as she tried to regain them. The track curved left; she'd never negotiate a turn like that—not at this speed. With awesome dread she aimed the bicycle at a vine-covered bush on the far side of the curve. At the last possible moment she let go and covered her face with her arms.

The bicycle stopped with a loud, rustling *SKISH*. Its handlebars hooked her legs and kept her from flying. She slammed forward and down into a million jabbing, scratching branches. Some loud-mouthed bird sounded the alarm high in the trees, and other voices picked it up.

She lay there she knew not how long, too spent, too tired and hurting, too frustrated to move. *Silly goose, Samantha. You have to right yourself eventually.* Her legs and skirt were tangled in the branches two feet higher than her head. She maneuvered, trying to extricate herself without getting dumped harder on her ear. Her bottom half dropped level with her top half and she could at last stand up.

She ended up crawling out from under the tangle of vines and branches. She yanked the bicycle free. Several of the wire spokes in its front wheel were broken, a few more bent. Did it still work properly? She wasn't about to find out. She would walk, at least until she hit level land. She gripped the errant vehicle by its handlebars and started down the road.

At least she couldn't get lost, even though she didn't really remember this particular curve. One road, thus one way. A quarter mile of walking downhill and she noticed there were no horse tracks in the mud. No bicycle tracks, either. That was logical. This rain would obliterate marks. Yes, but all of them? And yet, how could she miss the way when there was only one?

She stopped cold. Before her was a narrow, pinched *Y* in the road. Another track, just as muddy and obscure, was joining this one. She left the bicycle at the junction and walked a few yards down one leg of the *Y*. She turned and looked toward the bicycle. There was no way you could see the other track. Coming up the hill she could have passed a dozen *Y*'s in the path without ever seeing a one.

This was not the trail she had come uphill on. She must backtrack herself, discover her error and find the right way. She would follow the bicycle marks. She dragged the bicycle around and shoved it doggedly ahead of her, up the steep and winding lane.

Rain fell in earnest now. It traced little brown rivulets down the ruts in the trail. It turned the mud to slime. It pasted the loose strands of Samantha's hair down across her eyes and cheeks. And by the time she reached that infamous braking bush, it had washed away the faint marks from the bicycle tires.

She stopped and simply stood there, spent. Dense and alien greenery pressed in on her. These ragged hills were not Dagda's palaces that she loved so well. Unspoken fears, of everything from brown snakes to unknown horrors, crowded together, voiceless, in her breast.

Her sweet and gentle yesterdays back on the Auld Sod were driven from memory by the harsh and bitter today. She was alone. She was lost. And she was too, too tired to cry.

# CHAPTER TWELVE

# FOSSICKER

It was a lovely butterfly, vivid in the gloom. Its upper wings were a smoky gray; the back wings, red along the bottom, sported diagonal bands so white they nearly glowed. Samantha hoped it would alight, but it flittered up and around and away. She sat on a soggy, spongy log and stared at nothing.

It would be dark in perhaps three hours—maybe four. She might be twenty minutes distant from Cairns or perhaps eight hours away. The closest she could pinpoint her location was "Australia." She could be reasonably certain she had not left what was essentially an island continent. She sighed. So this was what all that blank white space in her atlas back home looked like.

The dripping forest hugged close around her. Whispering rain urged "press on."

She stood up and picked up that infernal bicycle. How could things get so mucked up? A few hours ago she had worried what Mr. Sloan would say. Now she didn't care a fig what Mr. Sloan said. She wanted only to reach human habitation.

Cairns lay at the bottom of the hills, flush against the sea. She could not go wrong, surely, by keeping to a downhill track. Two wrongs don't make a right, they say. She had gone wrong once, but perhaps if she took a second wrong, her trail would turn out right. When her track dwindled to less than a footpath, she tried to walk directly through the forest downhill. Even without a bicycle she couldn't do it. Dense, tangled growth clogged her every step, blocked her every move. She must stay to the trails.

She was stumbling now. The rain had ceased but the forest continued to drip. She was dripping, too, awash in perspiration. She still was not accustomed to the unrelenting heat of this country. She wished she could be certain she was working her way east, but the leaden sky gave her no hint where the muted sun might be. She could not even tell if the sun were close to the horizon yet.

She stopped. Something in the distant bush sounded just like a train whistle. The birds in this exotic land never ceased to amaze her. Again—low and mournful—

It *was* a train whistle! She was certain. But from where? The dense foliage sifted sounds so thoroughly there was no guessing the direction of that wonderful song of civilization. She walked faster, dragging the bicycle along. If the train whistled, it must have been nearing some sort of crossing or track junction. Trains do not whistle at random in the bush.

Also, trains follow rail lines and the lines do not merrily climb up and down hills as do roads and trails. Surely if she continued downhill along this trail, sooner or later it would cross the railroad grade. And once on the railroad grade she would enjoy a relatively straight, level walk to civilization and safety. Nor are railroad grades at all steep. Perhaps along the grade she could ride this bicycle without fear of it running away with her. Her spirits rose for the first time since she left that shabby little hut in the glade.

An hour later she was still walking along this endless track. She seemed no nearer anything. She had walked up and down hills and apparently over a saddle, though she couldn't see far enough in this thickness to know for certain. Things from time to time had rustled in the forest to the right or left, never close enough to see. And what about the dangers she could not see—brown snakes in the chocolate-colored mud of the trail, and poisonous plants known to aboriginals but not to her?

The forest seemed more open here, not quite a clearing, but almost. She let the bicycle fall over and set herself down on a soft, moss-upholstered something, whether rock or stump she could not say. Dusk. This was definitely dusk. She was bound to spend the night in this terrifying unknown.

All her life she had been praying to God on demand. When in church you recite this prayer, then that one. When pursuing private devotionals in school, you count off prayers by counting off beads. During your early childhood, you kneel at your bedside and rattle off the prayers expected of you, as Mum sits close and monitors for quality and quantity.

She should pray now. The phrase "A very present help in time of trouble" came to mind—or was that the exact phrasing? She could not pray. She was not in church or school now, the nearest bedside was distressingly far away, and Mum sat in her parlor in Ireland on the other side of the world.

Meg had told her once that the pastor Luke Vinson did not pray, either. That surprised the daylights out of Samantha until Meg went on to say, "But he talks to God frequently and intimately." Ridiculous. The good pastor was surely pulling the wool over his own eyes if he thought that. He was flummoxing himself just as Samantha had talked herself into believing that a pillow really does alleviate the discomfort of riding. If God existed at all, He was up there and we were all down here—hardly good positioning for intimate conversation.

Perhaps God did exist. Perhaps He did extend himself to the aid of His followers who were good and therefore deserving of His attention. That certainly wasn't Samantha. Everyone called her good. Even Byron Vickers today had used the word in reference to her. But she wasn't.

If she were truly good she would not be lost in the middle of nowhere—a very dangerous nowhere—on the brink of a sleepless, uncomfortable night. She would have handled the Amena/Vickers thing differently and much better. She would take a strong, moral stand instead of meekly trotting along behind Mr. Sloan, whatever he did. She would not berate Linnet so constantly, or find fault with Meg. She would not so eagerly back Mr. Sloan up as he trampled on human dignity and just plain did wrong.

No. In no way did she merit God's approval or deserve His help, if indeed He offered help. In fact, if deserts were at issue here, she probably deserved exactly what she was getting. And she was cast on her own resources, which were nil—no God, no leprechauns, no hill palaces, certainly no bright lights or merriment in this dark and dripping gloom.

Treetops rustled high above her. Large somethings were crawling clumsily about in the upper branches of the tall trees. They were grotesque creatures that changed form as they moved, bobbing, from limb to limb. But banshees were merely a figment of the fertile Irish national imagination—weren't they?

Someone coughed in the forest beyond. Coughed?! Four feet high, a small blue head moved by dots and dashes through the undergrowth just ahead. It paused. It stepped out from between dark green bushes. It was a bird, rather like an ostrich. A tall helmet sort of plate perched on its naked head. Dark hairy feathers covered its blob of a body. And those stout feet—it stopped to stare at Samantha. With surprising grace and silence for such a bulky bird, it slipped back into the forest.

Cassowary. That's what it was—a bird she herself had once cooked. Tough. Tasteless. But the bird dropped summarily outside her kitchen door had no head or legs. So that was what the whole creature looked like!

Something fell from above and plopped at her feet. It was a prune pit of some sort, the fruit meat all eaten off it. Those amorphous somethings away up there were eating fruit and throwing the pits at her!

She must go on; she couldn't spend the night here. She snatched up the bicycle, that infernal bicycle, and started forward. Would she never find a railroad grade? She doubted now she had ever really heard such a thing as a train whistle.

On sudden impulse she called out. The somethings in the treetops shuffled and flittered like giant bats. She cried out again, as loudly as she could muster. A pause . . . again. *How stupid! You're taking leave of your senses, Sam lass. The first step on the short road to madness. Get hold of yourself!* She shouted "ouch!" involuntarily when a pedal came winging around and slammed into her leg. Just as she thought her situation could get no worse, it was rapidly deteriorating.

The bicycle stopped so abruptly it pulled her off balance. Now what? It was getting too dark to see well. Her skirt hem was caught in the bicycle somehow. She let the machine down and groped in the gloom. The chain that linked pedal to back wheel—it had just eaten her skirt. She tugged. Nothing. The chain would not give, her skirt would not tear, the bicycle would not move.

She sat in the wet slop in dire need of a good cry, but she was simply too tired to muster tears. She should curl up right here and try to get some sleep. Wait until morning and better light, then try to make the bicycle chain disgorge her skirt hem. Soft rustling on the trail ahead changed her mind instantly.

What was it this time? Another impossible-looking bird? More yard-wide amorphous somethings? Some eerie aboriginal myth-monster that really existed after all and absolutely adored devouring innocent maidens?

She shouted, "Go away! Shoo! Scat!"

The forest dripped silence.

She pulled her knees up and crossed her arms upon them to provide a prop for her weary head. She thought of what Amena had found, and what Meg was apparently finding, and how she herself was so totally, abysmally alone.

The rain had ended long ago, and the leaves were about done shedding water, but Samantha was as soaking wet as ever—rain and sweat both. She'd mildew before she got out of this horrid wilderness. She tugged again at her skirt hem. Stuck. And night was here. In moments she would no longer be able to see her white blouse, let alone her black skirt.

Frustrated beyond words, she screamed the sort of tantrum-level shriek she had not indulged in since childhood. She pounded with both fists on the stupid bicycle and bent another spoke.

"Can't be all that bad, surely."

Samantha screamed again, but this one was fear.

The voice surely belonged to the dark form on the trail ahead. Matching sound to sight, Samantha guessed it to be an older white man, bearded, somewhat stocky and paunchy, wearing a broad-brimmed hat of some sort. He hadn't bathed for a while.

The form stepped up closer. "Heard your cooee and thought I'd come see who it was."

"Heard me coo—what?"

"Cooee. Shout. Call."

"Aye. Of course. Be there perchance a railroad grade near?"

"Very near. You 'spect to call in a train maybe?"

" 'Twas hoping to dispel some of the many frightening wild things about." She glanced upward, half expecting the huge amorphous somethings to start throwing fruit pits again, but leaves and darkness painted the overhead a uniform black. She would refrain from mentioning that this strange man was one of the frightening wild things she worried about.

A sulphur match flared as the fellow lighted a candle. He knelt close and held the candle near her. His bushy moustache reminded her a bit of Papa, and some of her fear faded. How ridiculous! *Fie, Sam! You cannot trust him. Can you not feel the menacing air about him, a strangeness?*

"Never heard of such a thing. One of them bicycle doovers. Out here beyond Woop Woop." The bushy head wagged. This man was just as hirsute as Byron Vickers, and yet he in no way gave her thc impression of a bear. Perhaps it was the glistening gray in his sideburns and beard. "Stuck in it, eh?"

"Aye." She scooted a bit to give him room.

He studied the chain and the cogged metal wheel, waving

the candle slowly here and there. "Hold this here." He thrust the candle into her hand.

She would have cautioned him that the bicycle was not hers and must not be further damaged, but it somehow didn't seem to matter anymore.

He produced an absolutely giant knife with a blade the size of a butcher knife. He poked at the chain. "Closer with the light, eh?"

Obediently she twisted around to hold the candle low. It dripped wax on the cogged wheel. With the tip of his knife he popped some little thing. The chain fell apart and he lifted it away. She pulled her skirt hem free. At last. She climbed to her feet slowly, for she was very, very stiff.

He coiled the chain and stuffed it in a pocket. "Put it back on when you can see. Less you want to ride it some more."

"Nae, I've ridden it quite enough for one day, thank ye."

He retrieved his candle and blew it out. The dark seemed darker. He picked up the whole bicycle in one smooth handful and set it on its wheels. The man was amazingly strong for one so gray. "So you're headed for the railroad. I'll walk along with you awhile if you like. Had a partner once, out fossicking. Irishman, talked the same as yourself. Irish?"

"Aye, County Cork. Working for a plantation owner in Mossman."

"Railroad's not gonna take you to Mossman, missy."

" 'Twill go to Cairns, will it not, or somewhere close?"

"That it will." Despite the dark this fellow was able to walk comfortably along the muddy track. Ridiculously, the bicycle seemed to behave better for him. He gripped it in the middle of its handlebars and by sheer force of arm made it come along smartly. "Where in Mossman?"

"Sugarlea."

The bushy face studied her in the gathering gloom. "Sloan."

"Aye. Ye know him?"

"By name and odor. Never met him."

Samantha could see nothing, but this man was moving

along at a normal pace. He wasn't bumping into anything, so he must be able to see something in the blackness. She ought to get a conversation going, or at least introduce herself. She dropped back a pace and reached out to put a hand on the bicycle seat. She felt much better touching something actual in this world of shifting shadows and palpable darkness. More flummoxing of the mind.

They slipped and slid along in silence, and he seemed not at all inclined to talk. Samantha finally began a conversation just to be polite. "Foss—ye were what, did ye say?"

"Fossicking. Seeking minerals. Digging."

"Ah. Be nae such in Ireland. Nae even coal that anyone's found."

"Australia's rich, lass, rich as can be. Gold and silver, and I'll wager only the least of it's been found so far. Tried some of the strikes myself, here and there. Fitzroy River was a little before my time, but Charter's Towers. Croydon. Gympie down south by Brisbane. Woulda wandered over to Kalgoorlie when they struck there ten years back, but it's too far. I'm an old man to be chasing dreams out beyond the black stump."

The sky turned gray suddenly; they had emerged from the forest.

"Anywhere in particular along the railroad?"

"Nae. The grade be good enough."

"Then here you are." He let go the bicycle so abruptly that it nearly pulled Samantha over; she gripped the seat with both hands. He reached in his pocket. "And the chain and the clip what holds it. You'll see easy enough how it goes on, come daylight."

"Wait!" She let the bicycle fall and snatched at the darkness. She caught his sleeve. "Er, me name be Samantha Connolly, at your service, sir." She extended her hand.

His huge warm paw wrapped around her hand, and she could feel the strength in it, even though he didn't squeeze hard, as some do. "Abner Gardell. If you mention me to Sloan, tell him you were talking to McGonigan's old partner."

"I shall. Tell me: how'd ye happen so far out here, that ye could come to me aid?"

"Live out here." His voice dropped to a rumble and she could not tell if he were explaining something very dear to his heart or feeding her a merry line. "Seeking the biggest gold strike in Australia's history. This here's the new Ballarat. It's right here; I'm certain of it. Y'see, quite a few years back—near forty years—some miners found a reef in these hills . . ."

"A reef. A vein of gold."

"A rich lode." The gray head bobbed in the darkness. "And they marked the way to it with a boulder—a rock about this high. I find the boulder, I'll find the lode. Keeps me healthy and honest, the search does." He chuckled in the hot and humid darkness. "You're a good woman, Samantha Connolly, to keep your courage up like this. G'night now, and God bless."

"And yourself, sir. Thank ye so very much for—"

But he dissolved in the gloom, gone like the steam from a teakettle.

The wet steel rails glistened in the gray sky light; she could see them lose themselves in curves in both directions. She could hear a river, too, though she could not see it. It must wind its way through the trees alongside the tracks. She climbed the weedy bank and stepped with her battered bicycle onto the grade.

She settled onto the seat. The disconnected pedals didn't operate the bicycle, but neither did they swat her in the ankles. Perhaps . . . Experimentally, she pushed with one foot, then the other. It bumped dreadfully on the ties until she got a little speed up and the ride smoothed out somewhat. Rough and choppy as it was, it was faster and easier than walking—especially walking while dragging the bicycle along. The front wheel made a rapid tictictictic sound—the broken spokes, no doubt.

She stopped suddenly. The bicycle bumpbumpbumped to a halt. A rock. A boulder this high. Sudden doubt engulfed her. When she sat down to rest there—when the amorphous somethings threw pits at her—what did she sit down on? It was moss covered. But she could not for the life of her remember whether it was an old rotting stump or—

—or a boulder this high.

## CHAPTER THIRTEEN

# OBSESSION

*What a mess. What a royal mess!* For the hundredth time, Luke Vinson berated himself violently for his foolishness. He should have known why those energetic little boys were romping around so cautiously. Even if they didn't, he should have known. . . .

Hindsight. Would that his foresight were one tenth as good as his hindsight. Luke snickered. Were man's foresight that good, the children of Israel wouldn't have suffered all the problems that came of their departures from the straight and narrow. He certainly wasn't alone in foolishness, when one views the cataclysms of history.

He studied himself in the mirror and tried to decide how to shave the blond stubble emerging from the coral cuts on his face. Prudently, he withdrew the razor. Hudson Taylor, Dwight L. Moody, Chinese Gordon—the giants of the faith—all sported beards. Actually, he wasn't certain about Gordon, but the bushes on the other chins made up for any lack. The matter was decided. He would let comfort rule the day.

His left arm and shoulder still seeped. How long did Burriwi say it took to heal? Forever? And the little shark didn't even taste all that good.

Someone knocked and he recognized the light touch. He really should cover up this mess before opening the door. If she saw his arm in this condition . . .

"One moment! I'm coming." Cautiously, gingerly, he

pulled on the baggiest shirt in his clothes press. It set fire to every square inch of torn hide that it touched. He buttoned his way across the parlor and stuffed in his shirttail just before he reached the latch. Satisfied in mind if not in body, he swung open the door.

What Luke saw as the door opened was the sort of vision that evoked poetry from the romanticists and made wandering Greeks forget their homeland. Her russet hair was drawn up and back in a pile of soft curls. The smooth and tender skin, the limpid gray-green eyes brought the lovely face to perfection.

"Ah, Meg. Do come in!"

She stood transfixed, staring not into his eyes but into the gouges on his face. "Oh, Luke. . . !" and he regretted a thousand times over his brief moment of foolhardiness.

"It looks much worse than it actually is. Come in."

"However did it. . . ? And your arm. Look at your arm, with the blood coming through your shirt there. It must have happened just now, aye? Eh, Luke, me heart aches to see ye thus."

He planted a hand on her elbow and forcibly ushered her across the threshold. "Waste no sympathy on me, beloved. I richly deserve whatever befalls me, for not thinking. Morning tea is ready. Have you broken fast yet?" He closed the door and planned for a moment to kiss her properly. Prudence, not modesty, prevented him. Were he to kiss her she would embrace him, squeezing his poor rib cage, and . . . A peck on the cheek sufficed; but then, she seemed preoccupied anyway.

He conducted her to the kitchen, popped open the biscuit tin and dug a plate out of the cupboard.

"Breakfast? I be nae hungry, thank ye. But, uh . . . meself would be pleased to sit with ye."

"Ah! The verandah? I'll be right there." He watched her move ever so gracefully across the kitchen and out the door.

His fingers fumbled, things escaped his grasp, tea slopped from the teapot spout . . . Why did he turn into a bumbling schoolboy whenever she was near? He gathered things more or less willy-nilly, paused long enough to rehearse the breakfast; was he forgetting anything major? He carried the tray out the door.

She sat on the edge of her chair and stared unseeing at the nanny goat out in the paddock. She was visibly upset, and he loathed himself for being the author of her unhappiness. Drat his clumsy thoughtlessness!

He put on a cheerful mien. "So. Did the slave driver give you the day off?"

"Mr. Sloan be out of town on business. Luke, whatever could've happened to ye so early in this day?"

"Yesterday. I was romping around on a coral reef and took a dive. We were trying to catch a shark, you see, and—" He stopped. He had just said about a mouthful too much.

"Shark!" Her whisper was barely audible.

"Not a real shark. I mean, not a man-eating sort. This was just a—what did Burriwi's nephew call it? A wobbegong. Rather a humorous little thing, actually. Funny shape, funny fins. You would have liked it. It wasn't . . ." And he quit trying to keep the air light. He sighed. "I'm sorry, Meg, that my accident upsets you. Now please disregard it, as I am disregarding it. It was a moment of carelessness and worth no further mention."

Her eyes were brimming over. "Luke, I have to get away from here. I want to get out of here. Anywhere. A town, a city, this country, some other country. Back to Erin. 'Tis the worst mistake I ever in me life made was coming here. Please help me."

He abandoned thoughts of breakfast. He swung his chair around and plunked it down hard beside hers, right leg by right leg and pointing the opposite way, that he might talk to her face to face. "What's wrong, Meg?"

"Everything! I hate this place. It destroys all the things I care about. Look at ye! This place did that to ye. A shark! And the crocodile. Kathleen was such a happy lass, Luke, the kind of girl the world needs more of. And Sam. Sam was such a good girl until she came here. It destroyed her, too. And the jungle. It closes down all around yer ears and presses ye to death."

At the seminary, Luke had received lessons in maintaining detachment while ministering to those who would seek his counsel. The lessons went out the window as he wrapped his arms around her and gathered her in. The vibrant warmth of her against his breast filled him with delight, even in the midst of this gloomy conversation. He let her simply sob and cling to him a few minutes.

"The nature of the jungle we can do nothing about. It's close, yes. Someday, Meg, you must see the rest of the land. All open. Wonderful panoramas, uncut distance. You feel hemmed in here; out there you may well feel exposed—the only soul left in the universe. I look forward to showing it to you, Lord willing."

"Take me now. Take me anywhere now. Please."

"I can't, yet. I'm not finished here with what I set out to do. Soon, though. Soon. What else did you say? About Samantha?"

She shuddered. "Ye did nae know her back in Cork. Sensitive and p—pure. A sort of sister ye might fight with and tease, but one ye would look up to. Ye know? And now. She be obsessed, and it's ruint her, the obsession."

"Obsessed with what?"

"That Sloan. She ranks on poor Linnet: 'Work harder. Do more. Mr. Sloan expects more of ye.' Never a kind word for the girl, or for me either. 'Tis always the same complaint. We never do enough to please her. And all for her Mr. Sloan."

"She seems to be a person with a strong sense of responsibility. That may well be—"

"In Cork she would've mourned the likes of Kathleen, and here it seems nae to bother her a bit. Kathleen dies horribly one day and the next day Sam's in the kitchen as if nae more has happened than a stubbed toe or a hangnail. She was the one packed up Kathleen's belongings, for I could nae bring meself to do it. 'Must be done,' she says, and never a tear.

And now . . . and now she's—" Her voice broke.

"You said Sloan's out of town. Samantha is as well?"

The gorgeous head bobbed against his breast. "May me aged parents never hear the truth." And she began again to weep.

A rush of bitter disappointment flooded his thoughts for a moment. Meg's sister seemed to exude integrity and honor. She was good from the inside out. How could she so quickly let her high standards slide? How could she present such a miserable example to her younger sisters?

The disappointment subsided, replaced by anger. *Sloan. What chance has even the most upright of young women if her master decides to take her? So long as she remained enthralled to that lecher, Samantha had no real options, moral or economic or otherwise.* But neither did Meg, and the sudden thought chilled him.

"Tell me the truth, Meg. Has Sloan ever made improper advances toward you?"

The head shook, *no*.

"Or Linnet that you know of?"

"She lives in a little world of her own, but methinks she'd mention such. I dinnae believe so. Why should he? He's got his pleasure now." The beautiful head lifted away, that the beautiful eyes might meet his. "Ye said ye care for me, Luke."

"I do!"

"Then take me away. Let us go a-marrying and start again some other place. Please, Luke?"

"I can't. Not yet. When—"

"Ye're the most important thing in the world to me, and the only person meself trusts. Am I nae just as important to you?"

"Yes! But it's not that simple."

Her voice hardened. "Then perhaps ye might explain."

"I'm committed to the work of Jesus Christ, Meg. He is my master, far more than Sloan is Samantha's master—or thinks he is. I've been given a task, an important task, and until it's done I can't just up and leave."

"This parish, or whatever your church calls it, can find another man. Ye can preach wherever; it need nae be here."

"That's not the only task I have. And the other's far from finished. I'm sorry, Meg. I understand your burning desire to get away. To escape. But right now I can't—"

"Luke, I will nae stay. Do ye ken? 'Tis all I can think about, getting away. Will ye take me?"

"Yes. As soon as my work here is completed. It won't—"

"Now. I'm leaving now."

The thought of her going away—the mere thought of it—robbed his mind of its ability to think straight. He grabbed her arms and held her tight. "If you walk out now you'll be abandoning me. Is that what you want? I'm the one who must stay. If you care about me as you say you do, you won't leave me destitute. I need you. I desire you. And I want to get out of here as much as you do, believe me. But I have no choice. You're the only one of us with a choice, so whether we part or remain together is up to you. I love you, Meg."

She stared at him the longest moment, those huge eyes pouring tears. "Ye're no better'n Sean Morley or any of the others. Ye care nae to understand." She wrenched free suddenly and leaped to her feet. She bounded off the verandah and strode away across the goat paddock.

He really ought to catch up to her. He really ought to try to press some sense into her. No. There'd be no sensible persuasion so long as she was this distraught. Let her cool off.

Was she right? His task was next to hopeless; he knew that before he ever came here. He'd given it a hard try and so far nothing good had come of his efforts. Was it time to give up? Was God telling him through Margaret Connolly that it was time to move on? Or was she a stumbling block set up by the Evil One to deter him from his goal? He lacked the gift of spiritual discernment that enabled the Apostle Paul to say, "Satan did this" and "God did that," and never did he feel the lack more than now.

She disappeared into the back door of the church at the far side of the goat paddock. Instantly the sunshine lost its gleam. Never had a young lady affected him as this one did.

He unbuttoned his shirt and slipped his right arm out of it. He tried carefully to peel it away from the other side, but the warm breeze of morning had already done its work. The shirt had dried fast to the seeping wounds.

Samantha. Sloan. Sharks and coral reefs. Crocodiles. He could well see how Meg might feel somewhat disoriented, having left an orderly little European city not in the least like this splendid savage land. He sat down at his lonely table and stared at the biscuits.

No! Faint heart ne'er won fair maid. He could not leave without completing what he had begun, but perhaps with God's help he could speed things up somewhat. He pulled the shirt back on his right arm, buttoned it on his way across the parlor and stuffed in his shirttail as he bounded out the front door.

He stopped by the wharf long enough to borrow Jason Wiggins' roan gelding, sent a telegram to Brisbane, and rode up the shore to Burriwi's village. He should be enjoying this superb day with its fine weather and cooling breeze. But Meg's possible defection clouded his thoughts and his appreciation. Surely she wouldn't—would she?

*Village* was perhaps too structured a word for the aboriginal settlement by the sea. The most makeshift of crude rain shelters leaned against trees and bushes, tilted at crazy angles above props of boards and stumps, huddled shoulder to shoulder along the shore. Dogs lolled about or stood to growl as children played in the smoldering ruins of this morning's fires. Aged and ramshackle as the settlement might appear, it was brand new, for the previous one had been swept away by the typhoon.

People of all sizes and shapes lounged about, none of them under a shelter. Every pair of eyes watched Luke approach. Adults masked their interest behind a glazed look of indifference. The small children, without pretense, froze in place to gawk. Their satiny black skin and blond-streaked hair never ceased to amaze him. Three brindled dogs bounded forth to worry his horse, but an old woman whistled them back.

Luke dismounted near two young men he knew. He smiled and hunkered down beside Burriwi's nephew. "Your uncle around?"

The nephew paused in his whittling. He waved his work of art, a tortured yellow stick two feet long. "Up in the hills, him and Dibbie. Gonna tell Dibbie about the cassowary people. Dib's father was a cassowary."

"The clan totem, I assume you mean."

"Huh?"

Luke shrugged. "An idle sociological guess. Do you know when he'll be back?"

"Naw. Prob'ly he don' know, either. Wurraoona's with him, so they'll do some hunting and some loafing and tell Dib the stories and maybe stop by Sugarlea, see if there's some work."

"Pick up some extra money?"

"Money!" Black eyes sparkled deep beyond that primitive brow. "Never get no money out of Sugarlea."

"But your uncle, Fat Dog—a lot of aborigines work there."

"Eh yeah, sometimes. Fat Dog 'specially." The boy set himself again to the task of whittling. "Turps and tucker, sometimes a shirt or something. That's why they work there. Good tucker, 'specially since that brown-haired lady been cooking."

"Your uncle, Fat Dog, Wurraoona—they're wise men. Elders. I can't believe they'd consent to work for someone without pay. It's so foolish."

"I'm giving you the drum. What they do with money, anyway? Food and grog, tha's what they need. When my uncle does good, Mr. Sloan butchers him a steer or a sheep. Feed the whole clan."

"You said turps. Sloan supplies liquor?"

He paused his whittling to frown at a word apparently new to his vocabulary. "Liquor. Grog, y'mean? Y'see, a whitefeller buys something in the bottle shop; it costs money. Abo buys the same thing, it costs more money. So they do better, the blackfellers, if they get the turps direct, 'stead of money to buy it. Don' get—oh, wha's the word?"

"Cheated?"

"Tha's it. Mr. Sloan or Mr. Wiggins or Mr. Rudolph or Mr. Baylor, when they pay with something you can look at and hold in your hands and use, tha's worth more than money. Unnerstand?"

"I understand your point; I don't agree with it."

The whittler giggled. "Tha's what my uncle says. He says, 'That boy Luke, he can see real good, but he has such a hard time nodding his head!' " And he continued his whittling.

"You're being exploited."

The dark face clouded momentarily as it encountered still another word outside its vocabulary. He must have guessed close to the meaning. He shrugged. "We do what we gotta do."

"Don't we all." Luke sat back on his haunches and crossed his arms across his flexed knees. Beyond them out there sparkled the sea. Somewhere within it, that amazing, dangerous, unending reef with its myriad life forms went about its mindless business. Did man degrade man, murder him, take unfair advantage? None of that mattered on the reef, where death struggles were cast in black and white and there were no moral dilemmas. His arm and side still burned white hot. No moral dilemmas, maybe, but carelessness certainly commanded an exacting price.

His anger burned white hot as well, and that commanded a far more exacting price. *Greed. Exploitation. When wolves circle each other you stand back and let them work it out. But when wolves prey on sheep, you intervene. When a wolf like Sloan extorted free service from the likes of these people—or the Sloan harem, for that matter*—Luke paused, reining in his thoughts. He must control his anger.

One natural damper on the fires of his rage was plain fear. When he so glibly surrendered all he had to God, preparatory to coming north here, he didn't have much. Now he had Meg—or used to. Could he surrender her as well, if called to do so?

Maybe not. And that frightened him most of all.

## CHAPTER FOURTEEN

# KANAKA

"What a mess. What a royal mess." Samantha studied the remains of her poor beleaguered body in the mirror. Scuffs and scratches from that braking bush marred her face, but the very worst part didn't even show—the aches and stiffness from all the tortuous activity she had forced herself to undergo of late. Bicycles are every bit as abusive as horseback.

She had washed her hair and bathed, so she was as presentable as possible under the circumstances. Someone knocked at the door of this little garret room. Only one person knew she was here. "Come in, Mr. Sloan."

He pushed the door open and actually smiled. "You look a little better." He wandered over to the single wicker chair by the window and plopped down. "Ready?"

"Aye, sir. The bicycle business?"

"The lad won't press charges and I've given him the readies to fix it. The fact that you insisted on returning it to him personally—handing it to him face-to-face with your abject apologies—really impressed him. Impressed me, too."

"The least I could do. I took advantage of him."

"Sam, the reason he was so eager to give you a ride was that he was trying to take advantage of *you*. Don't you realize that?"

"Aye. I understand his motives clearly. That hardly excuses me own behavior."

He wagged his head. "The Connolly honor."

"Be that so bad?"

Mr. Sloan laughed aloud. "No, Sam, that's not so bad. Keeps you loyal to me." As he stood up he dug into his coat pocket and handed her a small paper. "Ticket home. There's a tramp steamer docked down at the wharf, going to Port Douglas this afternoon. You can sail that far and take the sugar tram on home. I'll take the horses."

Samantha gripped the bit of paper, that beautiful bit of paper, in both hands. No fifty miles on horseback! No pillow! No days of pain and discomfort! "Mr. Sloan, 'tis pure wonderful ye be!" Without thinking she leaned up and kissed him on the cheek.

Then she gasped and recoiled. She clapped a hand over her mouth and wheeled away from him, lest he see her cheeks turn red. "Me deepest apologies, sir. I forgot . . . for the moment . . ."

He gripped her arm with a grasp surprisingly strong and firm and pulled her around to face him. Nor did he let go while he studied her a long, long time. She tried to read something, anything, in his face. She could not.

Then he pulled her against himself, pressed her close, wrapped his arms around her. And he kissed her—not a mere peck on the mouth or a noisy little *smack* on the cheek, but a soft, warm, luxuriant kiss such as she'd never before known, though she'd been kissed many a time.

When at last he lifted away and relaxed his embrace, his eyes were twinkling. "If you're going to do something, Sam, do it right."

She stood transfixed, her heart and mind muddled together into one confused glob. He turned and headed out. She hurried after him, closing the door behind her.

The streets of Cairns seemed as busy as ever—which was not particularly busy. The cobbled lanes and thoroughfares of Cork were much more crowded. Irish feet moved more quickly, too, it seemed. These people of the far north in Queensland pursued life with such a casual air. Nothing was so important today that it couldn't wait until the morrow.

They hailed each other on street corners and stood about talking. They lingered over tea in the tearooms and over beer in the taverns. When neither beer nor tea appeared before them, they simply lingered.

Samantha smiled to herself. She had assumed she would be following her master about on business. Instead, they were entering that little cafe on Grimshaw Street. Good. She was ravenous. She'd been missing too many meals lately for one reason or another. They sat near the window. White muslin curtains filtered the tropical sun but barely muted its brightness. After all these months Samantha still was not accustomed to the sheer brightness of this land.

"Bit early for lunch, but we both missed breakfast." Mr. Sloan signaled for tea.

"I slept through me own, but I cannae imagine yerself sleeping in."

He chuckled. "You looked like death in a chamber pot when you pounded on my door this morning—obviously weren't going to walk another step. I couldn't expect you to take me back there."

"Sure'n I doubt I could've found it again."

"Bet you could if you weren't so tired. However, it was past two and our lovebirds had surely flown the cage by then anyway, but I didn't want to go back to bed, making what might be a false assumption. So I saddled Sheba, took a stable lantern and rode north and west into the hills, out the tracks you described."

"Ye found the shanty?"

He nodded. "They were long gone, of course. I spent most of an hour searching about the place, trying to find some clue as to where they might be going. Nothing." He spread his hands and let them fall. "Got away clean."

"And ye missed breakfast."

"Then there was the bicycle to take care of. Asked at the hardware store that sells them; he knew the whereabouts of your Bob Wilkins. You know, I must have beaten on your door five minutes to get you up so you could talk to the lad. I should have let you sleep."

"Nae, I'm glad ye honored me request to get me up. Helps me sense of guilt if naething else. I had nae trouble falling back asleep again when I returned to the room."

"Don't doubt that."

Tea came, and shortly thereafter soup and sandwiches. Samantha should have been eating her lunch with single-minded purpose, but other thoughts kept intruding. That kiss. His embrace. He was being jocular, that was all—making fun of her unthinking, forward gesture when he gave her the ticket. And yet . . .

"Why did ye bring me?" she asked suddenly. "Instead of Fat Dog, perhaps, who no doubt can ride well and follow footprints; or Mr. Gantry, who was Vickers' foreman? I'm next to useless."

"Hardly. It's O'Casey I want back, not Vickers himself. I don't think you realize how many places a woman can hide that a man can't reach—and not just ladies' powder rooms, though that's one of them. Also, a woman thinks like a woman and I cannot. And, I need a faultlessly loyal aide-de-camp here, who's committed enough to stay to the trail relentlessly and not be soft-soaped by sweet words into letting her go. A woman like O'Casey can beguile a man; she can't beguile another woman."

Samantha's ears burned. When Byron Vickers came out of that shack she had already determined to let them go—no beguiling necessary. Soft-soaped by sweet words? Hah. Soft-soaped by her own foolish dreams and yearnings. So much for loyalty.

He wiped his mouth and laid his napkin aside. "In a way, I took a chance on you, I agree. But you came through for me; a splendid job. Stayed with him after I lost him, used your head, wouldn't give up. You're good, Sam. The best."

Her ears burned all the hotter for knowing she deserved none of that praise. "Mr. Sloan, why be ye so anxious to retrieve Amena? Ye could hire any of the cane-cutters ye let go; ye could've hired on Byron Vickers and mayhap avoided all this. And there be girls here in Cairns, in Mossman and Port Douglas—"

"Hiring someone else means paying a salary. I can't afford it. Amena's already bought and paid for."

"Then if ye be counting bob and quid so close, meself erred badly. I lost ye money with that bicycle."

He grinned. "When they told me they had Vickers here, I saw a chance to get back what's mine. I knew there would be costs involved—bed and board if nothing else—but the risk was worth it if I succeeded. I can repair a good many bicycles and pay a lot of hotel bills for the price of two years' salary paid to O'Casey's replacement." He waved a hand. "It was a gamble. I lost. I accept that; I'm a gambling man, as is every planter."

She had not as yet mentioned Abner Gardell or his part in her return. The omission had not been deliberate. When she arrived at Mr. Sloan's room at two in the morning, she was too tired, too befuddled to give any more than the essentials. And there had been no opportunity since. Was this the time?

She drained her teacup. "Who is McGonigan's partner?"

He turned rock-hard instantly and glared at her. "Where did you hear that?"

She sat back, involuntarily wary of the anger in him. "Abner Gardell introduced himself to me; asked if Cole Sloan be still with Sugarlea, and when meself averred ye were, he asked me to extend his regards." She frowned. "Nae, that's not precisely it. Actually, he offered nae greeting atall, as I recall."

"He's a fool and quite possibly a murderer. You stay away from him."

"As ye wish, sir." This was definitely not the time to learn more about Abner Gardell.

They spent the next hour checking and re-checking places the Vickers newlyweds might be, were they still anywhere around. The Cobb and Company stagecoach had left for Brisbane and points south at eight, bearing three passengers—none of them of the right description. Samantha asked in the hotels on the south side of town. She checked from desk to desk, not just looking for names on the register but describing the couple. Nothing.

The hotel chore didn't take long. Half a generation ago, Cairns had been a booming transportation head, the staging area for the gold rush to the west. The gold was spent now, the rush slowed to a trickle, and Cairns sat under the tropical sun with little to show for the boom save memories of glorious yesterdays and a lot of boarded-up buildings. Most of the hotels stood vacant. Some had burned. The few still open were showing their years.

Nothing to do now but go home. Mr. Sloan had lost his gamble. Back to cooking and constantly beating the forest away from the door and trying to extract an honest day's work from Linnet. Much as Samantha's put-upon body ached, she rather hated to see this adventure trickle to such an inglorious end.

Mr. Sloan headed north on Gypsy with Sheba in tow, and Samantha took her time wandering down to the wharf. Weary and past its prime though Cairns might be, it was still civilization. And much as Mr. Sloan tried, Sugarlea was not. Samantha found herself dreading to leave. Perhaps, after she had put in her requisite three years, she would come down here to seek employment. That is, of course, if she had not yet found a man.

*His kiss . . .*

The docks smelled of fish and left that unique taste of the sea that lingers on your nose and tongue. A swarm of black flies covered a pile of fish entrails; someone had caught something. A few old men and a boy were fishing off the pier. A small cormorant with white front and black back was fishing, too. It bobbed in the water beyond the pier, looking every which way but down. Suddenly it would dive, then pop to the surface moments later. Sometimes its beak held a little silver fish to bolt down, sometimes not. At least it was enjoying better luck than the human fishermen.

When Mr. Sloan said "tramp steamer" Samantha foolishly envisioned a boat similar to the one that had brought her from Ireland—big enough to take a walk on deck. This one was hardly long enough to stretch one's legs out. It was more a launch than a boat, dingy yellow-gray and in need of attention from stem to stern. The Irish, whose seafaring ways extended beyond the mists of farthest time, took great pride in their craft. Apparently Aussies, johnny-come-latelies in the stream of national identity, did not. Samantha surrendered her ticket and boarded, her feather pillow tucked under her arm.

Mr. Sloan had left Cairns about two hours ago. He'd be six or seven miles up the coast road by now. She spent the first hour of her voyage scanning the coast, trying to pick out where the coast road hugged the shore, watching for a rider with two horses. Silly. This boat was too far off shore for her to hope to see him, and trees obscured the road most of the time anyway.

She suddenly felt embarrassed to be wasting her time thus, but she was not so embarrassed as to stop. Eventually they were too far north of where he might be and she stretched out with her pillow on a canvas-wrapped bale by the forecastle. They docked at Port Douglas at suppertime. Far from easing her weariness, those two hours' rest left her stiffer than ever.

Samantha delighted, if that be the word, in the sugar tram between Port Douglas and the Mossman mill, from the moment she first saw it. It was a charming miniature of the trains that wound their way among Ireland's velveteen hills, and tugged just a bit at her memories of home. The Irish and English railroads were already hoary with age, most of them over sixty years old. This tram, though, was a youngster, in operation for only five years. Between May and December, and sometimes January, the little steam engine chugged patiently between the mill and the port, hauling cane, hauling raw sugar, hauling various workers and semi-important officials and inspectors in both directions.

Except now. The blowdown had damaged so much cane that the mill stood idle and the train ran sporadically, if at all. Today was not one of the days when it ran. Perhaps a brisk walk would loosen Samantha's aching muscles. It had better; with the boilers on the sugar tram sitting there cold, she saw no other immediate way home.

She was a quarter mile along the road from Port Douglas to Mossman when a rickety wagon approached from behind her.

The driver, a pleasant-looking young man the color of coffee with cream, tipped his floppy hat. "Bound for Mossman, mum?"

"Aye. And yerself?"

"The same. Hop aboard if y'd wish a ride."

She didn't have to ponder the opportunity long. "I'd be most pleased, lad. Thank ye." She scooped her skirts aside and clambered up over the wheel into the seat beside him.

He clucked to his dreary little horses and off they went. For want of someplace better to carry the pillow, Samantha put it under her.

He glanced at her. "Up from Sydney?"

"Cairns."

"Looking for work, eh? Wrong direction. Sugar and tea failed up here. You'll do better down Cairns and below."

"Already employed, but thank ye for yer interest. Ye be a waggoner by trade?"

"Aye. Most of my business is when the tram isn't running. Usually, mum, I charge passengers, but since ye didn't ask to ride, I'm happy to take you for the company."

"Very nice of ye. I'm obliged." How could she phrase this delicately? "One of me chief vices be an embarrassing curiosity, so here I go embarrassing meself again. I find meself intrigued by the color of your skin; a wee bit darker'n honey—a most marvelous, lovely shade. Be ye from this area?"

The young man laughed. "I was just planning myself how I could ask you where you're from. My guess is Ireland, but I'm not sure. Lot of Irish in Victoria and New South Wales. Most of them who's born here, though, don't have trouble with their nose peeling. I'll trade facts if you will."

Samantha laughed. "Ye were right, and most observant. I'm born and bred of County Cork in the south of Ireland; came to these shores but a few months ago."

He nodded, apparently satisfied. "I was born at Bundaberg. I'm half Kanaka, since you asked about the color."

"Is that an aboriginal group?"

He turned to look at her. "You don't know about Kanakas. My father came from Fiji, brought down here to work in the cane fields. There were thousands of islanders brought into the north here to work cane. Fiji, Samoa, Java. Kanaka. It's a Hawaiian word meaning 'the man.' "

She frowned. "As laborers? Or slaves?"

"Eh, them who opposed it—the stickybeaks and stirrers—said slaves. Sort of in between. The planters were as cruel as any slaver in the American colonies, and they bought and sold Kanakas, don't think they didn't." He smiled a sad sort of inside-joke smile. "No real difference between the sugar fields of Queensland and the cotton fields of America."

"You seem to have made something of a study of the matter. As I recall, slavery caused a war of secession in America. Not here, though."

"Almost. At first the north end of Queensland here wasn't going to federate with the others; talked of breaking off from the rest of Queensland, all because they wanted to keep their colored field workers. At least, that's what they say. I got a different theory."

"What's that?"

He grinned. "Football. Queensland plays rugby rules. All the other states, they play Australian rules. Now, how you gonna get two places together when they got a rift like that?"

"Impossible, of course, if Australia cares for her football as Ireland does for her horseracing."

"More, even."

"Can't be. So ye grew up in the sugar fields."

"No, my father did. Then the machines took over. Donkey engines and clanking doovers handle everything about cane now except the cutting. That's the only job left to do by hand.

Nothing for me in the sugar fields anymore so I took up hauling."

"For which I be grateful, being very weary and quite sore. Ye speak as one well educated."

"Reading. Ciphering. Then on my own I've been reading history. Kanakas, we're smarter than a lot of folks give us credit for. You said you have a job here."

"Aye, housekeeper and cook at Sugarlea."

He turned and stared at her. "One of Sloan's harem. I should've guessed; fresh from Ireland." His voice dropped. "So you work for Sloan."

"Ye sound as though ye regret offering me conveyance."

"Regret? Naw. Don't hold anything against you. In fact, got some goods here for the man himself—tea from England."

She twisted in the seat to look at the crates in his wagon bed. "Fortnum and Mason! Splendid! But ye do, however, hold something against Mr. Sloan. Your voice betrays ye."

"Back in the seventies his father planted some of the biggest fields around here."

"I see. Which made him one of the biggest slavers, so to speak." Samantha frowned. "I thought the present Mr. Sloan came from Sydney. A city boy turned planter."

"Aye, he comes from Sydney. His mother didn't want him growing up out here in the wild hinterland. Not good enough here for a high-class white boy. Bit snobbish, the Sloans."

"Why is he here now?"

"You said I made a study of these things. You're right. History interests me. There's a lot of complex reasons for it, but basically, after a land boom when prices got all inflated, Australia went through a bust. About fifteen years ago—falling land values, labor strife, and strikes. Panic. Sorry mess. One of them who panicked was elder Mr. Sloan. Thought he'd lost everything and committed suicide by defenestration."

"Defenes—" Samantha pondered it. ' "Fenestra' be 'window' in Latin. Ye mean he jumped out a window?"

The young man chuckled. "The only good long word I know. And you'd be amazed how hard it is to work into a conversation. Two of his sons ran away to dig gold in Kalgoorlie. Still there, so far as I know. And the other decided to save the plantation. Re-financed through the Queensland National Bank Limited, played sticky-wicket with what capital he had left, and presto."

"I admire his courage and determination."

"Courage and determination maybe. Not his methods. He was the last planter in the state to go mechanical, because he'd managed to arrange things so that his colored field hands worked for nothing, or just about. Ignored the Imperial acts that protect Kanakas. Talk about a slaver—he really was one." The man shrugged. "Saved his plantation, though."

"At a high cost of others' sweat, so to speak."

"So to speak. Sweat—and lives. He must be sitting pretty now, though—putting in new fields, raking in the cash from his old ones. Went mechanical finally, and that takes money."

Samantha sat silent.

"All that's past now, though. Australia's bound herself together into a new nation. Civilized. Organized." The young man shifted in his seat and leaned forward, his elbows on his knees.

"Four years ago, aye?"

"Yep. In 1901. Lot of similarity, our Australia and that America. Started as colonies. Devoted to freedom. America lived through her war, and Australia, she's about done with her bleeding, too." He smiled. "Freedom."

*Ye care naething for freedom.* Edan's words echoed in Samantha's mind.

"Sad plight, aye? Australia be not much more'n a hundred years old and me Ireland lay in the mists before time was. Yet after all her centuries, I fear, Erin's bleeding has just begun."

# CHAPTER FIFTEEN

# BUTTING HEADS TOGETHER

They were not called chickens in this country; they were chooks. No matter. By either name they tasted quite as good, and jumped around just as wildly when you decapitated them. Mr. Sloan would be home by dinner time and roast chicken would greet him.

Samantha tied the second rooster's feet together, suspending him from the clothesline. Never in her life, until she came here, had she ever prepared chicken from absolute scratch, so to speak, but she was getting pretty good at it. Both roosters hung upside down eye to eye with her. She knew to keep her face out of pecking range. She grabbed both heads in a grand swoop, applied the knife and jumped away. She turned her back on their floppy death throes and returned to the kitchen.

*When the cat's away the mouse will play*, and when the master of the house is gone the kitchen descends to chaos. Samantha looked around in dismay. Dirty pans and dishes, dried, caked-on food, not a piece of flatware left clean . . . a fly-blown heap of parings . . . stinking fish heads in a bucket on the sink . . .

"Meg? Meg!" In a sudden fit of pique Samantha stormed from room to room, her poor stiff muscles complaining at every step. She pounded on the door to Meg's little room. "Open up!"

"The door's not locked. I've naething to hide."

Samantha pushed the door open. Meg was slipping into her silk blouse, the one with all the ruffles and the white-on-white silk embroidery.

She glanced at Samantha and turned her back. "Button me up; there's a good girl. I use the term loosely."

"What've ye been doing for two days? The kitchen's an unholy mess!"

"So's your face. Good thing Grandmum isn't around to see it; ye'd be up to your hairline in goose grease. Button me blouse, eh?"

"Not unless ye're planning to clean up the kitchen in yer best clothes. I didn't make that mess, and ye'll not stick me with it."

"I didn't either. Linnet did the cooking." Meg turned around and twisted her arms behind to button her blouse herself.

"Yerself was in charge in me absence. Ye're responsible, and ye'll have the place in order before Mr. Sloan gets back."

Meg stepped in close and her eyes crackled. "Whatever makes ye think ye can order me about? Ye've nae the authority and heaven knows ye haven't the respect." She snatched up the black velvetta hat with the aigrettes and pushed past Samantha out the door.

Samantha bolted after her; she had to run to catch up. She grabbed an arm and dragged Meg to a halt. "And where do ye think ye're going?"

"To visit a gentleman—who *is* a gentleman. Dinnae fret; I'll be back before yer lover returns."

"Me lo—" Samantha stepped back. "So that's how the wind lies."

"May yer dear parents go to their graves never knowing any better. Ye make a grand show of being so darlin' good, but give ye the chance and ye're right out there in the bog with the other frogs a-spawning."

*Blind rage* had always been but a catch phrase to Samantha until this moment. She literally could not see. In her wild fury she swung at that haughty face, but Meg was too quick. Meg ducked away and through the parlor and ran out the door, clamping her fancy hat against her head.

Samantha followed—almost bumped into that hideous stone statue of a face in the parlor, she was so angry—but she stopped at the front door. Her stiff, sore body would never carry her far enough or fast enough to catch the snippet. And what good would it do? Meg was beyond her control or anyone else's.

She wheeled. Linnet stood beyond the stoop, staring at her. The girl's hands were chocolate brown with dirt, her hair disheveled.

With great difficulty Samantha brought her voice into obeyance. "Meg says yerself has been cooking. 'Tis time the piper be paid. Get to the kitchen and start cleaning up."

"Mr. Sloan's last orders to me were to weed the garden. He said naething about the kitchen."

"For two days ye been weeding the garden?!"

"That and other things, aye." Linnet cocked her head and her smoky gray-green eyes danced. "And what has yerself been doing?"

Samantha drew a deep, deep breath. "Me honor's intact, as had yer own better be. Ye've more than the name Linnet to protect; ye've the name Connolly. I've not sullied it and neither shall yerself. Mr. Sloan might've said naething about the kitchen but I am. Get to it, and without delay." She turned on her heel and hastened back inside lest Linnet decide to challenge her as well.

She should have expected this, particularly from Miss High and Mighty Margaret. After all, appearances—

But what now? If she remained here she would end up in the kitchen scouring pans. Linnet was extraordinarily good at wangling that sort of thing. Trail-weary as she was, it would never do for her to merely sit about twiddling thumbs.

Luke Vinson. He was the official who married Vickers and Amena. Vickers was friendly enough to refer to him on a first name basis. Samantha entertained no doubt that the words Vickers spoke regarding indenture and slavery had come first from Vinson's mouth. That man was the key. He might even know where the Vickers newlyweds had fled to.

Meg was going calling, eh? Instead of attending her duties, eh? Samantha would go calling as well, but for different purposes. She hurried to her room, glanced at her hair (and this poor scratched face!) in the mirror and snatched up her little black beaded hat. She had no money but she took her matching beaded reticule anyway.

Vivid sunlight dappled the path down to the road, intense bright spots in intense dark shadow. She must remind Doobie to pass through here with his machete soon. Branches brushed her on both sides. She marched smartly down the road toward the little chapel half a mile from the house. She almost hoped Mr. Sloan would appear early along the road here and either join her in this confrontation or send her home. Trouble came on its own frequently enough that one ought not buy into it, and here she was, eagerly purchasing grief by the handful.

The little chapel-church was nothing like the solidly built churches of Ireland. No ornate Celtic cross graced its dooryard. No leaded glass beautified its windows. Indeed, it looked no different from all the other light, ramshackle buildings that perched along the road. Only a skeletal little spire on the roof invited the passer-by to lift his thoughts heavenward.

Samantha almost forgot one need not knock to enter a church. She stepped inside the main sanctuary, if this could be called that, from brilliance into shade. And yet, it was a soft and gentle shade, a bright gloom of filtered light from floor to ceiling. More amazing was how stark the room appeared to her who was so accustomed to draped pictures and icons and the fourteen stations. There hung a cross but not a crucifix.

She should be horribly uncomfortable in this travesty of a proper church, but somehow she was not. Perhaps, what with her frenetic adventures these last few days, she was simply ready for some serenity. This whole building radiated peace.

It was also quite devoid of life. She crossed the room to a far door and stepped out back into a little fenced-in garden. Or perhaps it was a goat pasture. Yes; in fact, there was the goat, a gentle-looking brown nanny with floppy ears.

On the far side of the goat enclosure stood the manse, a tiny hovel every bit as informal as the chapel. It did, however, sport a verandah full length along its front. And on the verandah sipping tea sat the lovebirds. Samantha certainly would not like to have caught them *in flagrante delicto*, but she had secretly hoped for something a bit more compromising than teatime.

Luke Vinson saw her instantly and came down off the porch to greet her. He extended his hand. "Miss Connolly. Join us."

Samantha accepted the squeeze of his hand; it was somewhat less than a full handshake. "Thank ye, but I cannae stay. Me sister's glare be withering enough from this distance. Ye married Amena O'Casey to Byron Vickers, is that correct?"

"I did."

"And they be yer close acquaintances."

"Close. Yes."

"Then ye might know where they plan to take up housekeeping. Where they're headed for, having left here."

"Of all the despicable tricks!" Meg leaped to her feet. "To do Mr. Sloan's spying for him!"

"Hardly. Amena decamped owing her employer a sum of money. He is just now returning from Cairns in vain pursuit of that sum and I'm testing other waters. 'Tis a financial matter."

"All slavery is." The Reverend folded his arms loosely in front of him. "Financial expedience, exploitation, whatever you wish to call it. Ah, but here." The long arms undraped. One waved toward the verandah as the other wrapped around Samantha's shoulders. "Do join us for a spot of tea. You needn't consider it a social obligation." He piloted her toward the porch. "Frankly, I want to see you get out of the sun. Your nose looks burnt."

If angry looks were hammers, Samantha would have been pounded into the ground paper-thin. Meg fumed in silence as the minister brought another chair and teacup.

He sat and poured. "Close acquaintances. Well put. Byron and Amena are recent converts; I led them to the Lord."

Samantha frowned. "I would've thought Amena was born into the church. Never spoke of it, but I assumed—"

The minister paused. "I'll rephrase. No, I'll do better than that; I'll explain. I knew Byron socially for over a year. He's been a long-term employee here. We talked of spiritual things, and one conversation led to another until he committed himself to Jesus Christ. That is, he declared Jesus to be the ultimate ruler of his life. When Amena arrived, he was instantly drawn to her, and she to him. He told her about his renewed life in Jesus and shortly thereafter she, too, gave her heart to God."

"And to Byron Vickers."

"And to Byron." He nodded. "When the cutters were dismissed, he wanted to stay around, but there was no work. He appealed to Cole Sloan and was rebuffed. He asked to buy Amena back and was again rebuffed. It was not their preferred choice of action, but they decided to elope. They couldn't see any other way to be together, what with neither of them earning any money."

"And of course yerself had nae part in all this."

He shrugged. "I married them. That's my job. I helped them grow in the faith as best I could with teaching sessions—classes in discipleship—and gave them a Bible. That's also my job. So I suppose that's some part in it."

Samantha toyed with her teacup a moment, assembling and rearranging thoughts. They weren't coming together well at all. "The words he spoke to me—Byron Vickers—sounded as though—"

"Ye talked to him?! Just now?" Meg stared at her.

"Aye. He fled and I found him. But he got away clean, he and his bride, if that's yer worry." Samantha turned her face back to the Reverend. "The words he used would've come yer own mouth, Mr. Vinson. Calling—"

"Call me Luke. Please."

"As ye wish. Calling indenture slavery. Words from a man who can see only one side of the thing."

"We discussed it frequently after he met Amena. He knows that I feel very strongly about labor injustice in this region. But I didn't counsel him. I didn't suggest he take one action or another."

"I cannae believe that." Samantha waved a hand and very nearly bumped her teacup over. " 'Tis all so very one-sided, and very much a man's opinion. The views of a do-gooder who wants to revise the human race along lines more to his own liking. Make the whole world perfect."

The minister should have been angry with her. Instead, he threw his head back and laughed. It was a delighted, happy laugh, too, with no derision in it. "You got all that out of some speech Byron gave? Please explain."

"That be hard to do. I see—he said—" She stopped and started over. "He makes out indenture as an illegal sort of slavery, with Mr. Sloan taking unfair gain from poor Amena. He could see nae atall the other side of it—the good side."

"You mean there's a good side to exploitation?"

At last the brambles of her thoughts were clearing away. Her mouth was running off with itself again, and she didn't care. "Mr. Vinson—"

"Luke."

"Mr. Vinson. The auld sod's fallen on hard times, with scant opportunity and very little luck left, for a man, and for a woman even more so. There be more girls in Ireland who'll die an old maid than there are girls who'll marry. And none of them facing aught but a dreary life of hard work. I saw the pattern of me life and I dreaded it, yet I had nae means to change it. Then Mr. Sloan's notice appeared out front the butcher shop."

"An offer of indenture."

"Aye. He pays me way here and I return his kindness with three years' labor."

"You can pay back the cost of the passage in less than a year of very low wages. He's cheating you of two years. More. He's extracting two years' free labor from you, and that's slavery, illegal and immoral."

"Mr. Vinson, ye be nae hearing me. It matters not atall to me what the moralists and the law-makers think of the practice. 'Twas not a pound-for-pound business value I signed up for. 'Twas an opportunity. He gave me opportunity to change me life, something I could never do on me own. Without him I could nae break the sorry pattern me life was taking. I owe him far more than boat passage."

"You give away your freedom for an opportunity."

"Nae. Put me freedom in hock a few years, perhaps, with the hope of a far better life in the future."

The gray eyes stared at her; the pale lips broadened into a bright smile. Perhaps her argument was getting through! He turned to Meg. "There, Meg! She said it perfectly. You pawn the present as surety against a better future. That's the Christian faith! You enslave yourself to Jesus in this life, and reap the richest of rewards in the life to come. Indenture yourself now in order to reign with Him tomorrow."

He had missed the point completely. Samantha was talking not about the spiritual but about the practical, the everyday, from an Irish spinster girl's point of view. Nor did she feel like arguing any more at a brick wall.

She stood up, her tea untouched. "Mr. Vinson, clearly, I'll not change your mind. I meself be breaking nae law in black and white, and I've a clear conscience." She glanced at Meg. "In all matters, I might add. I best go now. There be chores waiting." She stared at Meg. *And there be chores waiting for you, too, sister.* "I thank ye for yer hospitality and yer ear. G'day for now."

He was standing, too. He grasped her hand again in that same warm squeeze. "Thank you for coming by. I'm sorry I couldn't be a better help to you."

She nodded to him and to Meg and stepped down off the porch. Her stiff legs complained painfully. She walked out across the goat pasture and through the little church, because that was the only way she knew in or out. Her legs loosened up as she reached the road and started home.

Fluffy clouds up there were taking turns blotting out the midmorning sun. She still had no luck predicting rain, but there must surely be some sort of rules to the game. Familiar hoofbeats behind her made her turn. It was Sloan, back already. He rode Sheba with Gypsy in tow.

He swung down from his saddle, apparently not the least bit sore. "You're just getting back?"

"Nae, returned last evening, sir. Pleasant trip up. Thank ye again for the thoughtfulness. Yerself wasted nae time."

"With two horses I could rest one and ride the other. It became something of a challenge to see how quickly I could make it. Care to ride the rest of the way?"

"Thank ye, nae, sir."

He grinned. "Still stiff." He glanced at the road ahead, thought but a moment and pulled the bridle off Gypsy's head. He gave her a swat. Her nose high, she bolted forward, surprised by the sudden freedom. At a loose-limbed canter she took off for the barn, quickly, no doubt, lest her master change his mind. Sheba nickered and waltzed in place.

He started walking and she fell in beside him comfortably, in rhythm, as if from long practice. He was the master, she the servant; if he wanted conversation it was for him to initiate. She spent the silence happily analyzing her feelings just now. She was enjoying this walk immensely. They were walking purposefully, striding the last few furlongs home. And yet this walk was akin somehow to the gentle stroll of a lass and a swain.

*That kiss . . .*

*Come now, Samantha. Let's not get sentimental and romantic.* She rebuked her wayward thoughts.

"If you got home yesterday, why are you out here now?" He didn't say it accusingly, but there was an edge to his voice.

"I took it upon meself, sir, to speak to Mr. Vinson—"

"You don't speak to Mr. Vinson a blooming thing! You

don't go near him. And that's an order."

The spell shattered. The conversation ended. He the master had spoken, and she the servant had pawned her freedom to reply. Humbly, silently, she followed him home to the messy kitchen and their dinner hanging on the clothesline.

## CHAPTER SIXTEEN

# DESPERATION

One expects trees in a forest, and of course this rain forest abounded in trees. Scores of different sorts of trees fought shoulder-to-shoulder for space and sunlight. A few of them, bold, tough fellows, managed to thrust themselves above the canopy, paying for the sunshine with the vulnerability of their unnaturally long trunks. Below the thick mat of branches and leaves grew myriad bushes, some gangly and some squat. Strangler figs and delicate vines tied top to bottom, branch to earth. And hidden in the cracks and crotches of all this, a hundred kinds of orchids bloomed.

With those millions of millions of leaves, one would think it a wonder rainwater ever reached the ground. It did. It poured from the sky into the forest, cascaded down the countless leaves and dripped off their specially pointed tips to the leaves next below. Tiny raindrops gathered thus into huge blobs of water, plopping finally into the mud or coursing in rivulets down the trunks and vines. Indeed, the ground never truly dried out.

Samantha stood under the back porch roof mindlessly watching the deluge. Irish rain fell sweetly, almost like a gentle mist at times. Not like this. Not like this at all. The only hearts gladdened by this downpour were those of the green tree frogs. Their piercing songs rang from all directions.

"The gnomes have been working overtime." Linnet's light voice at her shoulder made Samantha jump. The girl stepped in beside and leaned casually against a porch post.

"Gnomes? Sure'n we left them behind in Erin."

"Eh, nae. Fat Dog's wife says the gnomes here around swab the tree frogs' throats. They use some medicine mysterious and sweet to keep the poor things from going hoarse."

"Ye wouldn't want a frog to croak, now."

"The soul of a poet ye'll never have, Sam."

"Nae more than yerself'll ever have the soul of a worker. Be the carpets swept?"

"I would nae dare stand here if they weren't, would I?"

"Ye'd try." She felt damp, for want of a better word, all over. The pervasive humidity seemed to creep past her clothes into the very fabric of her being. Samantha turned and walked back inside.

A thousand little chores begged for attention. Samantha felt like doing none of them. Still, she ought—

Someone pounded on the front door. Samantha covered the length of the house at a jog to answer the knock.

Mr. Butts stood under the roof absolutely drenched. He stepped into the foyer and handed her his water-logged hat. "Is Cole around?"

"I'll go see, sir, if you'll excuse me momentarily." She curtseyed and hurried off down the hall.

"Tell him it's absolutely critical," called the half-drowned man to her back.

She rapped at the office door and entered. "Mr. Butts here, sir. Says 'tis urgent."

He sighed heavily. "I'll see him."

Samantha grabbed the brocaded wingback chair and dragged it to a corner. Quickly she pushed the leather-upholstered chair—the essentially waterproof chair—to the center of the room across from the desk. She nodded curtly to the gaping Mr. Sloan and hurried back down the hall to fetch his guest.

She ushered Mr. Butts through the office door and hastened to the kitchen for tea. She steeped the Fortnum and Mason black pekoe; Mr. Sloan looked like he could use it.

When she returned with the tray, Mr. Butts was perched on the edge of the leather chair like a crow on a fencepost, gesturing wildly.

"... Even though I explained to them. They insist I must honor the note now. I'm sorry, Cole, but I need the rest of your pledge. All of it."

"I understand, John. And I hope you understand that the money is not right here. I'll have to send for it. Be a couple days. Maybe a week. But it will be in your hands just as soon as I can gather it in."

"Of course. You don't keep a sum like that in your petty cash box. Uh, might I have some sort of written promise from you; you know, just to be able to hand them something?"

"Certainly. Least I can do, since I'm keeping you waiting. Miss Connolly, a snack tray."

"Not for me." Mr. Butts raised a hand. "Much too agitated to eat." He fidgeted and tugged at his necktie. "Cole, every time I think I can see the light, something else rears its ugly head. It's so bloody frustrating. Perhaps I'm not cut out for this business, after all. And yet, I do love it."

"They say the most gratifying relationships are those built on a love-hate basis."

John Butts laughed nervously. "That's it exactly!" He watched with hungry eyes as Mr. Sloan wrote across a letterhead and tucked it in an envelope.

"That should hold the wolves at bay a few more days." Mr. Sloan passed the envelope across to the distraught businessman.

Mr. Butts bolted to his feet. "Thank you, Cole. Thank you! I knew I could depend on you! Thank you!" With a few more expressions of eager gratitude he backed out the office door. Samantha saw him out.

When she returned, Mr. Sloan had melted into a sorry glob in one corner of his roomy chair. Quietly she dragged the wet leather chair back where it belonged and restored the wingback to its usual place. He had not touched his cup.

She paused by the tray. "Ye might feel better for a bit of tea, sir. 'Tis yer favorite."

He glanced up at her with a wan smile. "Butts is the one who looks like something the cat dragged in."

"Nae, sir. The cat would never let itself get that wet toying with its prey."

The smile opened into a grin. He leaned forward for his cup and sat back again. "Remember the promise of money I made him in exchange for title rights?" He sipped at his tea.

"I see. Now, if ye are to gain a solid claim to the land title, ye must produce the money. Which ye have nae."

"Which I have nae. If I don't come up with the balance of the amount promised, I lose any claim on his land plus what I've already paid him, and he loses everything—which makes it all the harder for me when the time comes to expand. Butts I can work with. These Sydney bankers I can't."

"Manipulate, ye mean."

He smirked. He sipped. Should she leave or stay? Presently he said, "There's a way, but it puts Sugarlea on the line. Do I take the chance, or let Butts and his tea slide away? Do I risk everything on a gamble that will three times pay for itself if I win?"

"Ye're asking a woman who left everything familiar behind her in order to gamble on a new life."

He studied her a long time with those deep dark eyes. "Pack my dark suit and the conservative shirts. Use the kangaroo-hide bag. And dark ties. Melbourne is chilly this time of year."

"Aye, sir." She paused in the doorway. " 'Tis the gamble, eh?"

"Nothing ventured, nothing gained." He snorted. "Or lost, for that matter. Yes, Sam, the gamble. Heigh-ho and away we go."

And away he went, leaving that afternoon through the pouring rain with his kangaroo bag and a cryptic instruction to keep the place from burning down in his absence. When Samantha asked Mr. Doobie what the master might have meant by that, Mr. Doobie replied that Mr. Sloan always said that when he left town.

The next morning Meg dressed up and walked out to have tea. With whom Samantha could easily guess. Not only did Meg's lack of responsibility irk her but also the snippy way she said, "Mr. Sloan may have told ye not to see Luke, but he didn't tell me." Linnet was supposed to have the weekly housecleaning done, and she had barely started. It was going to be a long day.

Was Samantha feeling lonely and at loose ends because Mr. Sloan was gone? Hardly! How foolish. It was her sisters, her sisters who so casually shirked their duties—that was what irritated so badly.

At midmorning, Mr. Gantry, the mill foreman, thumped on the kitchen door.

Samantha invited him in and waved toward the chair by the kitchen table. "Might I fix ye a sandwich and tea?"

"Don't mind if you do. Mr. Sloan coming back soon?"

"Methinks the man himself doesn't know. I surely don't."

"But it'll be awhile."

"Aye." Samantha flapped a sliver of goat cheese on the slab of roast mutton and dropped the second slice of bread on top. She gave the whole creation a bit of a squeeze, just to make certain all the parts kept their places. She set it and the tea before him. "Can I do something more for ye?"

"Sure you can. Come sit on my lap here."

She took a deep breath. This sort of thing cropped up with distressing frequency, but it always caught her off guard. "I prefer not, *Mr.* Gantry."

"And why not, with the old man gone? Nothing for you 'til he gets back anyway." His hand snaked out and seized her wrist.

She grabbed his cup and splashed the scalding tea in his face, leaping back as he yelped. "I'll thank ye, Mr. Gantry, to maintain a gentlemanly decor. There be naething between the master and meself regardless what gossip ye may be hearing, and there'll be naething between yerself and me. Are we clear?"

"Pretty uppity for a bondservant, ain't you?" He stood up.

She held her ground. "I strongly recommend against trespass, sir. Now. Be there anything I can do for ye regarding the business of Sugarlea?" Was her bluff good? Apparently. He stared at her a moment, then sat down and whipped out a handkerchief.

He mopped off his face. "I was hoping to catch him before he left. We have enough good cane coming I can open the mill part time. Need some cutters."

"Be they not all employed elsewhere by now?"

"That's the trouble. He shouldn't have sent them all packing like he did."

"Be yerself a cutter, Mr. Gantry?"

"How I got my start. Best cutter in Queensland once. Caught the eye of the old Mr. Sloan and got the mill job. I'm a real man, lass; worth taking a second look at."

"Ye see? There's one cutter. Now, how about that Mr. Dakin?"

"Eh, he's still around. But he works the crusher; ain't no cutter."

"Train him. Then ye can show Mr. Sloan how efficient ye've made yer operation. Men who can work any job needs doing. If the mill operates part time, ye've time enough yerself to cut. Put Mr. Doobie to running the field tram. As cutter and foreman, ye can pocket two paychecks in the place of one—nae a bad thing."

"Did Sloan put you in charge whilst he's gone?"

"Now, who'd let a woman handle such a task? More tea?"

"I didn't miss your meaning with that trespass remark." He stood up again. "No tea, thanks. Nor have I forgotten the way he scooped ye up when we went crocodile hunting back there. I'll be on my way. Go find Dakin. Get Doobie to firing up the donkey engine. Oh—I'll need a draught if I'm to start hiring."

"He took the checkbook with him. Sorry."

"Then I'll just have to put it on account. G'day. And consider reconsidering, aye?" He winked lasciviously.

"G'day, Mr. Gantry."

She watched him shove out the door with the last bit of his sandwich in his hand. It was sinful to feel so smug. Her feelings went far beyond smugness, too. For a few moments, at least in Mr. Gantry's eyes, she was mistress of this plantation. For a few precious minutes her freedom was out of hock and she had the answers.

But only for a few minutes. Almost immediately, nagging doubt displaced the smug satisfaction. What if Mr. Sloan didn't want the mill reopened? Quite possibly his answer to Mr. Gantry would have differed greatly from hers. And when he demanded of Mr. Gantry an explanation, the chooks would quickly come home to roost. How could she have let petty pride urge her to this?

She had no time to dwell on her mistakes. Here was Fat Dog at the back door.

He pushed his black face against the fly net. "Mr. Sloan back soon?"

"Not for quite some time. What's wrong? Come in. Come in."

He stepped inside and instantly appeared somehow out of his element. He shifted his weight from bare foot to bare foot nervously as his sunken eyes darted about. "Burriwi and Wurraoonah, they back. Gone hunt, come. There be lone man, one man, up in the hills behind here. Whitefeller."

"In the forest? Doing what?"

"Bushranger. Fossicker. Nuthin. Sumpin." Fat Dog shrugged. "Walkabout. Just walkabout."

"Did he just come recently or has he been up there a time?"

"New. Since full moon. Just come."

"Did they see him or only his tracks?" Samantha might be new to the country, but already she knew that the aboriginal hunters could look at a single faint footprint and tell you whether its maker was male or female, young or old, black or white.

"Both. Him. Signs. This big; gray beard this shape." Fat Dog gestured with his powerful hands. "White-feller clothes—white shirt, pants like fossicker. Boots like fossicker."

"And walkabout." She nodded. "I'll tell Mr. Sloan instantly he returns."

Fat Dog bobbed his hairy head. "See more, he does more, I'm back, tell you more."

"Thank ye."

The wary aborigine bolted for the door and swept himself outside with a look of immense relief on his face.

Samantha called after him, "Would ye saddle Sheba, please?"

He waved a cheery *will do* and strode off toward the stable with that marvelous, loosely swinging gait of his kind.

She left a note for Meg to start dinner, left a second note with instructions for Linnet, and hurried to her room. She changed from this straight black skirt to the full one with sufficient fabric for her to straddle a horse and remain modest.

If she was going to play the role of plantation mistress, she would do it in grand manner. She would ride down to Mossman, and if what she needed was not there, on to Port Douglas, as if she had every right to do so. She could likely be done with her business by midafternoon.

Would Mr. Sloan approve of this latest idea of hers? She was certainly overstepping the bounds of a simple housekeeper. And yet, he didn't seem to mind gambling against formidable odds. This was certainly less a gamble than his, whatever he was doing. This was merely a shrewd move.

By the time she got back from Port Douglas that night, the clouds were piling up against the mountains to the west, promising another drenching rainstorm by morning.

Those gnomes had better get busy with their swabs.

## Chapter Seventeen

# Up and Down the Hills

The moment she heard the front door slam, she knew who it was. She left her book face down on the kitchen table and ran the length of the ell to the parlor. He was standing there shaking his drenched hat, trying to reshape the brim.

"Welcome home, sir." Samantha snatched up the kangaroo-hide bag. "I've mutton stew on, just mayhap you'd be coming this night and had nae eaten yet."

"Thank you. Is the table set?"

"Nae, sir; I'll get to that directly."

"Don't bother. I'll eat in the kitchen."

"As ye wish, sir." She put the bag down in order to catch his soaked jacket as he shrugged it off his shoulders. She shook it out. "And how did your business go? Well, I hope."

"The fat's in the fire. We'll see what happens next. The mill's operating. I saw the smoke and steam beyond the trees as I was coming in."

"Part time. Mr. Gantry says there's good cane coming on, to make it worth your while. He knows his cane, aye?"

"Ought to. Grew up with a cane knife in his hand. Set my place. I'm coming."

"Aye, sir!" She draped his jacket across a dining room chair to dry out and left the kangaroo bag at his bedroom door. This was absolutely ridiculous. Why did she feel so bubbly? She had rather enjoyed the absence of the master—less pressure to keep the place in perfect order, fewer chores, less service. Now here she was bouncing about like a schoolgirl in the throes of a first crush.

She stopped cold. That couldn't be what it was. Surely not. She forced herself into motion again. By the time he came into the kitchen, she had black pekoe steeping for him in the flowered teapot.

He paused to pick up her book and glance at the front page. "*The Passenger from Scotland Yard.* H. S. Wood."

"Mystery tale written perhaps fifteen years ago. Five men board a train in Paris. One is murdered and ye must figure out from the clues who is the culprit. 'Twas in that little used-and-abused shop in Port Douglas. A great fan of used books, meself."

"Been shopping in Port Douglas?" He sat at the place she had laid and snapped his napkin open.

"Hardly the most of it." She ladled stew into his bowl. "Your humble servant here has been overstepping her bounds again, sir. We can discuss it now or later, but there's things ye must know."

"Now's better than later. I need a good laugh. You've eaten, I take it."

"Aye, but meself can join ye with a bit of bread." She pulled the towel off the plate of muffins and was pleased to see they were neither hard nor cold yet. She set the muffins and butter before him, poured his tea and sat down across from him.

"Overstepping your bounds. What now?"

"Not long after ye left, Fat Dog appeared. His trackers, out hunting, came upon a white man in the hills to the west of us. A fossicker, it appears. He described the man and the description fits the fellow I met near Cairns; Abner Gardell."

He stared at her transfixed, the stew forgotten. "Here! Did you see him?"

"Nae, sir. Burriwi and Wurra Whoever are keeping an eye on his whereabouts and daily doings, at me request. That's one of the instances where I took it upon meself to give orders."

"So far so good. You're sure it's Gardell?"

"Nae atall, sir. But Mr. Gardell does occupy himself with tramping about the mountains in search of a particular gold strike, and your trackers seem to think that also be the intention of our mystery fellow here. Walkabout, they call it. On the chance it is . . . and by-me-by he should find some gold here . . ." She licked her lips. "I, uh, er . . . took the liberty of going down to the land office and filing for mineral rights in the hills behind Sugarlea. On your behalf, of course. Brought the papers home, forged yer signature and took them back. Uh, there be costs involved in it, and something about squatter's rights . . ."

"You forged my signature on state documents."

"Aye, sir."

"And filed for mineral rights without my approval."

"Aye, sir."

"Just on the spare chance that some drongo back in the hills is a half-mad fossicker who might, million-to-one, find gold."

"Aye, sir," she muttered. Her grand notion had always seemed foolish to a degree, but the way he described it now revealed her splendid idea for what it truly was—absolutely asinine.

"That's it?"

"That's it, sir. Plenty, I warrant."

He bolted to his feet, grabbed both her upper arms and yanked her out of her chair. He kissed her harder, more violently, than she thought ever a man could. With a triumphant "Ha ha!" he plopped her back into her chair and returned to his own.

"Sam, you're a beaut! I love you!" He scooped his napkin off the floor and tackled his stew with renewed exuberance.

Her heart would have pounded to hear those words but for his tone of voice. He was using the word as does one who loves to ride in a carriage in the park, who loves iced desserts, who loves a good brouhaha at the bear and bull pits. "Ye be nae angry with me?"

"Angry? You acted in my best interests and acted quickly,

as the situation required. And it was blooming clever of you." His voice dropped a notch. "You really think it might be Gardell?"

"Possibility. I only met the man briefly on one occasion, and sure'n there be a thousand fossickers out there somewhere, all fitting the description. But possibly."

He waved a hand. "Regardless who it is, if he finds anything yellow I automatically get part of it." He abandoned his stew again. "Come out on the front porch. I have something for you."

Samantha followed him through the darkening house. Linnet was coming down the hall, carrying an oil lamp, as he passed.

She curtseyed. "Welcome back, sir."

"Hello, Linnet." He hardly glanced at her. He scooped the lamp out of her hand and continued without breaking stride. Samantha heard Linnet fall in at the rear of the parade, but she said nothing.

Out on the porch he handed the lamp to Samantha and wrenched the lid off a wooden crate. He lifted the gift out and plopped it on top of its box.

"A saddle." Samantha smiled suddenly. "A saddle! Look at the scoop seat; not atall like the seat I rode to Cairns on. And it feels softer—more padded." She ran her fingers across the smooth-grained leather. Clearly it was shaped for comfort. "What a lovely gesture." She could feel herself glowing as she looked into his eyes. "Thank ye so very much, sir."

He seemed quite as pleased. "I was all set to buy you a sidesaddle and the shopkeeper advised against it. Says they're passing out of fashion and difficult to ride in hilly country. Uphill fine, downhill no. This style is popular with drovers, who spend day upon day on a horse."

" 'Tis a fine thing to do, but ye needn't have."

"If I needed to, it wouldn't have been as much fun." He rummaged in the bottom of the crate. "This goes with it. You can open it later." He handed her a parcel tied with string and turned to Linnet. "I've brought a load of shrubs up, too.

Bottle brush it's called; nice bloom, pretty foliage. I want you to plant them along the south side of the house tomorrow morning."

Movement down the road caught Samantha's eye. At the worst possible time, here came Meg back from an afternoon with the object of her affections. Luke Vinson walked with her. Obviously she had forgotten her umbrella and obviously he was walking her home under his. How touching. Samantha glanced at Mr. Sloan. He glared at the two of them.

If Meg was perplexed, she hid it well. She curtseyed. "Welcome home, sir." She slipped out from under the umbrella and bounded up onto the porch. Vinson acknowledged Samantha and Linnet, offered Mr. Sloan a few cheery words and headed home.

Mr. Sloan scowled at Samantha.

"Meself can do things both legal and illegal in the land office, but I cannae control me sisters, sir. I'm sorry. I thank ye again for thinking of me so nicely." She dipped her head and walked into the house.

Behind her she heard him snap, "Meg. In my office." She stepped into her own room and closed the door.

The parcel was a pair of bloomers. No, it wasn't. It was a divided riding skirt, nicely tailored. Splendid. Samantha hated bloomers—she'd not wear those ugly things to her own funeral—and she was nearly bound to wear whatever Mr. Sloan gave her.

The next morning, immediately after serving Mr. Sloan his breakfast, she donned her new riding skirt and tried out her new saddle. Comfort. Bliss, compared to Sheba's flat saddle. He had said something about sidesaddles and hills. She would try out this superior saddle on hills. She rode north out of the stable clearing and then turned west onto the forested mountain.

The saddle felt marvelous; the track was a wreck. Within half a mile she was off Sheba and walking, fighting her way through tangles and low-hanging branches. Enough of this. She turned around and headed back.

The nicest part of riding locally here was the horse. Samantha could not become lost so long as the horse knew how to get home. They came out into a more open park of pandanus and stately white-trunked trees. She climbed back aboard. Her saddle wrapped gracefully across the back of her bottom, cradled her in snug comfort. Almost certainly she would get stiff again, but equally certain, it would not be nearly as bad. And she felt much more secure.

And she knew now what a forest horse was. The mare picked her way safely through tangled growth. She didn't wipe Samantha off under low-hanging branches. She had a feel for the trail and could follow it along those stretches where Samantha saw nothing.

Here was a track, now overgrown, that seemed to go straight up the mountainside. She turned Sheba away from her beeline home, and dug in her heels. Her nose nearly touching ground, the mare scrambled up the track. They topped out on a knife-edge ridge. Through breaks in the ubiquitous vegetation, Samantha could glimpse afar the patterned sea. Dark green and light green blotches marked, she guessed, coral gardens beneath the surface. The lucid blue-green melted into gray haze that melted into the filtered blue of distant sky. How bright and beautiful—how peaceful—especially when compared with dear Erin's dark and turbulent shore.

They followed the ridge for a quarter mile. These narrow trails must once have been logging roads wide enough for a team of horses to pass. Flat-topped stumps betrayed the use of axe and saw. They descended a tortuous old trail, topped a little hump and angled eastward toward home.

Sheba strolled out into a clearing so open a few sickly blades of grass could survive here. She wound among low, gangly bushes and was about to reenter the forest when Samantha stopped her. Over there along the edge of the opening was a camp. A lean-to of woven ferns and palm fronds provided protection from rain. The firepit in front of it, lined with stones, still sent stray wisps of smoke up now and then.

Burriwi and Wurraoonah? Their mysterious fossicker? Aborigines simply passing through? She wished she knew more about such things, and could read the signs invisible to her now. She urged Sheba forward, her eyes still on the little camp.

Sheba jolted to a stop.

He leaned against a tree not ten feet in front of the horse's nose and he was smiling. "First a bicycle, now a horse. You need some instruction on how to get through forests, lady."

"Mr. Gardell—the top of the morning to ye! I've a brand new saddle and I'm trying it out."

"I'm disappointed. I thought you were spying on me, too."

"Hardly, sir. Ye know as well as anyone that I be useless outside the city limits." She tilted her head. "As I recall, ye were seeking a rock so high, marking a gold mine."

"Still am. You've a good memory; particularly as flustered as you were that night." He nodded to the east, toward nothing but forest. "So there's Sugarlea."

Samantha smiled. "Ye'll have to ask me horse, sir. She knows the way better'n I. Where she takes me, aye, that's Sugarlea. Do ye care to visit us, ye being so close?"

"No. Thank you for the invitation. Since I talked to you, I've learned that quite possibly the hills I want to search are west of Port Douglas, not Cairns. So I'll sniff around here awhile."

"I wish ye all luck, sir."

"Thank you. Enjoy your new saddle."

"Sure'n I am, Mr. Gardell. G'day."

He dipped his head. Sheba shoved past him into the forest eagerly, homeward bound. Branches splacked Samantha in the face, mostly because she was not concentrating on her ride. She was thinking about the strange man, McGonigan's partner. She should have asked him about the significance of that. She probably should have asked him many things, having unexpectedly gained his ear. But what? At least she was certain now of the identity of their mysterious fossicker.

Even Sheba's shuffling trot, her most jarring gait, failed

to shake Samantha dangerously loose. They plop-plopped into the stable clearing and Sheba parked herself in front of her makeshift stall. Samantha slid to the ground.

Fat Dog chuckled. "You grin your whole face. Big fun, eh?"

"Marvelous! Sure'n I'll pay for it tomorrow, but today was lovely." She hurried down to the house. It ought be very close to lunchtime and she must make soup yet.

She burst into the kitchen.

Meg sat at the table lackadaisically cutting up carrots. "I'm to make lunch and you are to go help Linnet plant the bottle-brush bushes. He says they're going to die before she gets them buried. His words."

"I planned lentil soup and cold mutton sandwiches. That's enough carrots. Add some onions and plenty of garlic and a can of tomato juice. There should be several on the pantry shelf."

She really should change out of her riding skirt before groveling about in the dirt, but she didn't. She found Linnet out on the south side, surrounded by droopy plants with feathery silver leaves.

The limpid gray-green eyes looked up at her, woebegone. "I dinnae understand why he sends me out to the gardening. I cannae do this sort of thing."

"Ye're a natural, Linnet; ye have nae fear atall of being covered with dirt head to feet. Ye've got dirt streaks on yer face even though yer head's supposed to be the farthest thing from the shovel."

"Make fun. How far down do I dig? How deep do they go? He told me naething."

"If he had to explain everything, he'd as well do it himself, aye? Go up to the stable and bring a barrow of manure—the oldest ye can find at the back of the pile. Meself'll dig the holes. And be quick. These poor bushes may croak quicker than the frogs."

Linnet made an unappreciative noise and disappeared around the house.

The bushes had been pruned back severely. Samantha

studied the cut ends and tried to imagine how big they had once been, and therefore how big they were likely to get again. She measured by eye and by guess how far out from the wall to set them and began to dig.

The window by her head gritched open and Mr. Sloan leaned on the sill. "How does the saddle work?"

"A genius ye be, sir, a sheer genius."

"I've been called many things, but never that before. Where'd you go?"

"Up and down the mountain to try out the seat." She paused her digging. "Ye told me once to stay away from Abner Gardell. I disobeyed ye, sir, and conversed with him, though not by intent. I stumbled onto him, so to speak."

"So it is him."

"Aye, and he's aware he's being watched. He claims to be seeking his gold mine and allows it might be west of Port Douglas instead of farther south. He declined an invitation to call. Sir? What might a gold seeker carry in the way of tools?"

"Pointy hammer, small shovel, a pickaxe, ropes perhaps."

"He had nae such. Carried naething on his person and had nae tools atall in the camp. Not so much as a water pail. Nor did I see a gun, though I'd expect him to carry one if only to bring down fresh meat."

"You're saying he's not seeking gold?"

"Meself be saying he's not equipped for it."

He looked at her awhile, but there was no reproof in his gaze. At length, he nodded. "Don't go back up there."

"The abandoned trails all about there—logging tracks?"

He nodded. "My father logged the hill extensively, soon after he arrived. Ebony, mostly; a couple of kinds of gum-wood. There isn't much left back there in the way of costly timber, but there's some cheap and middle-priced wood. Might bring a nice penny if shipped to England. Heard from your father yet?"

"Nae. Mum writes, but he dictates. Soon, I'll wager."

He waved a hand toward his bushes. "Think they'll make it?"

"Aye. A bit to eat—Linnet be bringing it now—a cool draught to drink and they'll be soon chipper and fit." But the holes wouldn't dig themselves, so Samantha set to work. Minutes later she realized he was still watching her. She stood erect. "Sir?"

He shook his head. "Just noticing that the skirt fits." He stepped back and closed the window.

## CHAPTER EIGHTEEN

# SWEET SAVOR

A cricket, the town crier of Sugarlea, chirped its review of the day's news from beneath the baseboard in the hallway. Across a wall in the darkness rustled a house gecko intent on seizing some luckless multilegged thing. Samantha doused the light in the parlor. The frogmouth outside the glowing parlor window would be deprived of its private smorgasbord soon, once the moths decamped. Sullen, humid darkness. Night. Sounds. In Ireland when night came, most everyone except mice went to bed. Here in the rain forest, nightfall brought most of its denizens to life.

She paused beside the somber stone face to glance down the side hall. A light shone out from under the office door. The door opened and a familiar shadow stood in the yellow gleam.

"Sam?"

"Just closing down, sir."

"Come." The door swung to: darkness, but for the line of light.

She came, entering quietly, shutting the door behind her.

He sat on the edge of his littered desk. "So you're Gantry's boss now."

"Ah. Methinks I see the road ahead. Nae, sir, though I did offer an opinion, one servant speaking with another."

"A housemaid on a major business decision. Some opinion."

"I recall some time back, when first ye made Mr. Butts his offer, ye said to the effect that if a simple housemaid can see to the core of it, a businessman should be able to. That's all I see, sir, is what a simple housemaid sees."

"Gantry came to you for an opinion."

*No, Mr. Sloan, that's not what the rascal came for; that's just what he left with.* But Samantha would not mention the mill foreman's transgression. She'd learned a little something in her years as a servant. "He came looking for yerself, not knowing how long ye'd be gone, sir. I gave him lunch. 'Twas about that time."

Mr. Sloan gazed at her with the strangest expression on his face. "That's not what he says."

"I speak the truth, sir, and have nae interest in what he may or may nae say. 'Tis between yerself and himself."

His voice rose. "Gantry and Dakin logged themselves in as cutters as well as mill workers. Two men drawing four paychecks on an account with a minus balance to start with! Gantry's not that smart on his own, Sam. He can see only in one direction—straight ahead, like a horse with blinders. Nothing devious. That's why my father hired him—for his stupidity. That idea came from your head, not his."

"His problem was finding cutters, for they've all gone elsewhere. I suggested how he might solve his problem, for he seemed fair perplexed and though I dinnae tell him, I knew ye were headed for Melbourne—days and days gone. He's the experienced sugar worker, and I'd expect him to weigh me advice against his own experience."

"Gantry belongs to me and I expect him to do whatever needs done without getting paid double for the honors. He accepted that until you opened your mouth."

*Belongs to me.* Yes, the man actually said that. Samantha held her peace. She was saying too much already.

He lifted himself off the edge of the desk and wandered over to the darkened window. He stared out at faceless night, then turned. "You're spending the night with me. Get along. I'll be in shortly."

So here it was. She somehow knew it would come eventually. She dreaded facing the question and yet, in a curious way, she welcomed it. She yearned for it, for closeness. The yeses and noes tore at each other inside her. She was twenty-eight years old, with never a . . . and now this man who attracted her so . . . *his kiss* . . . And yet, her honor . . .

"Nae, sir." Samantha kept her voice low and even.

"You belong to me, too. I own you."

"Ye own me labor, which meself is giving without reserve." On impulse Samantha stepped forward until she was practically nose to nose with this haughty and handsome man. "Sir . . ." She studied the floor a moment, trying to keep the flowering thought in her mind from losing all its petals in her speech. "Ye're aware of me somewhat checkered record of employment. Two positions, and in part a third, which I left hastily because of the master's advances. When first ye commented upon the Connolly honor, as we strolled along the beach– ye remember?"

"I remember."

"Ye laughed that it builds a fire under me, or however ye said it. Aye, it does. 'Tis the most important thing I have, and the one thing I can keep, though luck and money slip through me fingers uncontrolled. I dinnae compromise it yesterday, nor shall I today or tomorrow."

"What makes you think you're different from all the other housemaids in the world?"

"I'm a Connolly, sir."

He burst into laughter, a hollow mocking laugh, and wagged his head as he walked away. He wheeled. "You're a Connolly. No, Sam, that's not what makes you different. But something does and I wish I could figure out what. Your first day here you were different." He smirked. "Sloan's harem. You've heard that."

" 'Tis a term been bandied about, aye."

"A jibe with the ring of truth to it. It's one of the reasons I hire a woman. I have no compunctions about taking up with any woman in my employ. Comes in the package."

*Kathleen Corcoran!* She saw now the deeper reason behind his rage, and it was not just economic, what the croc had stolen. The truth shocked her; she'd not suspected.

"I dinnae answer ye lightly. Ye're a splendid man, Mr. Sloan. Were it not for honor . . ." She licked her lips and turned to leave. She opened the door and paused, leaving it ajar. She turned, that she might meet his eye squarely. " 'Twould seem nearly everything ye have is purchased, and usually with money that is nae yers. A sorry way to romp through life, sir—exciting, nae doubt, but hardly honorable. G'night, Mr. Sloan."

"I'd be more inclined to believe your lovely little honor speech if you hadn't offered yourself to Gantry."

Her heart went into her throat. Gantry's word against hers, and Mr. Sloan would believe whatever he felt like believing; men are like that, she'd long ago learned.

She stared at him until the silence got loud. "Ye once, in so many words, painted John Butts as a fool. If ye actually believe meself would invite Gantry, when I deny Sloan and shall continue to do so, ye be a far bigger fool than he."

She swung the door open, stepped out—

—and very nearly ran over Meg! She gasped and Meg gasped and they stood staring at each other.

Samantha recovered first. "If ye've filled yer ears with enough slander that be none of yer affair, perhaps ye'd best hie yerself to your room now."

"Ye dinnae . . . I mean, ye were nae . . . uh . . ." Meg took a deep breath. "I came to speak with Mr. Sloan—"

Mr. Sloan leaned out the door. "Meg, get in here!" He pointed at Samantha. "And you stay."

"Be a private matter, sir." Meg stepped inside.

"She stays. What is it?"

Meg swallowed, turned a bit pink, and then drew herself up as tall as five foot five allows. "I wish to be relieved of me duties here, sir, that I might go a-marrying."

Mr. Sloan looked past her to Samantha. "The Connolly honor."

"Ye forbade me speak to Luke Vinson. Rescind the rule, eh?"

"Go."

Samantha turned toward the door but Meg grabbed her arm. " 'Tis not so simple as it appears, Sam. I'm a Christian now."

"And what were ye before, a pagan Hindu?"

"He said ye wouldnae understand. When ye talked to him about how indenture is pawning yer freedom now with hope for the morrow, I saw for the first time what Luke had been trying to tell me. And what it means to be a bondservant of Christ. 'Tis your own words helped me see the light."

"Light! A dark day for the Connolly name and ye call it light." Samantha yanked free and slammed out the door.

She didn't bother with her little beaded hat. The matching beaded reticule stayed behind. All she took was the punched-tin hurricane lamp from the kitchen. She lighted its candle as much to notify the mysterious night creatures that she had mastered fire and was not to be messed with as to see through the black gloom.

She approached the manse the only way she knew—through the little chapel and the goat pasture. A light in the window under the verandah told her he was still up. She hopped onto the porch and rapped smartly.

He opened the door smiling, and he was much closer to handsome in this soft yellow lamplight than she had given him credit for. "Miss Connolly. Good evening. Please come in."

She stepped inside his little kitchen. It was nearly as spare as the chapel, without so much as curtains at the window. She obviously had interrupted study or sermon preparation or something. On the kitchen table with the oil lamp were an open Bible, an earthenware mug, a teapot and a scattered sheaf of papers.

Without so much as by-your-leave, he grabbed another mug from an uncurtained shelf and poured. "Sugar?"

"This be nae a social call."

"Perhaps not from your viewpoint, but it is from mine." He grinned disarmingly and swung a chair around for her.

"Sugar. Thank ye." She sighed and blew out the candle in her tin lantern. She regretted that instantly. Either she must beg a match off him or stumble home through the dark, for she had not thought to bring matches. She would stumble before she'd ask a boon. She sat down and stared morosely at her mug, wondering all the while why she was not feeling more uncomfortable. She ought to be.

"How can I help you?"

"Me father and his father before him held the family honor sacred, Mr. Vinson, and he taught his children to do the same. Now me sister's about to sully it and I believe 'tis at yer own behest. Regardless what ye may think of the matter, she made a written promise, which she wants to break. Yerself is the only one who can sway her, for she listens nae to me. I've come to beg ye yield to honor and change her mind."

"Do you pray, Miss Connolly?"

She froze, wary. "I've heard yerself does nae."

He sank back all relaxed in his chair, chuckling. "I've said that, yes. But it's not properly true. I pray many times in a day. It's just that I hate using that word because people so often misconstrue its meaning. Let me ask this: have you ever simply talked person-to-person with God?"

"I be a humble servant girl, sir, and dinnae presume to know God that well. He's up there and I'm—" She stopped, her mind awash in recent memories. She almost giggled. "I was considering this same thing one night quite recently. Amorphous somethings in the forest were throwing fruit pits at me."

His eyebrows shot up. "Oh. Fruit bats."

"Nae, sir, bats be wee things, and these were—"

"About three feet across. Crawl around in the treetops using those wings for hands. They especially like damson plums."

"Bats," she whispered and her spine tingled. "Nae, Mr. Vinson, I dinnae pray. Thought about prayer, but dinnae do it. There be considerable difference, ye know."

"Perhaps not. The book of Romans tells us the Holy Spirit intercedes when we don't pray as we ought. We struggle to speak, particularly when we don't know the person of God well, and the Spirit reroutes it; makes it right. God listens to your heart, you know, not your words."

Until now she had not felt uncomfortable about talking to him. Now her mind began to squirm a bit. "How did we get off on this? The question at issue is me sister, who—"

"Who has made an important step. The *most* important step. She's gone from knowing about God to knowing God himself."

"She's been in the church since birth. Twisting words around makes your mumbo-jumbo nae easier to swallow."

"How do you like your new saddle?"

"Stop it! Ye change the subject at will, for nae reason."

"Oh, I do have a reason. How do you like your saddle?"

"Well enough, thank ye. Much improved over previous."

He leaned forward and made an imaginary horse and rider with his hands. "Faith is what carries us along, ultimately to heaven. Faith in Jesus. Faith is the horse. This. You are the rider. This. The saddle—that's the church. Any church that points a person to salvation in Christ. Yours. Mine. The saddle's purpose is to make you more comfortable on your horse, and to keep you from falling off. The church helps you stay with the faith. But it is not, itself, the faith. You can throw the saddle across a rail fence and ride it, and feel very safe and secure. Of course, you won't go anywhere. Not an inch. Meg still has her saddle, the church, but it's now on the horse. And she knows God person-to-person."

Samantha stared at the hands, at the two-finger rider perched on the flat-hand horse. "And what has that to do with keeping the promise she made half a world away?"

"That is between her and her God and Sloan. Neither you nor I can make her decision for her. She carries the Connolly name as much as you do, Samantha."

"Ye can advise her."

"And so can you. But the final word must be hers."

"So ye will nae intercede. Of course ye wouldn't. 'Tis to your advantage, if marriage be your notion, for her to break away from her commitment unbetimes. I dinnae see now why I came, except 'tis so important to me. But nae to yourself, nor, apparently, to her." She stood up. "Me apologies for breaking into yer studies there."

He tapped his open Bible. "Second Corinthians two. 'We are to God a sweet savor.' In the Old Testament that term was used in reference to sacrifices. In the New Testament *we* are the living sacrifice. Crops up again in Ephesians five. Fascinating study."

"Nae doubt, if ye have interest in such things."

"Every person should. Several years ago I realized I was giving God, essentially, my leftover time and efforts. I was pursuing what Luke Vinson enjoyed doing, not what needed to be done. I recommitted myself, gave myself to Him wholly as a living sacrifice. A sweet savor. I want to be always a sweet savor to God—to leave a sweet taste in His mouth."

"Then why do ye interfere? Had Byron Vickers not listened to ye, he'd probably have a job as a cutter now. And Meg . . ." She sighed.

"In essence, the sweetness comes in sacrificing personal desires in order to please God. Can you see that?"

Could she see that? She thought of the personal desires she had sacrificed this very evening, and all in the name of honor. Was honor of itself a sweet savor? She was pretty sure chastity was, but . . . "Sacrificing the self. Aye, I see."

Vinson dug into a matchbox by the stove and brought two barn burners to the table. Unbidden he lighted the candle in her lantern. "Cole Sloan seven years ago was convicted and fined for illegally using Kanakas. For slaving, pure and simple. He is still at his old tricks, but calling it by a new name." His gray eyes met hers and she could see cold steel in them. "Jesus was the ultimate theologian, but He also bore the ultimate social concern. I'll not bend in the matter any more than you would. May I walk you back?"

"Nae, thank ye. Methinks I prefer to be alone. I trust 'tis safe."

"As safe as anywhere, I suppose. But you don't have to go through the goat yard, you know." He led her out to his front gate, gave her hand that squeeze of his, and she was on her way.

She took her time returning. This meeting had gone nothing at all the way she would have expected, though she had no clear expectations for it when she came. He had taken it exactly where he wanted it to go and said exactly what he wanted to say, and she had achieved nothing.

When is a Christian not a Christian? His hands burned vivid on her mind. Person to person. Prayer. Talking. Fruit bats. The sweet savor of sacrifice. Her wildly diverse thoughts waltzed in and out in her mind and left her in total confusion. One thing was certain. She had let Mr. Sloan down.

All was dark as she entered the house; there was not even a bar of light under the office door anymore. She blew out her candle and retired to her own room without lighting a lamp. The saddle picture—so vivid. Sweet savor—nicely put.

Whatever spiritual dimension the preacher operated in, it was one Samantha had never suspected existed. He intimated that Meg now walked that road. Was this some sect such as the priests were constantly belittling in their homilies back home? Was Meg truly finding solace in a new relationship with God, or was she streaking toward hell on a greased pole, hard behind the seducer of her soul?

What words were spoken in Mr. Sloan's office after she left? What was Meg's fate—to be hounded and followed after like Amena? The thought of pursuing her own sister as if she were a fugitive chilled Samantha's heart. For long, long hours she lay alone in the humid darkness, wide-eyed, and listened to the house geckos scurry along the walls.

## CHAPTER NINETEEN

# EXPLORATION AND DISCOVERY

*Luke's wrong. He's misleading you.*

Leaves rustled. Tiny feet riffled through the duff of the forest floor. All familiar sounds.

*Here, right here, everywhere around you, is the truth you heard from your fathers. Here is reality.*

Occasional sun-dapples intruded on the brooding gloom. He parted the leaves and branches as he moved forward. Whispering, they closed protectively behind him. Safe. Cradled in the past.

*Listen to your ancestors and the spirits that guide you. The sky is but one of many. He's an outlander, a babe. He's proven that. What can he know?*

Burriwi stopped. The forest voices had fallen silent up ahead to the northwest. He moved forward without parting leaves, letting his dark, naked body slip from here to there. He became yet another shadow in a forest of shadows and shapes that may or may not really be. The eye sees not half of reality.

There was the reason the spirits were silent. Waist deep in ferns, the intruder stood on a rocky little spike jutting from the steep hillside. He peered through a long black tube down toward the coast and Sugarlea. Burriwi moved in close and watched the man a few minutes. This fossicker, this white–

feller with the hoary beard, was not one with the forest; only blackfellers achieved that unity; but he came very close. The spirits all around him did not embrace him, but neither did they cry *Stranger*! They tolerated him and allowed him to be comfortable. That much Burriwi could feel.

Sloan hated and feared this man. Burriwi had sensed that the first time Sloan questioned him about the man's whereabouts and activities. Sloan's own spirit was malign, though Burriwi felt no real discomfort around him. What made this fossicker an enemy of the lord of Sugarlea?

The man lowered the long tube from his eye and collapsed it somehow to a third of its length. Remarkable. Burriwi would have guessed it to be made of some very hard substance. He watched the man pick his way across the fern-clad ledge, then followed at a discreet distance as the fellow crunched through the forest, quartering up the hillside.

The man stopped. He sniffed loudly. "I smell you out there. You been eating too much whitefeller tucker. I can't smell you when you eat off the forest. Prowl around and watch me or come walk with me. Don't make no difference to me, either way." He ambled on carelessly.

Burriwi followed silently until the fossicker had topped out on the ridge and seated himself on a rocky little outcrop. Why not see what this man has to say? Burriwi could judge later whether to reveal to Sloan that he had spoken with him. He stepped forward far enough to be visible.

From somewhere within that graying bush a smile emerged. "Welcome, friend. Have a seat."

Burriwi leaned against a tree trunk and cocked one leg against the other. He folded his arms and waited.

"You're not the same blackfeller was following me around a couple days ago. They were youngsters; not very good at it yet. But they're learning. Gonna be fine trackers someday, the both of them. You're all working for Sloan, though, I expect."

Burriwi waited.

"Sloan say why he's so interested in me?" He paused for

an answer, then answered it himself. Burriwi would not have expected impatience from this man who roamed the forest in so leisurely a fashion. "Naw, he wouldn't tell you a scrap more than you need to know. I'll tell you. My father and his father were partners once, out seeking gold. Them and a third, McGonigan. They started out the best of friends and ended up at each other's throats, and me in the middle. I've a score to settle with Sloan and he knows it. Bet he's mentioned none of that to you."

Burriwi considered several courses of action before choosing to speak. "That why you're here?"

"Seeking gold, friend. You and your chums been watching me long enough to know that."

"Don' find gold looking at Sugarlea through a tube."

The fossicker roared his laughter and clapped his hands, stilling the voices of forest birds for a mile around. "Here. You ever look through a telescope? I'll show you." Without standing up he snapped that long tube out to its full length and extended it toward Burriwi. "Point it at the treetops there and peer through the little end."

Burriwi lurched forward. He could feel nothing hostile in this man; no spirits warned him. He accepted the tube and looked in the narrower end as instructed.

"Now sort of push it in and out—make it longer or shorter—until you can see the treetop clearly. See what it does?"

Amazing! Burriwi lifted his eye away momentarily. The man was not moving. Away out there, barely within sight, a wedge-tailed eagle perched near the top of a great gum. It took Burriwi a while to find the gum tree, and there to find the eagle. He restrained himself from reaching out to touch the bird. This was illusion. This was not reality, not even spirit. But what a fascinating illusion, to eat distance so cleverly!

"I cannot hear the gum leaves. It brings forth the sight but not the sound." He handed the tube back, satisfied that it was harmless. *You look down upon Sugarlea, strange fos-*

*sicker, but you hear nothing*. The tube posed scant danger to Sloan; no need to mention it.

"You're right, obviously," the bearded man went on. "Poor way to seek gold, through a tube. Aye, I have more than a passing interest in your Cole Sloan. He shares his father's sin. You can tell him that or not, as you like."

*Sin*. He had just used one of Luke's favorite words. Burriwi considered further. Here was an independent opinion, the point of view of a man with, apparently, no direct ties to Luke Vinson. Even more important, unlike Luke, this man was not at odds with the voices of the forest and the sea, the way Luke was. The spirits Burriwi knew did not scoff at him as they scoffed at Luke. This man surely saw things Luke could not—spiritual realities in Burriwi's book as well as Luke's.

Burriwi leaned against a stump near the fossicker's arm and tucked his leg up again. "Tell me 'bout Jesus, eh?"

"About . . . what? Jesus?" The fellow studied Burriwi with the most perplexed expression. He chuckled. "Bet Sloan never talked about Jesus. This must be something else, aye? Jesus." He wagged his head. "Lost contact with Jesus, friend. Sorta drifted away from Him."

Ah! The man referred to Jesus in such a way that it was clear the fellow actually existed. That answered one question: Jesus was indeed a reality. Burriwi waited.

"Went to church when I was a tad, before I turned twelve and McGonigan made me his partner. After that—after all that—when I was roaming on my own pretty much, I tried a couple times to get religious again. Used to read the Bible a lot. Didn't work, though. Me and Jesus, we're not good friends; hardly even know each other anymore. But I know what I gotta do. Got that from the Bible."

"What's He like?"

"Well, let's see. Son of God, but He also called himself the Son of Man. Half and half and both, all at the same time. Used to be a walking, talking man. Spirit now, though."

"And explain to me the word 'salvation' mebbe, eh?"

"You should be asking a preacher that one."

"The preacher's a good lad, but he can't hear a voice 'less it's in his book. My spirits tell me he's wrong, but they don' seem to mind you much. You tell me mebbe."

"Why not? Let's see what I remember. Been a long time."

And Burriwi sat down beside him to listen.

"She has a history of hard deliveries, but this one came in just under three hours. 'Course, it's her ninth. She oughta be getting the knack of it now, eh? Heh!" The portly shipper jabbed his elbow into Cole's ribs. "Here. Have a cigar. They're the best. Cuban. Only person I ever asked who knew where Cuba is was that preacher, Vinson, and I've asked lots of people. Something about a Spanish-American war a couple years back. 'Down south of Florida U.S.A. in the Caribbean,' he says, and by jove that's right! Smart bloke, Vinson."

"Yuh." Cole grabbed Wiggins' hand and shook it vigorously, lest he be given another of these stinking cigars. "So glad your woman gave you another son."

"Cole, I remember the look on your Papa's face when you were born. He was glowing. Glowing. And I thought to myself, 'Old Conal, he can't be *that* happy.' Now I know 'twas no put-on. This here's my third son and I'm just as happy as the first one. And the girls, too. You need a family, Cole, a fine one like your papa's. Every man does. Isn't anything comes close to it."

"For that I'd need a girl like Mum, and I haven't found one yet."

The man's face darkened, sobered. "Nor will you so long as you're mucking around with them coloreds and servant class. You gotta find yourself a good white girl. Maybe down in Sydney."

"I'll probably end up taking your advice, Wiggins, but right now I have a warehousc full of tea to move. What have you found for me?"

The man stared out his window a moment, either looking at the docks in the distance or perhaps looking at nothing at all. "Luke tells me there's a court injunction to deal with first."

"Dealt with. A judge in Brisbane overturned Bothner. I have legal possession now. And it's none of Vinson's legal concern anyway."

"Hah!" The man wheeled around and began rifling through the papers on his cluttered desk. "Now, I investigated a couple markets. America's out. They passed those good-tea laws and don't let anything through the door now, practically. Mexico's somewhat of a possibility, but it's only the wealthy class there drinks tea at all and there's precious few of them. But I scored big in South Africa. I've nearly a ton lined up with a jobber in Durban. And Argentina. Think I can get rid of the rest of it in Argentina for you."

"You're brilliant, Wiggins."

"Shipping's my job. I love it." He winked. "Almost as much as siring heirs, that is." Before Cole could speak he whipped out another of those big black cigars. "Here. Take two; cement the deal."

A handshake would have been sufficient, but Cole knew when to exercise diplomacy. At least, when he finally got out of there five minutes later, he didn't have a third one of those blasted things.

He paused a moment on the street until his eyes adjusted to the summer glare. There across the way stood Sam, as the proprietor of the dry goods store loaded a crate of something in her wagon. Crisp white blouse and black skirt, as usual. The blouse nearly glowed. And her little black beaded hat shaded all of her face except her nose—the part of her that needed it most. Would her nose with its peeling white skin and blotch of red never get used to the sun? On the other hand, it was kind of cute—it added a touch of vulnerability to her brick-wall demeanor.

Samantha exchanged inaudible pleasantries with Mr. Hamm and climbed into the wagon box. She gathered up the lines like a pro and away she went. The stereotype was true: the Irish did indeed enjoy a certain natural gift for handling horses.

He walked down the street to Gypsy and untied her from the rail. He mounted smiling as he thought about Sam's pillow. Game girl. Another wave of smug pride rolled over him as he remembered his stroke of thoughtfulness—buying her that boat ticket. If anyone should voice doubt about his largess, let 'em ask Sam about the boat ticket.

He sent a wire to Chestley. He called on Ian Carlson but Ian was out of town. Bereft of further business, he pointed his eager little mare toward home.

Half a mile short of the mill cutoff, it occurred to him that if he had any space left in that tea shipment, he just might be able to sell some turbinado without paying additional shipping. He reined Gypsy aside and headed for the mill. Gantry would know how much yellow was immediately available. Maybe he'd have to be content with raw. No matter; any kind of sugar sold was money in his pocket.

Sam's wagon was parked by the mill office, its horse dozing in the sun. Sam stood about by the office door looking impatient, but then that was a wild guess on Cole's part; he was too far away to read her face. Gantry came out and paused at her elbow. She took a deliberate step back. From the rear of the wagon, he scooped up a bulky parcel of what looked like office paper. He disappeared inside with it as she pulled a smaller package off the wagon and dropped it on the stoop. Did she seem reluctant to go inside?

She was climbing up over the wheel when Gantry reappeared, grabbed her arm from behind and pulled her down off the wagon. He yanked her around and gripped her other arm. Instant inexplicable rage flared in Cole's breast. He dug in his spurs; the mare leaped forward. He could hear Sam's voice, strident, above the clatter of Gypsy's full gallop.

So intent was he on stealing a kiss, Gantry almost failed to notice Cole in time. At the last moment he wheeled wide-eyed and dragged Sam around as a shield. Cole would have run him down; he couldn't now. He veered Gypsy aside and dived for the ratbag's throat.

Was it Gantry or Sam he slammed into? They all hit the

dirt in a heap. Cole got most of the wind knocked out of him, but surely Gantry wasn't feeling any rosier. Sloan rolled free and pulled himself to his knees facing what was left of the pile. Sam lay curled in a ball with her arms flung over her head and Gantry was struggling to—

A load of bricks drove Cole into the ground. Without thinking he tucked to protect his face and belly, then arched back and out, flailing arms and legs. The weight on his back dropped away. Cole wrenched around—Dakin! Cole was a pretty good fighter, Rafferty's rules as well as Queensberry's, but he had precious little chance of winning this one—not against two big, solid cane-cutters.

"Punch up!" Someone was yelling from the mill. Cole couldn't trust any of those galahs—what if they all came piling in?

Dakin's big brogan was flying at his face; he managed to grab it as he ducked aside. He swung it like a cricket bat, with all his weight. As Dakin flew past his ear, Cole took a wild swing at the ugly face, but he didn't connect well at all.

Gantry was on his feet and taking that first step forward. Cole mustn't let him get his balance; he must prevent him from squaring away. Cole charged him—he came at the mill foreman the way Gypsy had come at him moments before, full tilt.

Gantry was a strong man and wildly angry, but not nearly as enraged as Cole. Cole had that edge, that advantage. Suddenly he knew he was going to win. He didn't guess; he knew it, and pressed the attack all the more furiously.

He must put Gantry away quickly, for Dakin was surely right behind him. Fat chance; he was getting as good as he gave, fists and knees both. For a big man, Gantry could duck and feint with the best of them.

Gantry knocked him reeling against the front wagon wheel so hard he didn't feel the blow. Through the fog he saw Gantry's hulk coming at him. Cole twisted aside just in time as a massive fist hit the brake bar *whank*! and Gantry roared.

It was all but over. Cole pressed forward swinging. He got

a few back, but nothing really effectual. And now Gantry had both arms up, protecting his head, as he yelled something penitent. Mercy be hanged! Cole slammed a hard one into the man's belly and put his knee solidly where it did the most damage. Then when the arms involuntarily relaxed he punched that filthy, presumptuous face until the drongo collapsed like wet rags in the dirt.

Cole wheeled. Dakin. . . ?

The burly mill hand lay face down in the dirt, his big cane knife still under his limp hand. Sam's dainty foot darted forward and kicked the knife aside, beyond reach. Sam. Sam! Cole stared, incredulous. She was sucking in air in great choking sobs. Whether in fear or anger Cole couldn't tell. Her bloody nose was making a mess of what was once a crisp white blouse . . . not a bit ladylike. But Cole would have been chopped like ripe cane had she remained a lady. She stood over the inert Dakin with her weapon, a singletree still gripped in her two hands.

The grip loosened a bit as her hands began to shake. She watched Dakin a moment longer, then let the singletree fall from her grip. She covered her face with both hands and began sobbing in earnest.

One of the mill hands stood over Gantry, wagging his head. "Done like a dinner. And lookit the brake bar—he bent it!" The man stepped back and shot Cole an admiring grin. " 'Twas a moral certainty ye weren't gonna come out on toppa this'n. What a ripper!"

Cole glared from face to face. "You people attending the theater or drawing pay? You"—he pointed at the mill hand—"hitch her horse back up."

The man leaped to the task with an enthusiasm usually reserved for quitting time. He snatched up the singletree and called for help to get the horse back in position. The gallery of spectators disbanded itself by ones and twos and threes.

Cole crossed to Sam and hoped nobody noticed that he was a little wobbly and close to collapsing. Not knowing just what to do, he simply wrapped his arms around her. She melted against him.

Her lovely red-brown hair tickled his chin as she spoke. "I tried to un . . . to unhook . . . the singletree—even before he . . . he pulled out that knife. But . . . the horse kept . . . kept jerking it." She swallowed a couple times and lifted her head. Those marvelous eyes . . . "You look terrible."

"Same to you." Was this the time? Yes. "Sam, I owe you an apology—for even thinking you might've invited Gantry. I'm sorry. Very sorry." He let his arms turn her loose and regretted having to do it. "Let's go home."

She nodded numbly and started wiping off her face with her sleeve. It didn't make much difference to the blouse anymore. She let him give her a hand into the box, and she scooted over to make room. She knew Gypsy would not only be back in her stall by now, but unsaddled. He pulled himself up by sheer force of will and settled in beside Sam. The mill hand gave him the lines and even sorted them for him.

All the way back to Sugarlea her warm body pressed against him, pressed harder each time the wagon jiggled. Sam. He thought a lot about Wiggins' heady joy. He thought of his own unspeakable fury when Gantry dared try to possess what was his, bought and paid for. But was that all she was? A possession? A few months ago he would have said yes. Now, though . . .

What was it he told Wiggins? He hadn't found a girl like Mum yet? Truth was, he wasn't looking for a girl like Mum. Mum loved parties and teas and balls and riding in her finery behind a team of high-steppers around Mrs. Macquarie's Point. Mum fainted dead away at the sight of blood. Mum would never in a million years find the presence of mind to unhook a singletree, let alone get into a fight with it.

No. This wasn't Mum. This was better. Just maybe he had found the girl.

## CHAPTER TWENTY

# ENCOUNTERS WITH HISTORY

Samantha balanced her tray on one arm, rapped on Mr. Sloan's office door and entered unbidden. "Tea and sandwiches, sir."

"Bring an extra cup for yourself?"

"As ye mentioned, sir, and I thank ye."

"Ever use one of those typewriters?"

"Me sisters have, Meg especially. She's proficient at it—employed thus back home. Don't know that meself would be coordinated enough." Sam set out his plate of sandwiches, cup and napkin.

"Looks like I'm going to have to give in and go mechanical here in the office, too. Only businessman around, just about, who stills writes it out."

"Secretaries cost quite a penny, aye?" She poured.

"Not if I use Meg." He sniggered. "You know, if much more happens to your nose, you're going to have to trade it for a new one."

"Eh, the swelling's gone down a bit." Samantha settled in the wingback chair with her cup of tea. "Burriwi stopped by the kitchen asking for tucker. Said something strange about how whitefeller food makes him smell but he'd like some anyway. I gave him a joint of beef and those squash. Yerself voiced a certain resistance, ye'll recall, at seeing so *much* squash at meals."

"What's he say?"

"He's been up in the forest. Yer Mr. Gardell be there still and seems to be paying closer attention—looking nae so much for gold as at Sugarlea." She cleared her throat. Then she went on. "Me curiosity be me worst vice. Who is he, Mr. Sloan?"

"I've never met him. Heard of him indirectly a couple times. He's the son of my father's former partner, Winston Gardell. Win, my own father Conal, and a Clancy McGonigan were together."

"Wait . . ." Samantha frowned. "He called himself McGonigan's partner. He's old, but nae near old enough, for yer father's surely of another generation."

"Let's see if I can keep the dates straight. They met in 1850 and went over to California together. America. Gold rush there. Earned barely enough to get a boat home again. Minute they got back they went to Ballarat, where the gold boom was just getting started. Win married but spent more time chasing gold than staying home. Abner was born a couple years later. His father died when he was just a toddler."

"Winston, ye mean."

He nodded. "Cave-in. Foully assisted, some say. McGonigan sort of took over responsibility for the mother and child—sent money, dropped by now and then. When Abner was twelve, McGonigan took him in as a full partner—over my father's objections."

"Surely he couldn't be harboring hatred for that."

Mr. Sloan shrugged. "You spend all those years scratching around in the bush, your mind does funny things. McGonigan died soon after, which took care of the partnership. My father brought his body out, but the boy disappeared. Not too long ago I heard someone mention the name, and I recognized it. So I knew he was alive, and apparently around Cairns. Then you ran into him."

Samantha wagged her head. "So many who sought gold found death instead. Here. America. That affair in Ballarat. All over. In a way, Erin's blessed that she has nae precious minerals."

"Oh, Papa found his gold, all right. How do you think he financed Sugarlea? Built the plantation?"

Samantha laughed suddenly. "I cannae imagine that! In Erin the farms and the hamlets and cities have always been. Ireland be almost like God—nae beginning and nae end. I cannae conceive of starting a farm from naething; change a boundary, mayhap, or a dry stone fence, but nae a whole farm."

"Cairns was built as a staging area for the gold boom inland—in sixty-seven, I think. Brand new town and looking down at the heels already."

Samantha counted. "Thirty-eight years old. A whole city only ten years older'n meself! Ye have a history, Mr. Sloan, but 'tis such a short one. Me own native city? Why, Cork was old when the Vikings rowed ashore, and that was a thousand years ago. More."

He poured himself a refill. "Cairns and Cork. Whether their history is marked in hours or millennia makes no difference. They're both here now, and that's all that matters. It's the now I'm concerned with. History doesn't affect me, and I'm not the least bit interested in it."

"Eh, nae, sir. We be carried along on our history—'tis a part of us—we be enslaved to it and never once do we realize what it does to us, nor ever suspect we're making more of it as we go along. Me brother Edan died months ago because Henry the Eighth and Elizabeth and James the First planted Protestants on the auld sod three centuries ago. Englishmen who never did belong there. And now Arthur Griffith and his *Sinn Fein* are making more history. And more trouble."

"You see?" Mr. Sloan put down a sandwich to spread his hands wide. "You have Vikings and Henry the Eighth on your neck. I don't. A couple of black savages chasing cassowaries and spearing fish, until my father's generation arrived; that's all."

She drained her cup and stood up. "Aye. But ye've that, all right—yer father's generation to contend with. 'Tis history, all the same, be it short or long. Me very point first made."

His face washed dark like a tropical storm. What had she said? She no doubt would have found out, but Meg rapped earnestly at the door.

She burst in. "Mr. Butts here, sir."

John Butts barged in right behind her. The storm in his face made Mr. Sloan's scowl look like a picnic in the park.

Meg disappeared instantly.

"You foreclosed! You took my whole plantation! I trusted you, Sloan."

"No need to stop doing that. Let me show you something." Mr. Sloan nodded toward Samantha. "Another cup for Mr. Butts."

Samantha darted to the kitchen at a dead run, snatched up the first cup that matched its saucer, and raced back. Mr. Butts had never frightened her before. He did now. He was normally such a mealy man, uncertain of himself it seemed. Today he boiled and roared like a runaway train.

She plunged into the office and set the cup hastily before him. He didn't even see her.

Mr. Sloan thrust a paper in his hand. "That tea the typhoon rained on—I have it sold, John. It's not a total loss. But I couldn't have done it until it was mine, and I didn't have time to work through you with all the releases and signatures and all that mess." He smiled winningly. "You're right I undercut you. But it was to our mutual financial advantage. An opportunity with a close deadline."

Mr. Butts studied the paper, perplexed. "Durban. Wiggins told me he couldn't find a market."

"I put him onto some connections—friends of friends of my father's. People my father knew back in his gold-digging days."

*So you're not influenced by history.* Samantha caught her master's eye, but she couldn't tell if he understood her thought.

Did Mr. Butts sink into the wingback chair because he was feeling less tense or because his knees collapsed? He wagged his head. "I—I guess I didn't realize when I signed that . . . " He shuddered. "It's so hard seeing my land—*my* property—in someone else's name. Under their control. Your control, that is. Harder than I thought. I admit you have a head for business. And heaven knows I don't seem to. Still . . ." His voice trailed away.

"I can imagine how hard it would be for me, were it Sugarlea," cooed Mr. Sloan.

"I built the place, Cole, from nothing. Less than nothing. The century was in double-aughts when I started, and I thought surely within five years . . . Well, it's five years, and . . . and . . ." He looked near breaking down. "I almost think I'd rather have the place back and keep making mistakes, or whatever I was doing, than to see it . . . understand, not that I don't think you, uh . . . you know . . ." He licked his lips.

Samantha's heart wrenched. The man, so ominously wild moments before, seemed more like a disappointed child. Disappointment? Wrong word. Consternation was closer, a child denied the one single thing in the world precious to him. She proceeded to do the only thing she could do—she went back to the kitchen for more tea.

Here came the brash young preacher whom the spirits mocked. Burriwi smiled to himself and watched the man come riding into the settlement on Wiggins' roan. The boy was ignorant about relationships and how to greet friends, relatives and strangers, but he did ride well. Burriwi must remember the preacher was from a wholly different world, and be tolerant of his lack of culture and politeness.

Women, children—Luke greeted them all by name, those names he knew, and dismounted by Burriwi. With a grin and a handshake he hunkered down beside him.

"My nephew said you came by."

"Dibbie all caught up on the cassowary people?"

"Caught up. Learn about. Yeah. Now he knows the stories about his people in the time gone."

"The Dreamtime, you call it, I believe."

"Eh, that, too. But he has to know lots of other stories,

too—lots of times—since the Dreamtime. His fathers dead and all the others."

Luke smiled. "Oral history. I understand that people without a written history can literally recite their oral history word on word for days at a time. The historian, so to speak, tells it to the next-generation historian, and that person has it memorized." Luke snapped his fingers. "But once they learn to read and write, they lose the ability to memorize large quantities of information exactly."

Burriwi shrugged, grinning. "Now Dibbie knows his fathers."

Luke studied him a long moment. "You don't happen to know how many teeth you have, do you?"

The laughter exploded out of Burriwi. It was not the least bit polite to laugh so at what was clearly a sincere question, but its absurdity delighted him. Besides, this young man didn't know politeness from a coral cod, and he didn't seem bothered by Burriwi's infraction in the least. "Sometime we count 'em mebbe."

"I'd love to."

Burriwi wagged his head. Hopeless. He sobered. "If Dibbie learns to read and forgets his fathers, don' you go teaching him to read, eh? Fathers more important'n reading. Oh, and I found out about your Jesus yesterday. Not in your book. My book."

Luke's ears didn't snap erect literally, but he perked up like a dog who first notices a chunk of fresh meat. "Tell me!"

"I asked a whitefeller you don' know, he says about Jesus same as you. Now I know it's not just you and your book."

"And what have you decided?"

"Eh, what you said. That Jesus is real, and He's stronger 'n the spirits I know. He's the best way. We talk a long time."

"Burriwi, that's wonderful. Who is this man?"

"Here. Why not you come along? Bet we can find him, talk to him more, mebbe, eh? Name's Abner Gardell. Wise man; wise about the forest."

Luke bounced to his feet with the kind of grin Dibbie

saved for acknowledging special treats.

"Besides," Burriwi smiled with all his uncounted teeth, "he keeps good eye on Sugarlea. Watch out for your lady friend."

Luke's face hardened. "He works for Sloan?"

"Ask him." Burriwi was not about to get all mixed up in the various machinations of these outlanders. But then, Luke claimed to be very close to this Jesus fellow (in His present spirit form, apparently), and Abner Gardell admitted losing contact with Him. Burriwi would simply put the two men together and sit back to listen. The encounter ought be informative—at the very least, entertaining.

It was logical that the spirit world should extend far beyond the realities within blackfeller ken, just as did the physical world. This might provide Burriwi insight into the spirit world of the whitefellers, if indeed there was any, and he could pass what he learned on to the others. It might even help explain the whitefellers' strange, inhuman drives and hungers.

Luke Vinson had the same effect on the forest that a sugar tram has on a quiet conversation. It took Burriwi most of the day to locate Abner Gardell, despite the fact that the fossicker was not at all trying to hide. Burriwi finally left Luke sitting—the man got tired easier than Dibbie did—located Gardell, and brought him to the preacher with as few words of explanation as possible.

Burriwi knew that whitefellers, having no custom for finding out how to greet one another, tended to be guarded and formal at first. But he certainly didn't expect the feeling of just plain hostility that bristled between these men who purported to know Jesus. Nor did their talk go the way he had thought it would.

"I understand you work for Sloan." Luke studied Gardell warily.

"No. Never met him. Seen you around his place now and then, though."

"We're not friends. I've formed a friendship with one of

the young women in his employ."

"Yeah? From the looks of your face there, I'd say you were out kissing a reef."

Silence. Glaring silence.

Burriwi broke it. "Abner, friend, how do you smell me like that?"

The man burst out laughing. "Burriwi, I was leading you on. Since I realized Abos were keeping an eye on me, I've just been shouting that at the forest now and then. Couple times a day. If the boys are following me, they step right out and walk with me; I feel better keeping an eye on them. Didn't think it worked on you, though."

Burriwi snorted. Embarrassing, but the hostile spirit evaporated. He settled against a pandanus trunk and waited.

Either Luke didn't catch on or he was good at hiding it. "Burriwi says you keep an eye on Sugarlea. May I ask why?"

Gardell snapped his head around to Burriwi. "You said he was a man I'd be interested to talk to. About Sloan?"

" 'Bout Jesus. He big-notes Jesus and you don' talk to Him no more." Burriwi shrugged and grinned. "So whata you say?"

"Ah!" Luke recovered his boyish grin and the feeling of hostility fled. He settled down cross-legged on the ground and explained to Gardell what he had told Burriwi. Then he recited what Burriwi said and what he understood Gardell to have said. . . . And in all this Burriwi plucked the men's words from the air and shook them through the sifting-basket of his own thoughts.

He perceived how barren and colorless is the spirit world of whitefellers. Only four entities need be considered seriously. And yet, those entities were each so powerful, they performed by themselves all the blessings and curses that in the world of the blackfellers' spirits were assigned to a host of specializing entities.

Amazing, too, was the black and white nature of their spirits—wholly evil or wholly good. Gardell seemed particularly concerned with the effects the evil one had upon him.

He spoke of an unforgiveness, a smoldering hatred. Both men agreed this came from the evil spirit, a single entity called by either of two names. They agreed that this unforgiveness erected a barrier to intimacy with Jesus.

These two men, diverse in many ways, agreed completely on the powerful influence of their few spirits. Burriwi dismissed any doubts about the reality of Jesus, God the father, His Holy Spirit and Satan, whom they referred to as the devil now and then. And yet, if the three good spirits were so powerful, why did they exert so little influence on whitefellers, on Gardell especially? In a contest of three against one, how could Satan prevail? He must be powerful indeed.

Perhaps the raw strength of the evil spirit explained the whitefellers' common traits of insane greed and callousness. Perhaps Burriwi felt this malign spirit directly when he felt Sloan's spirit. But Luke's book said man himself bears an evil nature. Burriwi thought about the petty jealousies and power plays within his own clan, much less these men. Luke's book was probably right on that point. So then, how does one discern between the evil spirit's malign work and the evil within the man himself? That was not coming out in this discussion at all.

Good thing he was listening with one ear, at least; Luke addressed him directly. "Burriwi, I'm glad you brought me. After conversing here with Abner, I realize I have to reexamine my own motives for confronting Sloan. Am I truly interested in the higher morality of freedom and human dignity, or am I exercising vindictiveness toward a man with whom I disagree, who doesn't approach life as I do because he doesn't have the light of God to go by?"

He had just used five words not in Burriwi's vocabulary. Since the little speech didn't add anything to the questions in Burriwi's mind, he let it go by. "Glad you're glad, Friend."

Gardell chewed pensively on his lower lip. "What you're saying, Vinson, at the core of it, is that if I want to get back together with God, I'm going to have to forgive and forget."

"In essence, yes, if you want wholeness with Him."

"I can't."

Out of curiosity, Burriwi asked, "Who is strongest, really? The good spirits or the evil spirit?"

Luke glanced at Gardell. "Strength for strength, God, of course. But God does not impose His power on us. He doesn't make us obey Him. We have to want to, to do it voluntarily." He translated his own long word. "On our own."

"Sometimes we can't." Gardell scowled, somber.

Luke nodded. "It may seem so. Satan knows how to use the wrongdoing and evil within ourselves to add to his own strength. He's able frequently to get the upper hand that way. Abner here has that very war going on within him—Satan using Abner's own nature to keep him away from God."

That answered the question exactly, and the way Luke sometimes talked a long trail to reach a short destination, Burriwi was mildly surprised. Gardell might have problems, but the matter was clear in Burriwi's mind.

He would transfer his trust from the many spirits of sea and forest to the great God who was more powerful than all of them. That meant, he knew, that he must also believe about Jesus. No problems. And that surely meant, too, that the evil spirit would try to separate him from God, as it was doing to Gardell. He saw that he must guard against that.

Gardell was wagging his shaggy head sadly. "The past, Vinson. The past. It makes slaves of us all."

## CHAPTER TWENTY-ONE

# DISASTER AND TRAGEDY

Brilliant late-morning sun set the rippled sea to glowing, bluer than blue. Dazzling sand and bright water made Samantha's eyes hurt as she walked the narrow strand below the house. She sat for a few moments beneath a small, gnarled tree. She had to tuck in and hunch over to fit beneath its low, spreading branches.

Out over the water a large white sea-eagle came soaring. Its gray-tipped wings dipped and spread; it looked more like a monstrously huge butterfly than a bird of prey. It coasted low to the light-dapples, its long white legs hanging down, then dropped suddenly. When it rose with mighty wingbeats, a silver fish flapped in its talons.

From above the trees here on shore—from out of nowhere—a dark wedge-tailed eagle zoomed by. It made a menacing pass at the sea-eagle. The second threat worked; the white eagle dropped its fish and angled away from the danger on its huge spreading wings. The dark eagle had the fish in its own claws before the trophy could touch water.

Why did this primitive act of avian piracy enrage Samantha so? It probably happened frequently; indeed, it had occurred quickly, as if rehearsed. And it was certainly none of her affair. Nature has its own rules for heroes and villains.

She'd best get back and commence luncheon preparations. *That is one sorry thing about being a cook,* she thought wearily. *Your creations disappear three times daily—or oftener—and must be constantly recreated.* She squirmed out from under her shady retreat and started home.

She was within a few rods of the house when hoofbeats came clattering from up ahead. Here came Mr. Sloan on Gypsy, wearing a city suit. She stepped out of the way.

He pulled up beside her. "I won't be back for lunch. Have a supper waiting late."

"Ye look upset, sir. Meg? Something meself can help with?"

He smirked. "Bankers I can't manipulate. Don't let the place burn down while I'm gone." He twisted Gypsy's head around and cantered away.

He did not get back for supper, though she kept it waiting for him until past eleven. He did not return at all that night. When he finally did ride in, grim and weary, the sun was ready to set on the next day.

Samantha put her pen down, her letter to Mum only half finished. She watched him through the flynet on the back door as he pulled Gypsy's bridle and let her find her own way up to Fat Dog and her manger. He washed his face off perfunctorily at the ewer and basin on the back porch, shoved through the kitchen door, and flopped into the chair by the table.

"What do you have from dinner? Sandwich, maybe?"

She tied on her apron. "Fish chowder. Linnet's friends brought us some very nice rock cod. And perhaps a bit of lamb."

He nodded, not a bit enthusiastic about rock cod chowder.

She ladled a serving of the chowder into a smaller pot so that it might heat more quickly. "Ye don't appear to have fared well with yer recalcitrant bankers."

He laughed wryly. "Recalcitrant. Love it. I'm one step ahead of ruin, but at least I'm still that step ahead." The forced cheer melted into gloom. "Ever use a telephone?"

"Aye. They have some in Cork. Hard to hear from—dim and scratchy—but 'tis a grand improvement over running 'cross town."

"They have 'em in Sydney, too. Also in Melbourne, and their telephones caught me, Sam. The bankers got together and discovered among themselves that I've encumbered the same land twice."

"Meaning?"

"I took out a loan using land as collateral that already had a mortgage outstanding on it. Now they want their money. All of it. Or else proof that if I go under they'll get what's theirs. That there's enough real estate for all the vultures to feed on."

As she sliced a slab off the leg of lamb, Samantha added two and two and came up with Butts. "Ye're going to foreclose on the tea lands, hoping to impress the bankers with your real worth."

"Tried that approach." He sighed and rubbed his face. "I thought my clear title to that, plus Sugarlea, would convince them they shouldn't call in their loans. No luck. So I managed to sell the tea land to a starry-eyed emigrant from Liverpool who hopes to make his fortune here in the brave new land. Gave the bankers a hefty sum; let 'em talk about that on their telephone. Now I wait to see if that'll hold 'em."

She turned and stared at him. The anger boiled up in her. How could he do that to. . .? *Hold your blabbing tongue. You're a servant and no more.*

"When will ye know their mind?"

"You ever hear of the sword of Damocles?"

"Aye." She set the lamb before him and dished out the soup. "I'll steep ye a fresh pot of black pekoe. This old tea be strong enough to roll up the sides of yer tongue."

"Gardell still up on the hill?"

"I presume so. Fat Dog's nephews look in on him now and again, and Burriwi keeps an eye out. Meself has heard nae new."

"Like a bloody carrion bird he sits there. A vulture. Watching me, waiting for the carcass to cool off."

"Or mayhap simply scratching about in search of gold and dinnae know or care ye exist."

"He knows. And believe me, he cares." Mr. Sloan poked absently at his soup with his spoon, but his interest picked up when he tasted it. Rock cod makes an exceptional chowder.

Samantha sat down at the table, the better to meet him eye to eye. "Mr. Gardell distresses ye almost more than yer bankers. Why?"

"None of a housemaid's business."

"True enough, sir." She stood up in part because she knew when she wasn't wanted and in part because someone was knocking at the front door.

Meg was just ushering Constable Thurlow inside as Samantha got there.

Thurlow twisted his cap nervously about in his hands. "So Cole's not returned from business yet."

"Arrived moments ago, sir. Margaret may not have heard him come in." Samantha turned back toward the kitchen. She would have preferred the man wait in the foyer until summoned, but he followed on her heels. She got to the kitchen three steps ahead of him. "Constable Thurlow, sir, to see you."

Mr. Sloan stood up slowly. Neither man offered a hand. "Percy. G'day."

"Cole, I hate to do this, believe me. Not my cup of tea atall. The papers came to me from Brisbane in the afternoon post, to be served in person." With that preamble completed, he groped a moment in the inside pocket of his tunic and produced a very official-looking envelope. Samantha could not see it clearly, but she glimpsed the return address in part.

Mr. Sloan received it, opened it, studied its contents.

The constable hastened on. "I need a signature here, a witness that I did in fact deliver it to you. Sorry; bit of paper work, y' know, but must be done."

Mr. Sloan pushed past without hearing him, it appeared, and roared off down the hall.

"The signature? Cole?" Mr. Thurlow turned to pursue him, but Samantha grabbed his arm.

"May I see the paper, please, sir?"

"Well, I don't see why you should." He shrugged. "Or shouldn't." He let her take it from his hand.

She picked up her own pen and scrawled Mr. Sloan's signature across the line provided for it. "There ye be, sir."

He stared. He sputtered. "Miss, this isn't right. It—"

"Did ye deliver the papers as ye were instructed?"

"Yes, but—"

"Into his hands as requested."

"Yes, but—"

"So ye did indeed do it, he's got his bad news, and ye've the proof right there that the deed be done. Now do ye suppose it matters to the judge and the court in Brisbane whether the name they see be penned by one hand or another?"

"Well, I . . ."

Samantha motioned to Meg over in the doorway. "The black pekoe is ready. Pour this gentleman a spot of tea, give him a bit of fish chowder; 'tis an excellent chowder; and see him on his way, aye?" She curtseyed to Mr. Thurlow. "G'day to ye, sir, and godspeed." She left him standing there blinking.

She ran the length of the ell and down the far hall. She was overstepping her bounds as a housemaid again, even more severely this time, but she didn't care.

She had seen his face.

She pushed open the office door gently. She stepped inside, closed it and leaned against it. "Ye need someone to yell at and throw things at, and a housemaid's as good as anybody for the job."

He lay draped in his chair, arms and legs askew. He looked at her the longest time with sadness from the very depths of his soul brimming up and over in his eyes. He tensed only enough to lean forward and shove the papers, those infamous papers on his desk, an inch closer her. "Read them. They pertain to you, in part. What's a housemaid's opinion of this?"

"Ye be mocking me, sir, and welcome." She picked them up and perched herself on the edge of the brocaded wingback. Wading through the florid legalese took a while. One was a desist order enjoining him from using servants obtained by indenture. Another was a summons to appear in the state court in Brisbane. There he was to show cause why he should not be arraigned for violating state, federal and Imperial laws regarding the use of imported labor.

She looked into the sad, sad eyes.

He waved a weary hand. "You're free, Sam. You and Meg and Linnet. Amena, wherever she is."

"I can't believe an indenture be all that illegal."

"You didn't read the page with all the small print. It's the terms they object to, and a few other things."

"The labor laws, as I understand it, were designed to keep out colored labor more than prevent slavery. We Irish girls may nae be high society, but we be nae pagans, either."

"Tell it to the judge."

"I shall."

He looked at her with those deep, haunted eyes. "Straws and camels' backs." He sat there, numb. And sat there. "It's gone." So was any whisper of hope in his voice.

What should she say? She had no need anymore to worry about stepping out of bounds. The bounds had been removed by a court action in Brisbane.

She stood up. "Then 'tis gone. Ye did yer best. Ye played the game according to the hand ye were dealt. Now it's gone. Ye can pick up the pieces or ye can jump out the window."

He had been so loose a moment ago. Instantly every muscle in him tightened. "Who told you?!" He relaxed again. "Gardell."

"Nae the fossicker. A pleasant young man, a stranger seeking to work 'defenestration' into his conversation."

"He would've been seventy-five years old next month, my father."

She sat down again and waited.

He stared past her at infinity awhile. Finally he returned.

"Shouldn't you be packing or something?"

"Do ye wish I should?"

"Not my choice. Judge Winteringham there, he says to."

"And were it yer choice?"

His voice dropped nearly to a murmur, devoid of strength or resource. "Don't go, Sam."

A very distant, very strange splintering thunk—feet coming down the hall at a lumbering run—Samantha stared at her ex-master, too surprised to move. He stiffened in his chair, but that's all he had time to do.

The door flew open. Wild-eyed, John Butts filled the black doorway. "You!" He screamed at Mr. Sloan and pointed a quavering finger. "You betrayed me!"

Mr. Sloan sat back in his chair and folded his hands across his lap, totally composed. "Good evening, John."

Samantha stood up and stepped quickly aside. "Yer chair, sir. I'll be going now." She looked at Mr. Sloan. "Tea and that coffee cake, aye?"

"That would be g—"

"No! You don't leave!" The pointing finger swung from Mr. Sloan to Samantha. The man fumbled in his pocket and pulled out a pistol, a dark revolver with a barrel perhaps three or four inches long.

She should be terrified now. Paralyzed. Transfixed. Why was she so calm? This man did not bring a gun simply to brandish it in the air and make everyone uncomfortable. He was facing the wretch who had just ruined him and destroyed all his dreams. The gun was here for Cole Sloan. If she could move in close enough to seize his arm . . .

She stepped forward. "Mr. Butts, sir, I be but a serving girl, sir, but I am a lady, sir, and ye'll not wave that g—"

His free arm swung at her backhanded. She saw it coming, but she could not move in time. Even as it caught her in the neck and sent her wheeling, she could see Mr. Sloan come rising out of his chair in one great motion. She slammed against the wooden file cabinet and clung there as the room kept spinning.

The constable loomed in the doorway now, screaming orders, a dribble of fish chowder on his chin. The gun blasted, louder than any shout. Mr. Thurlow ceased his yelling and stood there with a look of most wondrous surprise on his face. Slowly, casually, his knees buckled.

With a howl Sloan came diving over his desk. He slammed into Butts, dragging him down in a deadly wrestling match. They rolled back and forth, struggling, kicking, and flailing. Cole Sloan was the younger, the stronger, the more fit. But Mr. Butts was powered by a pure hatred, a manic fury for which youth and strength were no match.

Just where Butts landed his lucky blow Samantha didn't know, but suddenly the madman was free and leaping to his feet. He screamed a frantic obscenity at Mr. Sloan; he was aiming the gun; Samantha flung herself forward. She was no fighter. She had nothing going for her but momentum. She tucked her head and legs and cannon-balled into the back of Mr. Butts' knees.

His weight came down on her as she buried her head in her arms. Then Mr. Sloan's legs thumped across her back. The gun went off; it fired again. She wriggled free barely in time to see Mr. Sloan lurching to his feet.

He had won. The gun was in his hand now. It was over. And yet it was not. In a flashing moment of time she knew what he was going to do, and she knew she was powerless to stop him. She screamed out "No!" but she was too late. The gun roared. Again. Again. It clicked. Mr. Butts's foot still lay in her lap. It jerked rapid-fire for several seconds and went limp.

*Now* it was over.

## CHAPTER TWENTY-TWO

# THE THEME OF TIME

Samantha sat in the wingback chair with her elbows parked on its arms and watched her fingers tremble in her lap. She didn't try to still them. Less than two hours ago her whole body had been shaking like that. Only the fingers? Why, that was nothing.

Meg flew about, remarkably in charge. Energy and organization had replaced her ho-hum attitude, and the transformation amazed Samantha. Part of the reason was surely Luke Vinson. He was here pretty much against Mr. Sloan's will, but Mr. Sloan wasn't actually kicking him out. Yet. In truth, the minister was a big help. He may not have been trained in medicine, but he seemed to know what to do until the doctor came. He had Constable Thurlow resting comfortably in Mr. Sloan's bed across the hall.

The Port Douglas constable was here now also, taking notes and scribbling elaborate diagrams in a tattered copy book. The man was a contradiction, no matter how you looked at him. He sported a manly, very bushy handlebar moustache, no doubt left over from the rage ten years ago. And yet the delicate *pince-nez* perched just above that moustache suggested a meek counting-house clerk. On the broad chest a silk shirt with a ruffle down the front; massive ham hands without a callous on them; a powerful stride, yet a delicate touch and small, firm handwriting—the body of a stevedore housed the mind of a college professor.

His assistant, a skinny little gentleman in a tunic a bit too large for him, scurried about measuring the distances from place to place and thing to thing. He would quote figures as his superior wrote frantically and demanded still more numbers.

Doobie and Fat Dog were in and out. Linnet floated on the periphery. And in the middle of the floor, like the centerpiece on a table of horrors, lay John Butts.

The pool of blood in which his whole upper body lay soaking was turning darker. His skin was taking on a bluish, ashy color. Samantha couldn't bear to look at him, yet she couldn't keep her eyes off him. Someone had closed his eyelids and his mouth, but the mouth kept falling back open.

"Excuse me. Constable Fish? Do you suppose you could cover him now? Linnet has a bedsheet there—"

"Few moments more, my dear." The hulking official paused in his ceaseless jotting. "Criminal investigation is no longer a casual examination of surface facts. It's a science. Here we are five years into the twentieth century. We must keep pace."

From the doorway Linnet announced to no one in particular, "The doctor has arrived. He's with the constable now."

Constable Fish flourished his pencil. "I'll need him in here for a death certification also."

Linnet curtseyed and disappeared.

The constable studied his pages of spider-web diagrams all riddled with arrows pointing to marginal comments. "I think that will do for the moment. You may cover him, miss—Where did she go?"

"I have it." Mr. Sloan brought the bedsheet from the leather chair and snapped it open.

A portly man Samantha had not seen before stepped into the room, toweling off his hands. "I want to take Thurlow down with me to Port Douglas, Sloan. Got a spring wagon or something comfortable for him?"

"Better. I have Doobie firing up the tram. Fat Dog will see that you both get down to the mill, then ride your horse home for you. You can take the sugar train with the constable."

The doctor nodded. He glanced at the corpse almost as an afterthought. "He's dead, Harry. Certified." He left.

Mr. Sloan smirked. "Now that's scientific." He draped the body. Instantly the bedsheet began wicking up blood, and Samantha knew who would ultimately clean this mess away. She shuddered.

Constable Fish snapped his notebook shut. "Sloan, had Butts put a bullet in your heart, I would have ruled it justifiable homicide. I know what you did to him. You're bloody lucky Thurlow saw everything and lived to tell about it, or I'd have you in irons now, and happy to turn the key."

Mr. Sloan eyed him, his head high. "What are you saying, Harry?"

"I'm saying the wrong man died tonight. And if I ever have the opportunity to lay something at your door, however trivial, I'll do it."

"I appreciate your vote of confidence."

"You insufferable—" The constable caught himself. Apparently he, like Samantha, had a tendency to overstep his bounds.

Mr. Sloan tightened up like an overwound watch spring. He exploded with an obscenity. His pointing finger waved toward Samantha. "He hit her! He came into my own home to kill me, and he hit her!"

Constable Fish studied Samantha curiously, as though he had never before considered her to be an actual person. He turned and marched out, his assistant tagging along at double-step.

She felt numb, absolutely unresponsive. She heard Fat Dog and his nephews in the bedroom, preparing to carry Constable Thurlow down to the waiting sugar tram. She watched vacantly as the local mortician and his assistant gathered the ghastly remains into a basket. The centerpiece of horror went out the door.

Luke Vinson asked what he could do for her and she assured him "nothing." A mechanical singsong was all the voice she could muster. One by one, each went his own way. The hubbub quieted until she could again hear the banjo clock beside the file cabinet. A few minutes longer, and its ticking was the only sound left.

She was not, however, alone. Mr. Sloan had sunk into nearly as complete a stupor. He sprawled all jammed into one corner of his chair and stared at nothing. She should move. She should leave. She should return to her room and beg sleep to come.

He stirred and shifted his gaze to her. "I owe you, Sam. If you hadn't dived into it there . . ." More silence.

"I feel like I felt when we learned Edan was—" Words failed her. She started over. "Ellis described it, and this, uh, this matches what he said so dreadfully well. Poor Ellis. To look on this, and 'twas Edan. And not yet fourteen years old he was."

"I'm sorry. For Ellis as well as you."

"I'm sorry also. But . . ." She stared at him. His face was drawn, almost haggard; but there was no remorse in it, no true sensitivity. How did she know? She didn't know how she knew, but she knew. ". . . but what I be sorry about is that I helped ye, I think. I've not yet worked it out in me mind, understand. Too much happened far too fast. Yet I know this. John Butts didnae have to die."

"Maybe, looking at it after the fact. But in the heat of battle, when all I could think of was defense, I did what I felt I had to do."

"Nae. Nae, Mr. Sloan, that's not it. Either Constable Thurlow be shielding ye or he did nae see as much as he thought he saw. Yers was nae an immediate response to danger. Mr. Butts lay vanquished and there was a pause, however wee. A fraction of time for thought. Ye pulled the trigger on purpose. 'Twas a considered action."

"That's not what you told Fish."

"I was sleepwalking when he asked me story. Still am, in truth. Me mind and me memories be just now starting to wake up. Nor shall I change me testimony. Fear not. How would I define a brief moment as being long enough to think in—or not, as the case may be? 'Tis only me feelings, at the very end of it, and that be nae enough to start a fight over. Or a legal action."

He chuckled mirthlessly. "Sam, you're a wonder."

"So I've heard, sir." She stood up. She didn't want to glance at the bloodied bedsheet, the mess on the floor, but she did anyway. "Ye might yerself tell Meg and Linnet to clean this up. When I give an order of that sort, they tend to ignore me. On the morrow meself shall send one of Fat Dog's nephews to the chemist for peroxide. That should bleach out the blood that's seeped between the cracks in the floor boards."

"You and Meg and Linnet no longer work here. Remember?"

"Ye did nae tell them yet, aye?"

"Not yet."

"If ye're wise, sir, ye'll not tell them 'til after the floor's been tidied." She walked to the door like an awkward wind-up toy and paused, turning. "Forgive me boldness, sir, but I suggest ye not jump out the window, either, regardless yer troubles. Ye'd drop three feet into those bottle-brush bushes. Ye don't want to look so stupid, aye?"

"Aye." His eyes managed to twinkle in the drawn face. "Good night, Sam."

"G'night, sir."

She walked down the cool, black, silent hall. The memory of her last view of him—asprawl in his chair, looking weary and in need of comfort—and the view before that—standing over the poor tea farmer with that pistol blazing—wrought chaos in her mind. It was like two orchestras playing entirely different pieces at once. Who was Cole Sloan really?

Before dawn the next day she put on her new riding skirt and walked up to the stables. She gave sleepy, stumbling Fat Dog the written request for a bottle of peroxide and wrapped it in a one-pound note. That was taken care of. She climbed into her new saddle and rode Sheba out into the wooded hills.

How could she possibly find that clearing again? Every

square foot of this forest looked just like every other square foot of it. It might be twenty feet from her and she'd never see it. Constant rustling, bird calls, chirps and croaks told her the night crew was retiring as the day crew took up the watch. The forest seethed with activity—birds, creeping things and others.

A mat of strangler vines like the pipes of a monstrous organ stretched from floor to canopy. She remembered this place. She urged Sheba on up the hill. Was she nearing the crest? The dense vegetation here blocked vision beyond a few feet.

She stopped Sheba and listened. She sniffed. Bacon? Couldn't be. Or perhaps it could. "Mr. Gardell?" The forest activity around her ceased instantly. Hushed, a thousand tiny ears listened with her for a response. "Mr. Gardell!"

Sheba turned her head slightly to the left. She could hear things Samantha could not. Samantha reined her aside and took off in that direction. She stopped and called again.

"A little to the right." The forest broke up his voice and she could not tell its direction. She gave Sheba a nudge in the flanks and the mare scrambled up the hill.

Here it was. Sheba stepped out into that sheltered glade.

He sat cross-legged beside his firepit, watching his bacon wrinkle in a shallow pan. Except for a shotgun laid casually across his legs, he looked peaceful. He smiled at her.

She tied the horse to a low branch and walked over to join him. He said neither yea nor nay, so she sat down by the firepit.

She watched the embers wax and wane a while. "I need ye, Mr. Gardell, for I be sore confused." She looked beyond the bushy eyebrows to the eyes within. "Prithee tell me about Cole Sloan."

"First you must tell me why you want to know so badly that you're up by dawn on this mountain."

"He's an attractive man, a strong man, who's seized me fancy. And yet, he's also—well, there be a whiff of evil about him that be just as fascinating as the good—and far more dangerous to a woman's emotions. Methinks he finds me attractive—or at least unusual . . ."

*You were different, Sam, from the first. . . . Don't go, Sam.*

" . . . But I know not where me heart lies, or his. I be hoping ye can straighten me thoughts around to where I can handle them."

With the tip of that huge knife he flipped his bacon over. "They were young men—twenty or so—and full of life when they heard there was gold in the hills of California. My father Winston Gardell, Clancy McGonigan and Conal Sloan, all from Sydney. They sailed to the goldfields penniless and returned with enough money to buy passage to the next gold strike. That was at Ballarat the very next year."

"What would that be, 1850?"

"Fifty-one. They say a man who had also been to California came back to Australia, sought out geologic features here that resembled those he saw in America, and started digging. Before you knew it, there were gold strikes all over. Fitzroy River in fifty-eight, sixty-seven here in Queensland. An exciting time it was, lass; a happy time to be alive. Zesty. Perfect time for young men out to seek their fortunes, and there's not been another time like it, before or since."

She smiled. "Sure'n these times be nae so bad. The telephone and the telegraph, steam ships, and I've seen a talking machine that plays a whole orchestra and a singing voice."

"Foo foos. Doovers. They add nothing to the stature of a man. The gold strikes, they tested men and made better men of them—or crushed them."

He pushed his bacon aside and broke a couple eggs into the pan. "My father married along the way, but Sloan and McGonigan did not. Then my father died during the height of the Fitzroy strike and was buried without my mother ever seeing the remains. I was three. Clancy McGonigan made himself a sort of father to me and took me along when they reported gold here in Queensland."

"At three?"

"Twelve. I was twelve. Sixty-seven. Now here it gets sticky. McGonigan called me a 'partner,' but Sloan of course would never sit still for a snip of a lad taking a third the profits. I knew that. Especially because Sloan treated me like a houseboy."

"Like a slave?" She watched the edges of the egg whites curl.

"Very astute. Aye, lass. A lackey. And tender as my years were, I thought I deserved a third part. After all, Clancy said I was a full partner. Now Sloan had this notion that down under all the ferns and tree roots and vine tangles in these mountains, there was more gold than in Sovereign Hill, if we could just scrape down to it. We worked stream cuts mostly, near waterfalls and in gorges."

"These very hills! Forty years ago."

He nodded. "You couldn't have had breakfast yet. Here you go." Without benefit of spatula or implement, he slid a strip of bacon and an egg onto a little tin plate and handed it to her. "Hot on the bottom. Don't burn yourself. We found a little color here and there. Promises." He gave her a fork.

He slipped his own breakfast onto a plate. "Sloan and I went crooked on each other constantly. One day he had me digging a drift in a gorge and I quit. Climbed out of my hole, and decided to walk home to Sydney and forget it. Didn't get far when I heard dirt sliding. Ran back and the drift I just came out of had collapsed. And there was Sloan throwing more big rocks in it!"

She stared. "Sure'n ye don't think he deliberately tried to bury ye!"

"Kept myself hid. When he left I worked my way around and back to our camp. He was gone, McGonigan was gone, and it was just me and the cassowaries. Took me over a month, with the help of some coast aborigines, to get home. North coast here wasn't developed then like it is now. Besides, I didn't want to be anywhere Sloan might be."

"What about Mr. McGonigan?"

"I learned years later that Sloan brought Clancy's rotting

body out, claiming he died in a cave-in. Ten years later, when I was twenty-two and old enough to take care of myself, I came back up here. Cairns was a real town then, and they were finding gold in the interior behind the mountains here. They started Cairns in seventy-six, but the road in from there was too steep to be useful. So they started another road in from Port Douglas up the way, and that one was better."

"I heard both towns were once booming."

"You shoulda seen Port Douglas in its heyday; early eighties. Eight thousand people, two dozen hotels and more going up every week. Dancing girls in every pub. Polished brass everything, from bedsteads to bars. Buy anything, if you had enough money. And a few of the men coming out of the interior had enough and then some. But that kind of glory never lasts. The gold slowed up from a rush to a trickle. Still coming out, but in measured amounts now. Then the railroad came to Cairns instead of Douglas, and that was the end of Port Douglas 'til the sugar got started."

"Sugarlea?"

"One of the first. I think old Conal Sloan got his start-up money from the very dig Clancy died at—and I ran away from. I think he made enough out of that hole for one man but not enough for three."

"You're talking murder, sir. Sure'n ye dinnae know for certain."

"It's happened more'n once, lass. Greed'll do that. Sometimes the reason need be no more than simple inconvenience. Sugar really got big around sixty-eight and there on. At first it took a lot of hand labor. Clear land, break it up, plant, harvest; every step by hand. They imported colored labor by the thousands for that, just to keep the sugar cheap enough to sell on the open market."

"Kanakas."

"You've learned the word already. Kanakas. Thousands and thousands of them. And hundreds of them in Sloan's cane fields."

"So Cole Sloan inherited more than just sugar fields. More

a whole heritage, ye might say."

"More than you know, lass. More than you know, he's inherited. Right away, white labor panicked and the do-gooders cried out 'slavery.' In ten years there was a whole sheaf of laws, out of Brisbane and out of London, to aid and protect colored labor. By the time the lawyers got done, the cost of colored labor was double, and it didn't pay any longer. Besides, by then the fields were all cleared and tended by machinery."

"Except Sugarlea."

"One of the last. Part because Sloan couldn't afford to change and part because he was too hard-headed to change. In ninety-two the Parliament of Queensland abolished black labor policies and Sloan's world fell apart."

"And he fell out the window."

The man chuckled. "Aye. That year and the next were bad. Very bad. Strikes, labor problems, people fighting and killing over working-class privileges. The young Sloan would've had an uphill battle under good economic conditions, and this was Australia at her worst. The birth pangs before her federation, you might say."

Samantha forced the last of her egg down because it was the polite thing to do. She nearly choked, for it lodged in her throat along with her heart. "Cole's father may have been a murderer."

"Not 'may have,' lass. Was."

"Ye dinnae know that unless there's more to't than ye've said. Circumstantial. Dreadful circumstance, aye, but circumstance. Sure'n the secret—the certainty, if ye will—died with Conal." Why was she defending the father? She felt nearly certain the son was a murderer. She had watched him, and the more she rehearsed that horrible moment in her mind, the more certain she became.

Abner Gardell was staring at her. "What is it, lass?"

She shook her head. "Yer story disturbs me so."

"More than that. Don't be devious with me. Your whole soul is vibrating."

It was common knowledge, or would be as soon as the gossips and the newspapers spread it. Why try to hide it? "A man named John Butts—do ye know him?"

"Know the name. Tea planter, I think."

"He's dead, sir. Last night . . . uh, a misunderstanding."

"Cause of death?"

"Gunshot, sir. He, uh . . . 'Twas his own gun."

"And Cole Sloan's hand on the trigger, whether suicide or murder. Which?"

"They were fighting."

The man darkened, as if a light went out—or a very black light flared on inside him. He withdrew into himself in an unexplainable way. "Of course. I should have acted when I first heard of him instead of waiting until after I'd run out that Charter's Towers claim. And then I wandered around for months, wasting time, dropping little hints, letting him stew."

Samantha drew in a breath. "Notes. Ye sent him hints in notes, about vengeance."

"You know about them. Didn't think he'd tell a soul about them. Aye. Let him know God's not turning His back. But I made a bad mistake. You see, I diddled around here doing what I wanted instead of taking care of the important business. I wasted a lot of time looking for the old claim. The big one. Wanted to be able to rub him with that, too—that there be gold right under his nose all these years, but it took McGonigan's partner to find it; and he the loser, y'see."

"Ye said, I recall, seeking gold keeps ye honest."

"Putting it off, was all. Dwelling on it. If I'd done what I was supposed to when I first purposed in my heart to do it—sacrificed my own desires for God's will—your Butts would be alive now. The sins of the fathers. Well, I know now what I have to do, and Luke Vinson be hanged." He twisted around to lock her eye to eye. "You run down the hill to Sugarlea, little lady, and you tell Cole Sloan he's about to die. Him and Sugarlea and all. And get your sisters out of there lest they be destroyed with him."

"Ye can't be . . . 'Tis madness!"

"Run!" His bull voice roared to heaven and rattled hell.

Samantha leaped to her feet. She snatched Sheba's reins off the branch and dragged herself into the saddle. She jammed her heels into the startled mare's ribs, not that Sheba needed added inducement. She lay forward, pressing against the horse's neck, lest the harsh leaves and branches slap her right out of the saddle.

She had learned what she came to learn—and far more than she wanted to know.

*The sins of the father . . .*

*. . . are the son's as well.*

CHAPTER TWENTY-THREE

# CRESCENDO

The merest breath of a morning breeze stirred the soft air here on Vinson's verandah. Martin Frobel had spent so long in the outback that he had almost forgotten the wind can blow in other ways besides lustily. He sat back, wiped his lips and folded his napkin. "Luke, lad, you bung on one grouse breakfast."

The boy-faced preacher grinned, and in grinning looked all the younger. "Thank you!" He poured more coffee—rich black coffee that started the old heart right up.

How long had Martin known this lad? Five years? Six? As long as the young Canadian had been in Australia. He was like family— practically like a son to the missus. And in those six years he hadn't aged a minute.

"Y'know, Luke, you ought to think about coming back to the Creek. The congregation there needs a strong head. Don't have that now, with that student preacher. We need you back."

"I have a job to finish here." Luke sat down looking pensive. "At least, I think I do; lately I'm not so sure. Getting mixed feelings. How much is stubborn me and how much is God's desires?" He sat erect. "Ah, but that's to ponder some other time. You're on holiday, Marty. What shall we do today?" He looked out into the yard at his brown goat a moment. "If I can find Burriwi, how about sailing out onto the reef?"

"So my face can look like yours? Break it down, mate."

"So you can see the most wonderful thing God ever made. You were born in Queensland and I'll wager you've never b—"

A very pretty girl bolted out the side door of the church over there. She came racing across the goat pasture, her skirts flying as the goat trotted nervously to the far end. Luke was on his feet so quickly that Martin knew this was *the* girl.

She leaped onto the verandah and into Luke's arms in one great athletic swoop. She was too winded to make sense. How far did Luke say Sugarlea was—half a mile? She surely ran all the way. "She will nae leave!" came out eventually.

Luke rubbed her back and purred platitudes. Martin watched all about. Something big, something dangerous, was in the air. She had brought this breath of danger with her. Must be something up at Sugarlea.

As she caught her second wind, she pushed away in order to look Luke in the eye. Even lathered in sweat her face was lovely. Old Luke had found himself a real bobby-dazzler. "Someone named Gardell is coming to kill Cole Sloan and Sam refuses to leave. She sent Linnet and meself to—but I came here instead. Ye have to make her leave before that Gardell gets there!"

"I was hoping I'd talked him out of it. How does Sloan know Gardell is going to—"

Her gulps were more like sobs than breaths. "Sloan's so—so defiant! Like he wants Gardell to come and—'Tis frightening! 'Tis so frightening, and Sam won't—" The wild sobbing won out.

"Who's there now?"

"I don't know." Her head wagged, and she gasped for breath between sobs.

"Any guns in the house?"

She sucked in air and tried vainly to speak. "I—uh. . . .Oh, Luke!"

Luke looked helplessly at Martin.

Martin shrugged as he stood up. "I married one of 'em, and after all these years I still ain't figured her out yet. You're on your own. Think I'll get my gun, though. How about a holiday at Sugarlea?"

Luke nodded. "Sorry, Marty."

"Sorry? Naw. Let's give it a burl. I haven't had any good fun for a couple years now, not since that cattle thief." He left Luke to figure out for himself what Meg was trying to say and returned to the little room Luke had provided him at the back of the house; sparsely furnished, but comfortable—the kind of life Luke was accustomed to, as was Martin as well.

He generally didn't carry his sidearm when he was close in to civilization, but Sugarlea didn't sound too civilized just now. He pulled it out of the valise where he'd tucked it as his train approached Brisbane. Gardell. Gardell. Nope. Couldn't place it. He was rather surprised "Vickers" wasn't the enemy named. Maybe she was mistaken in the name. He dug around in his valise for the extra shells, just in case.

Samantha listened to the banjo clock force its measured beat onto the murky silence. "Deathwatch beetles. Ye ever hear the deathwatch beetles?"

"No." Mr. Sloan, asprawl as usual in his chair, could not have appeared less interested.

"They make a tiny tapping sound in the walls or woodwork. Some say their ticking portends a death in the house. Others say 'tis only silly insects beating their heads against the wood. I suppose ye're to believe whichever strikes yer fancy."

"I'll take the silly bug theory."

"And meself as well." She glanced for the eighty-seventh time at the banjo clock. " 'Tis past ten and not a peep. Do ye suppose I misread him and he intends only to frighten ye?"

"He's coming. And not to say 'boo,' either." His dark eyes watched her a moment, as if seeking some sign. "Are you sure you won't leave? Your sisters are safe. You should be, too."

"Abner Gardell has aught against me. I dinnae think he poses danger for any save yerself."

He studied her with those menacing black eyes. "I think you're right." Samantha expected to see some sort of fear; she saw only a cold and flinty grimness. He was quite ready to die or to deal out death, and that look about him frightened her more than fear would have.

He stood up deliberately, almost casually, and cradled his shotgun on one arm. He picked up the ungainly pistol on his desk and tucked it away somewhere at the small of his back. "Stay out of harm's way, and don't let the place burn down while I'm gone."

"Where are ye going?"

"Out. I never in my life sat down to wait for trouble, and I can't now." Before she could phrase an effective protest he was through the door. Gone.

She was alone.

Now she must reach out to the desk and pick up her own pistol, the gun with which she was to defend herself—explicit orders—and perhaps help defend her former master and Sugarlea—implicitly expressed. She laid her hand on the cool steel and felt it suck the warmth out of her fingers. She wrapped around the unyielding grip and lifted. Its sheer weight startled her, despite the fact that she must have picked up this very weapon a dozen times already today. Mr. Sloan had been thorough in his instruction—so he wouldn't have to fear the troops behind him, he said. She laid it down again and folded her hands in her lap.

The clock ticked. Ticked. Ticked. Deathwatch?

Someone pounded on the front door. Samantha thought she was frozen in fear, but apparently not. She was standing at the door with that pistol in her hand and she couldn't remember rising, let alone picking up the loathsome thing. She hastened down the hall to the parlor. Outside the window stood Mr. Wiggins' old roan and another horse. That meant . . .

She opened the door an inch.

Mr. Vinson stood there smiling. "We've come at your sister's request to escort you to safety."

"We?" Samantha glanced at the stranger draped against a porch post. He dressed like a pastoralist and looked so casual leaning there, but the pistol in his covered holster betrayed him. He was as dangerous as Mr. Sloan, and probably just as ready to fight. Or kill.

Mr. Vinson was carrying his weapon, too—a big black Bible tucked under his arm. "This is Martin Frobel. When I first came to Australia, to a tiny congregation near Torrens Creek, the Frobels took me in. Got me started. Old friend, and trustworthy."

Samantha nodded at the man.

Luke dipped his head toward nowhere in particular. "I assume Gardell's not appeared yet. I would have been here sooner but I had to find Burriwi. Burriwi's gone ahead, scouting. Wouldn't let me come along; said he couldn't hear anything when I was with him."

"I don't know if I should trust ye—all the harm ye've done him legally. . . ."

Luke looked perplexed, a reaction Samantha would not have expected. "Done to him? I've achieved nothing! It's one of the major reasons I doubt that my efforts here are truly God's will."

"Mr. Vinson, when ye—"

"Luke. Please."

"Luke, he was near ruined before ye stripped away his indentures. Ye did nae see his face, as I did . . ." She shook her head, near tears. Too much was happening too quickly.

"Whatever magic you think I did with indenture legalities, it's not mine. I tried, but I couldn't file because I was not a party directly wronged."

"But who. . .?" A light dawned. "Byron Vickers! I'll wager he went straight from Cairns to Brisbane."

The stockman spoke in a warm baritone not the least in keeping with that cold pistol at his side. "Vickers. He's the one. Bashed the ear of every judge in Brisbane, telling what a slave merchant is Sloan, bad-mouthing him."

"Mr. Vinson. Luke. Explain the sins of the fathers."

"It's a phrase from Old Testament law—punishment for the sins of the fathers being visited on the children. I believe it refers to iniquities against God himself. Why?"

"Abner Gardell used those very words this morning; 'sins of the fathers.' Do ye know the man?"

"I met him very recently. That's why I think I can talk sense to him, assuming Burriwi can find him."

" 'Tis why meself shall remain here. 'Tis possible I can talk to him, maybe stay his hand. Where is Somebody's Tower?"

"Charter's Towers? West of Townsville."

"I believe, until recently, Mr. Gardell mined gold there. He feels Mr. Butts would still be alive if he'd followed his original intentions of bedeviling Mr. Sloan years ago, when first he discovered his existence."

Luke snorted. "John would still be alive now had he allowed me to follow through on that restraining order. But he was completely convinced of Sloan's integrity."

"I perceive Mr. Sloan may have misidentified his enemies." Samantha stepped back and swung wide the door. "Please come in."

The stockman lurched erect. "Luke, I think I'll prowl around the edges a little. Heard a lot about this place."

Luke nodded and walked inside as the pastoralist turned and headed down the sloping lawn at a casual saunter. The light of Meg's life sat down at the kitchen table as Samantha made lunch. He thumbed through his weapon, mostly the front end of the book, muttering occasionally, nodding.

The day creaked along. The stockman, Mr. Frobel, came in for lunch and went out again. Samantha tried to bind herself to dinner preparations, but she kept leaping up to pace the house. At a bit past three she stopped the banjo clock pendulum to still its infernal ticking.

At four she built the fire up high. It made the kitchen excessively hot but she wanted tea. She put on a lamb stew for dinner; not only would it feed just about any number, it would keep on the back of the stove and taste all the better for delay.

The tea, though, was the *raison d'etre* for her fire. Here was a drop of sanity in a sea of fear, a bit of the familiar in a world of chaos. She lingered over tea.

Near dusk, Burriwi appeared at the fly screen. Except for a plain headband holding his curly hair up and back, he was utterly unclad; yet he looked not the least naked or out of place. He had just walked or run many miles, no doubt, but he breathed and spoke with ease; he wasn't even sweaty. He leaned on a long decorated spear. "Fat Dog's nephews say he came off the mountains this morning. I looked around up there and he's gone. He's down here among whitefellers."

"Seen Sloan?"

"Now and again. Didn't show myself to him."

From the south side of the yard came Mr. Frobel's shout: "Luke! Heads up!"

Two guns fired out there, a large one and a larger one.

Burriwi disappeared, literally; one moment he was standing there propped up by his spear, and the next instant he was gone.

"Marty!" Mr. Vinson called. "Where is he?"

"Coming!"

Samantha heard horses—no, horses and a wagon. They were charging full tilt up the lane toward the house. The guns roared again. She snatched up her pistol from the kitchen table. The office window crashed. Had Mr. Gardell just gained entrance? His Bible still in his hand, Luke raced down the hall. Samantha followed, running.

She heard a kitchen window smashing, but before she could call out to Luke, Linnet's bedroom window shattered. The wagon clattered around the far end of the house. Samantha smelled coal oil. A kerosene lamp must have spilled in there. The pungent fumes assaulted her nose even out here in the hall. She paused beside Luke at the front door.

She still held this pistol in her slippery, sweaty hands, but at whom would she aim it? Mr. Gardell? She couldn't. No. Mr. Sloan's troops here were useless. Another window crashed on the north side.

Out the open front door she saw Mr. Gardell for the first time. He was just coming around the end of the house, shouting to his team of horses. He carried in one hand a smoking, flaring torch. From down at the end of the yard, Mr. Frobel blasted away again and again.

The far horse squealed and lunged high. It lurched aside into its teammate and dropped in its traces. Now the other horse was being dragged down screaming. The toppling animals slammed into the front porch posts and somehow just kept moving, a ton of squirming, kicking, flailing disaster.

The wagon ripped free of its front axle and came tipping right toward Samantha. She wanted to move faster—her legs weren't carrying her out of the way quickly enough. Luke slammed into her, dragged her to the floor, crushed her with his weight.

She felt the gun in her hand kick as it went off, but she hardly heard it—not for all the other horrible smashing noise. She knew when the wagon hit the house, for the floor beneath her shuddered. After one final creaking crash, silence.

"Luke? Luke, boy! You still with us?" Mr. Frobel's voice came from somewhere out front.

The weight on her stirred, shifted. She let go of that pistol lest it fire itself again. Luke rolled aside. Where was Mr. Gardell? She groped for the gun. She'd best hold on to it, at least for a while. By the time she was on her feet, Luke was outside.

It wasn't easy for him, getting outside. Debris from the splintered wagon box blocked the doorway; he had to climb over and through the wreckage. The porch roof had collapsed, forcing him to creep beneath it.

The living horse struggled mightily beneath the dead one.

Mr. Frobel waved his gun at the mess. "Hated to shoot the horse, but the bloody galah was gonna fire the house. I stomped the torch out. No danger now."

"He's gone?"

"Saw a glimpse of him ducking into the forest off that way. Quick as a cat, that feller, for as old as he looks. Didn't seem hurt. Or repentant."

Luke stared off at the forest wall. He grimaced. "Let's dig this horse out. Then . . . well, I don't know what."

Samantha clambered over and under splintered wreckage. With only half her attention, she performed her assigned task of sitting on the horse's head while the two strong men cut its dead companion free and rolled it aside.

Somewhere in that deadly forest, two men stalked each other. She knew them both. No matter who won, she would mourn. She could not win. The woes plaguing her beloved Erin were not limited to the Emerald Isle. They were here with her, now.

There is no such thing as escape to peace. Perhaps, there is no such thing as peace.

## CHAPTER TWENTY-FOUR

# FIRE AND FURY

Burriwi particularly relished that breath of time between day and night that is neither, yet both. With clucks and murmurs the birds of day settled themselves, as with rustling and flitting the creatures of night began to stir. The air paused between its rhythms of sea breeze and land breeze. The forest for these few moments dimmed without turning black; it gave him the time needed to reattune his senses from day-brightness to night-darkness.

He dropped to a comfortable squat and leaned his back against a plum tree. With noisy flaps and flibbers, a fruit bat arrived overhead and commenced its breakfast. Burriwi thought of Luke Vinson's first encounter with fruit bats and smiled to himself. Whitefellers have the strangest attitudes about bats. Luke spent half that night telling Burriwi about vampires, some doctor named Frank Stine who tried to be God. . . . Sometime Burriwi would have the opportunity to repeat Luke's own stories to him, word for word. Luke and his books. Burriwi smiled again.

A soft patter of rain began as the day dribbled to an end. This night would soon be here; the rain would dull Burriwi's ability to hear and the darkness was robbing him of vision. He must be especially careful.

Here came Luke up the path between the house and stable. Luke. Burriwi could feel him without following with his ears, though Luke made so much noise any child could tell you exactly where he was. The man with him, that Martin Frobel, made much less noise and bothered the spirits of the forest hardly at all. The man was a native of the wide open land out beyond Woop Woop; you could feel it in him, that different spirit all the outback natives, black or white, shared.

How strange, this. Burriwi could still discern the spirits, those of men and those not of men. But he no longer felt at one with them. Now that he had cast his lot with the great God of Luke's book, and with that God's Son, he was in some way separated from the old familiar realities beyond sight and sound. Whitefellers had erected a dog fence mostway across Australia, they said—to keep the dingoes out of the sheep. That's how Burriwi felt, like the dingoes must feel; they could see the sheep but they couldn't get to them. Was his own spirit somehow changed? He must discuss this new thing with Luke. Or perhaps with Abner Gardell. That man understood the bush.

Gardell versus Sloan. A difficult choice. Burriwi might well be called upon to declare his loyalty to one or the other. Sloan, while not generous, did provide tucker and sometimes turps. Sloan had given both his crocodiles to the clan when by rights he could have kept at least portions of each. But Gardell was much closer in spirit.

Luke and his Martin friend were far enough ahead. Burriwi picked up his spear and stood. Was the cook coming? No. She must be remaining at the house. She was a spirit at odds with the voices of the forest! She didn't just chill the spirits; she antagonized them, and they her.

The rain came harder and louder now. Gunfire erupted up by the stables—a shotgun blast, a large-calibre pistol, another shotgun blast. The shotgun would be Sloan's and it was spent now. He must have found Gardell.

Burriwi shinned up the poinciana tree just north of the stable area. From here he could see all the open lot, not to mention most of the forest wall around. This high up, he was relatively safe from wild shots.

Sloan, behind Sheba's hardwood manger, tossed his shotgun aside and yanked a pistol from his belt at the small of his back. There was Gardell, behind the big pandanus near the tin water tank. Bent over double, Sloan scurried like a crab down the length of the stable, from manger to manger. He dived around the far end beyond Gypsy and fired wildly at the water tank, three or four fast shots. In gracefully curved streams, water spewed from the neat round holes in the tank.

Gardell stepped out just long enough to return a couple shots and ducked back to safety. "More than time for the piper to be paid, Sloan. Your daddy left you a fine legacy of debt. A life for a life. Too bad you can't pay two lives, for that's what's owed. Maybe even three, if we count the Butts fellow. How does that go. . .? McGonigan's blood cries out to me from the ground."

"You're sick, Gardell. That generation's dead and gone. I'm not my father's keeper any more than I'm my brother's."

Luke's voice cut in from twenty feet behind Gardell. "It's God who said that, Abner, and you're not God. He's the only one can judge. Not you."

Gardell cried out, "Leave us alone, Vinson!"

Simultaneously, Sloan shouted, "You interfere and I'll be on your hammer just the same as his. You've done enough, Vinson."

Undaunted in the least, Luke called, " 'Vengeance is mine, saith the Lord.' Abner. Let Him take care of it."

"I'm doing God's will. The sins of the fathers are visited on the children unto the fourth generation."

Sloan popped out and fired twice, his pistol steadied in both hands. Was he shooting at Gardell or at the voice of the preacher in the forest? The gathering gloom of dusk dulled his vision; from his high angle, Burriwi couldn't really tell.

Luke's open-country companion swore and said something about being a fool. The forest rustled above the patter of the rain; its voices gasped.

And here stood Luke, like a shag on a rock, out in the clearing. He carried his book. No gun, no spear, not even a stone to throw. He stepped into the thirty-yard-long clearing between Sloan and the pandanus palm behind the water tank. His book! Even from the height of this tree, Burriwi could feel the hostility in the two white-feller adversaries. They were determined to kill and there stood Luke weaponless but for his book. The boy was a bit strange (why count teeth?), but Burriwi would not have guessed he was so utterly foolish and careless of life.

Luke's voice rang clear on the still and ominous air. "That's from Jeremiah, Abner. Know what else it says? 'In those days they shall say no more, The fathers have eaten sour grapes and the children's teeth are set on edge. But every one shall die for his own iniquity; every man that eateth the sour grapes, *his* teeth shall be set on edge.' " Gardell was using the lull to better his own position beyond the water tank. So, Burriwi noted, was Sloan.

Luke turned his back on Sloan. "I spent a little time making certain of the text, Abner. Deuteronomy clinches it. 'The fathers shall not be put to death for the children, neither shall the children be put to death for the fathers; every man shall be put to death for his own sin.' That's God's will, Abner, and you're not in it."

Burriwi could feel the tension from away up here. Sloan was bent over attending his pistol—reloading, no doubt.

Sloan exploded up and out of his hiding place. He fired at the pandanus and leaped the manger. He hunched down behind his big burly wagon horse now. The animal rolled its eyes and shifted back and forth nervously in its stall.

Luke wheeled to face him. "You, Sloan! I opposed you bef—"

Three steel chains stretched across the front of each stall to keep its horse inside. Burriwi himself had hooked and unhooked those chains many times when he helped Fat Dog with the horses. Sloan didn't bother with them. He came diving forward; he sprawled on his belly under the chains and fired at Luke!

Burriwi could hear the slug hit. The preacher staggered

backward—done in, or just ducking? Burriwi couldn't tell from here. Almost instantly Luke's friend Martin roared something and opened fire. Gardell screamed "No!" and blasted away. The clearing filled with drifting gunsmoke. That and the near darkness obscured Burriwi's view. Curious how driving rain fails to wash away smoke.

Sloan was on his knees now. His gun clicked; it clicked again. The gunsmoke began leisurely to lift away and dissipate. Burriwi could smell it up here now.

Gardell, with a wicked grin, stepped boldly out and stood before the water tank, his gun on Sloan. "I still have a few shells left. One from my father, one from McGonigan, one from Butts."

Burriwi expected fear on Sloan's face; darkness and some smoke still obscured his vision, but all he could see was defiance. Defiancc and hatred.

Movement in the haze—Luke regained his feet and planted himself squarely in front of Sloan, facing Gardell. "Here's where you choose, Abner. Your own revenge, or God's way. But they're not the same thing. Tell me to move aside and I will. I won't try to take your choice away from you. But you have to tell me to."

For once, Sloan and Gardell agreed on something. As one they shouted at Luke, "This is none of your business, Vinson!"

Luke wheeled on Sloan and pointed his Bible at him. "You stay out of this, Sloan!"

The planter knelt there in the stall door, the chains pressing his back, and gaped. The hatred faded to utter surprise.

Luke turned his back on the man who had just tried to kill him and faced Gardell. "It *is* my business, Abner." He wagged his Bible in Gardell's face. "You're doing what my Lord forbids and then trying to get Him to take the blame for it. It's your vendetta, not God's, and you'll pay bitterly for the lie, I promise you. I'm trying to save you from that."

"I waited for this too long, Luke. Set him up—sent him warnings so he could worry and fret, like my mum fretted all those years. His father destroyed both my fathers. Both."

"And you think God's going to let that sort of thing slip by Him? Crikey, Abner! You can trust Him better than that!"

"Don't ask me not to. You got no right to ask me not."

Luke's voice rolled on. "God said in Ezekiel that the soul of the father and the soul of the son are His, and the soul that sins will die. Don't you see? It's not you against Sloan, two boys scrapping in a back alley, or I'd stand back and let you both have at. It's God against Satan for control of *you*!"

Sloan broke his pistol open to reload. He glanced beyond the clearing to the pastoralist and at Martin's large gun. He laid his empty pistol in the mud.

"Let God take care of Conal Sloan's sin, Abner. Don't bring sin upon yourself by killing a man for someone else's crime."

What was wrong with Luke's book? Burriwi wagged his head. Bullet damage. It worked better than a hard kangaroo hide shield, for sure. Kangaroo hide doesn't stop bullets at close range.

The haze of gunsmoke nearly cleared before anyone moved.

Gardell stared at Sloan as if Luke were not there. His arm relaxed until his gun pointed at the rain-beaten mud by his side. "If you're destined to burn in hell, I leave it to God to strike the match." Wearily he walked past Luke and Sloan, across the open stable yard, and disappeared into the darkness and tangle of the forest. The voices accepted him instantly and said nothing to betray his route or passing.

Luke's book had won out over guns and hatred! Burriwi grinned. He'd chosen the right course, all right! An amazing and powerful thing, Luke's book about his God. And an amazing and powerful God, to give such strength to the preacher man whom the forest spirits ridiculed.

Martin moved out into the open, his pistol in his hand. "Now what?"

Burriwi sniffed and sniffed again. It wasn't the unique tang of gunsmoke. "Luke!" he called from his high roost. "Fire! Fire from the house!"

A splintering *crack* and the kitchen lit up orange. Samantha threw the tea billy, the last of her water, at the nearest flames. They sputtered and flared anew. She whipped the cloth off the table and beat at them wildly. That was an error; the cloth was soaked with coal oil no less than was the floor and wall. The glass from the kerosene jug Gardell had thrown crunched under her shoes.

The fire loved its tasty tidbit and ate instantly into the cloth. She threw it aside as flame rushed at her face. The kitchen was lost. She must retrench and fight it from the hall. If she could somehow cut it off at this end of the ell, the rest of the house would be safe. Even if it dropped brands on the roof, it could not spread—not with rain wetting down the tin.

Cole Sloan! *Oh, God, please don't let Abner kill him!*

Sloan, Gardell, Luke—the distant gunfire had ceased. What had happened? Were any left to return to help her? She mustn't cower now. She backed into the black, smoke-filled hall and slammed the kitchen door, cutting off the horror in there. The wall beside her, the wall of Linnet's room, radiated heat. She laid a hand on it; it was too hot to touch. She heard crackling overhead; the fire was moving through the rafters above the ceiling!

The eggshell of wall exploded in orange fury. The fire in Linnet's room had broken out into the hallway. With a shriek Samantha turned and ran through the darkness. She must do something to save the house, but she was helpless now. The only available water, the slashing, stinging rain, was not enough to stem the blaze. She heard a tin sheet pop and clang on the roof.

The hallway was so filled with smoke now, even were it noon instead of dusk, Samantha could not see. The smoke burned her eyes; they closed and filled with tears. The smoke set fire to her lungs and choked her; she couldn't breathe.

If the fire destroyed her now as it was destroying the house, no one would know until tomorrow, after the ashes cooled. Her mind was warning her "Don't panic!" even as her feet raced wildly down the hall toward the front door. Any moment her groping hands would fi—

She lay on the floor and the world churned, full of black smoke. The side of her head throbbed. What was. . .? The stone face! She had run squarely into that stone pillar. All was not lost. It looked out the front window. She would find the face on it by touch and escape by following its nose. Where was. . .?

Here. Kicking and groping, she found the cold stone, but it lay on its side. It had toppled and rolled. It offered her no clue, no hint in which direction safety lay.

The fire in the ceiling was igniting fresh tinder now in a room to Samantha's left. No doubt it found more kerosene to feed upon. Gardell had doused the rooms liberally with his jugs thrown through windows. She heard the wild flames crackling close by and overhead.

*God, help me, please! Send someone . . . do something!*

Her own prayer startled her. She was no good—at least, not good enough to warrant divine help. She was no good at all. Her heart was as black as Mr. Sloan's, in its own way. She knew it and God knew it. Honor merely for its own sake was not enough, not if God wasn't included in it. Hours ago she had doubted His very existence. That surely must be some sort of flagrant sin. She knew now. Yes, He was up there, and probably snickering at her ineptitude.

*God, please help me anyway . . . please!*

"Sam? Sam! Where are you?" The baritone boomed from . . . from somewhere in the thick and horrifying darkness.

"Here, Mr. Sloan! I'm here. Ye're alive! Thank God ye're alive!"

*Oh, yes, God, I mean that; thank you!*

She tried to untangle her legs and stand erect. No! The smoke and heat were much denser up there; she must stay down close to the floor.

"Can you move? Can you come to my voice?" That way! He was over that way!

She crawled clumsily, trying to keep her skirts from dragging her down, but her knees kept pinning them to the floor. "Keep talking! Where are ye?"

"Sam! Here." He was closer. . . . He started coughing.

A window shattered and a rush of hot air swooped past her. She heard tin popping on the roof, buckled by the heat. Her lungs were properly full now; she couldn't stop coughing; she inhaled deeply without really meaning to and coughed all the worse.

A hand slapped the top of her head. It grabbed her hair and hauled her to her feet. Strong arms locked around her and pulled her in powerful strides through the darkness. They were in the other ell now; through the murky haze she saw a line of orange light under the office door.

He slammed his shoulder against his bedroom door and they lurched into the room almost without a pause. With a muffled *fwump!* the office door ignited behind them. The yellow light flared bright; the whole room in there was afire. She could smell the black and oily kerosene smoke.

One arm let go of her long enough to fling a chair through the window. Howling fire and smoke gushed in the door at their back. He snatched her up in brawny arms and threw her feet first out the window. She hit the bottle-brush bushes, fell forward into the cold, rain-soaked grass, and rolled aside to her feet.

She heard him hit the grass near her. He was at her side again in the darkness, dragging her into the cool black air away from the horror.

They stopped. She turned to see. Tin roofing peeled back and lifted up into the air, illuminated from below. Metal sheets near the open holes in the roof glowed pink. Flames leaped treetop high back by the kitchen. Red light danced in the windows. The big front window with all its tiny panes shattered and spewed flame out across the wreckage of that wagon, across the poor dead horse. A minute ago she had been in that room, right there.

With a mighty roar the roof collapsed into the parlor and dining room. A brilliant spray of sparks and firebrands danced skyward on the billowing smoke.

His arm remained wrapped around her. She could feel him breathe and sigh. "There go my dreams."

She clung to him and sobbed, "I'm sorry. I'm so sorry. It's all gone."

"No," he murmured, "it's not all gone. You're safe."

# Chapter Twenty-Five

# IN ASHES

The sky was murky, overcast, obscuring the morning sun, but Samantha didn't care. At least it wasn't raining. She walked stiffly, every bone and muscle in her body aching. How fortunate she was that she could feel all those parts! Her hair was a little frizzled, one eyebrow scorched off, but she had escaped unscathed.

She paused near the south side of what had been one of Mossman's better homes. The black heap smoldered and stank. The ruins would probably harbor hotspots for days yet. Here were the bottle-brush bushes, shriveled black stumps in the loose dirt.

The west office wall had collapsed outward and reduced itself to fine gray ash. Mr. Sloan picked mechanically through the pile, poking here and there with a stick. He stood erect as she approached and cautiously worked his way, one step at a time, to her side.

She sighed. "Yesterday, after they left, I couldnae just sit while yerself and the others were . . . ye know. I was going to start cleaning up all that spilled kerosene, starting with the kitchen and just working back, room by room. He threw kerosene jugs through half the windows at least. It was something for me to do. I went out to the dunny first; wasn't gone but a couple minutes. When I came back in the house, the kitchen was . . ." She shrugged.

"That's when you should have run outside."

"I thought I could put it out before it spread. Sure'n I could stop it, aye? For the fire was aught but a few minutes old. And then some of the kerosene caught, and whoosh. I threw the dishwater on it, dishes and all, and the kettle . . . But it burnt so hot with the coal oil; it went up so fast and furious."

"Which is to say, if Gardell hadn't—" He chuckled bitterly. "You told me I couldn't get away from history, and I said I wasn't worried about it. Remember? You were wiser than I gave you credit for. My short little history got me after all, just as surely as your long history took your brother." He waved a hand across the ruins. "Hit me where it hurts most."

"We'll never know whether Mr. Gardell was at all justified in hating ye; whether yer father really did those things."

"We know." His voice rumbled, sad and quiet. "He told me, not long before he—what's the fancy word you used? Defenst—that."

"Defenestration."

"Yeah. Winston Gardell's death was accidental. McGonigan's was not. And my father was certain to the very end that he had buried Abner alive. That he'd left the boy to die a slow, agonizing death. I think that was what put him over the edge—what drove him to suicide. I'm sure he could have coped with the financial reverses if it hadn't been for the guilt."

"Mr. Vinson lectured Meg extensively on the subject of guilt and how to rid oneself of it. He discussed a commitment to God by accepting Jesus as . . . I be nae sure of the words, but the end of it is that Jesus alone can erase guilt. I dinnae understand it except to know that apparently there be a way out of guilt."

He frowned at her. "Thought you said you're not sure God exists."

"I wasn't, then, but I am now." She turned to look at him more squarely. Ashes smudged his cheek, and probably her face was just as dirty. "The storm, those months ago; 'twas God I called out to, even though I didn't directly think of doing so. And when 'twas yerself and Abner Gardell out in the forest somewhere, and each intent on killing the other, me heart was begging God to take a hand and preserve ye; keep ye safe. I pleaded with Him to save me from the fire, and moments later I hear yer voice. Aye, He exists. Me head may doubt, but me heart knows, and I've learned to listen to me heart."

"Good. Then you—" He turned, scowling, to look.

A freight dray behind two heavy horses came rattling up the lane toward them. On its bright red slab sides was lettered *J. Wiggins, Shipping* in vivid yellow. Luke Vinson drove and Meg, in the clothes she was wearing yesterday, pressed close beside him in the box. Martin Frobel was still around. He hopped out of the back to hold the uneasy horses as Luke climbed down. The pastoralist wore his pistol at his belt; perhaps he was not so sure the war was over.

Luke extended a hand. "Cole. Meg and I've set the date—this Saturday—and you're invited to the wedding."

Sloan declined the handshake. "Sam thinks you weren't the one who sent the notes or set the courts on me, so I suppose I should offer congratulations."

Samantha stepped into the silence. "Ye have me warmest blessing and congratulations, Luke. Meself will be by later this morning—aye, Meg?" She looked past the pastor.

Meg was beaming, a ray of sunshine on a dreary day. "I'll be at Luke's. I hope ye'll come along shopping with me. Trousseau."

"For a trousseau? In Mossman? Heh! But aye, I'll be along."

Luke's gray eyes met Sloan's fairly. "I was mad at God, the state, the federation and everyone else, because I couldn't act legally on behalf of John Butts or Byron Vickers. Now I'm coming to understand it's for the best if a third party can't intervene. My motives were misguided; I would have acted wrongly."

Mr. Sloan sniffed. "You apologizing for something?"

"No. Yes. For my attitude. It's a long business, and I won't bore you with details. I've examined my reasons for coming here, and I've decided they weren't very pure." The boyish smile looked pure enough.

"Just why did you come here, anyway?" Was Mr. Sloan's voice softening a little? It almost seemed so.

"To Australia? To serve Jesus. Found myself in a little ministry out by Torrens Creek, near Martin here. But there were problems and I got restless. I wanted to conquer injustice in big gulps, not little bits."

"So you came to pester me. Whacko." Mr. Sloan snorted.

The boy-face grinned sheepishly. "Aborigines, Kanakas, Orientals—Queensland has high numbers of such. And I was out to put the world to rights, so I decided to rip myself up from where I was planted, so to speak, and come here, to the sugar fields. You're about the biggest sugar grower around. I thought that if I could bring you into compliance . . ." His lips formed a thin flat line for a moment. "What I failed to see until just recently was my true motives. Christ acted from compassion. I acted because this sort of thing is fashionable at the moment. So I'm backing away—retrenching—as I realign myself. I want to be more like Christ himself, however that takes me."

Samantha smiled. "A sweet taste."

"A sweet taste. Sweet savor. Acerbic hatred is hardly sweet. I'm sorry, Cole."

The man obviously hadn't understood a bit of it. He nodded as if he did. "I'll be needing a housekeeper, assuming I get a house built again. Meg gonna be around?"

"No. We're moving to Torrens Creek. God put me there in the first place. I'll work there." Luke nodded toward Samantha. "On our way." He took a deep breath. "God bless you, Cole Sloan." He turned quickly and climbed back into the wagon. Mr. Frobel hopped up behind and off they went. Meg waved furiously. Samantha envied the glow in Meg's heart that so copiously spilled out into her face.

Mr. Sloan voiced her own thoughts: "Looks happy enough, doesn't she?"

"Aye. She's found her man. I daresay it appeared when I saw Amena that she found hers as well."

"And you?"

Samantha drew a deep breath.

Mr. Sloan turned her around to him, his hands on her shoulders. He laughed suddenly. "Your face is dirty, you lack an eyebrow and your nose is peeling. And you know what? You're still a beautiful woman, Sam. Also strong, honorable, loyal—all the things I knew I wanted in a woman. Besides that, I love you. I think I've loved you for quite some time, but last night was the first time I admitted it to myself. I don't have much to offer, and most of that's in ashes, but will you marry me?"

She must have hesitated a moment too long, for he closed his warm hands around the sides of her face and kissed her. That kiss in Cairns had been wonderful; this one was unbelievable. His fingertips traveled down her throat. His powerful arms, the arms that had dragged her bodily out of the fiery house, wrapped around her and fused her to himself. When at last he moved away, she felt so giddy and weak she could not let go.

She buried her head in his shoulder and clung to him. "Eh, Cole Sloan, sure'n ye be the world's most magnificent man. I find meself infatuated with ye. Mayhap 'tis love, as yerself admits."

"I've been infatuated before. This is different."

She stood erect and stepped back. "I told ye moments ago that I've learnt to listen to me heart. But me head doesn't do too badly either. Me heart would join itself to yer own in a wink, but me head cries 'Pause!' I cannae trust ye. Meself has seen yer devious ways and I've told meself lots of reasons to excuse them away. But in the end of it, me head tells me I've seen the man, the true man; beware."

"Sam . . . I told you you're different. I'd never hurt you or betray you."

She licked her lips and she could feel her eyes get hot. " 'Tis the hardest word that ever will leave me lips, but I say it now. Nae."

"That's why you came to Australia, to find a man and marry. Admit it."

"Aye. And here I've found the best, 'twould appear to most. But nae. I cannae marry ye when I cannae put me full trust in ye. I'm sorry." She whispered it again. "I'm sorry."

"I won't take that as a final answer."

" 'Tis the only answer I can give for now, or in the future that I can see."

His deep, dark eyes studied hers, and she could not tell if that was sadness or anger in the depths of them. Perhaps she saw both. He stepped back and nodded grimly. "I'm going into Mossman with the wagon. I'll drop you off at the chapel."

"I thank ye."

For the longest time he gazed at the smoldering ruins. "Tomorrow." Suddenly the lilt was back. "Tomorrow!"

"Aye! Tomorrow."

She watched him turn away from her. As he walked up the path to the stable, the old verve was back in his stride. She watched him disappear in the trees.

The lingering stench from the burn hovered over the area. The air hung still and listless, strewing the smoke and smell. A family of Aborigines arrived and with cheerful, unintelligible chatter commenced to butcher the bloated horse.

It started to rain again. Heavy drops plopped in the powdery ash, disturbing it without wetting it. They rang *pung* on the charred timbers. Hotspots began to whisper, *Psst. Psst. Psst.*

Somewhere in brooding, chilly Ireland, in Dagda's hill palaces, warriors and demigods feasted amid bright light and splendor, safe from mortal eyes. But here in Queensland's mountains, fantastic activity was limited to gnomes who swabbed the throats of little green frogs. The bright light and splendor was the land itself—brilliant, dazzling, sun-filled, a delight to mortal eyes.

The first of the frogs chirruped. Another answered. Others picked up the call, their voices in fine fettle. And now the forest beside her rang with tiny voices. Samantha decided she liked the frogs much better than Dagda's palaces.

What was that line from Robert Browning, the poetic optimist? *God's in His heaven; all's right with the world.*

Sure and the skies were open now. The rain came pelting in fast, cold splashes—cleansing rain, sweet rain, rain that heals the soul. Samantha tilted her face up and let the stinging drops wash away the dirt and the ashes and all the fears and tears from yesterday.

Tomorrow!

Aye. Tomorrow.